For Jan

With warmest

good wishes

Jack

Sept 08

REFLECTIONS
IN A TAR-BARREL

JACK HARTE

Scotus
Press

Author's Acknowledgements

Thanks to Pat Pidgeon, Colm McHugh,Michael Phillips, Vergil Nemchev, Toma Markov, Bernie McGinley, Mary Kelly, and many others who helped at various stages and took an interest in the long gestation of this book. Also thanks to Fiona, Paul, Paddy and Jimín for the barrel

For the next wave

Lara, Vanya, Fiachra, Aonghus, Audrey, Vince, Sandra, and little Celia

Published in Ireland by
Scotus Press
PO Box 9498
Dublin 6

First published in Bulgarian translation in 2007 by Altera
Publishers, 21 Hr Belchev Street, Sofia 1000, Bulgaria,
Published in India by, Banyan Tree Books, Rajkamal
Prakashan Pvt Ltd, 1b Netaji Subhash Marg, Daryaganj New
Delhi 110 002

ISBN 0 9547194 84

Set in 11pt. Century Schoolbook

Cover art-work and design Pat Pidgeon
Layout: Pat Pidgeon and Colm McHugh

1

DEATH IS A WALL. I'VE ALWAYS FELT THAT.
Now I frigging well know. A stubborn wall
against which the ripple of our days and years
washes, is halted, is reversed.

A moment is a wonderful thing. One moment of life.
Because one moment can contain all. Especially the
moment between seeing the wall and hitting it. That
moment is a day. Is a life-time. All the life-time you've
got, for frig's sake. Not that your experiences start
flashing before your eyes, like a newsreel gone
berserk. Not that at all. That's rubbish. How can I
explain it? It's just that a total and absolute awareness
of that one moment is the total awareness of a whole
day, of a whole life-time. Of the whole history of the
human race, I'm sure, if you were to concentrate hard
enough.

It's a bit like looking into a rock-pool on the edge of
the sea. Not a stranded one. One that still has the water
flowing into it and out of it. You stare into that rock-
pool, long and hard. Watching the little swirls of sand in
the bottom. The heaving to and fro of the tiny little
strands of wrack. Then you become conscious that this
is not just an isolated pool. It is part of the bay. And the
bay is part of the ocean. And the ocean is vast and sur-
rounds the whole world with water. And all of that
water is flowing into and out of this little rock-pool. Do
you know what I mean? What you're staring at is not
just a puddle of water, you're staring at the vast mea-
sureless bottomless ocean. Am I making sense?

What calm. Only a moment left. The wall looming.
But a moment left. A total moment. A day. A lifetime.

It began - the end, I mean - when I glanced through
the back door of the van. My mind splattered like an egg

that has been dropped from a great height, if you can picture that. That's how I felt. Shocked, confused, sick. But above all, utterly alone. I was a small boy again, and the teacher had asked me a question, some silly simple question that everyone had the answer to, had it pat, all but I, and I was standing in terrified awe before the sheer mystery of the question. And all were laughing at me, laughing because they knew the answer and belonged, laughing because I was different and outside and didn't know the answer, laughing because they wanted to remain they and not become me.

I was gutted. Angry. Disappointed. This was a state of mind I had been constantly trying to put behind me, constantly trying to exclude from the new me. But here it was once more. As if I was still that child. As if I could never become a normal person. As if the last couple of years had counted for nothing.

I slammed the sullen door. Bolted it. Jumped into the cab and accelerated away from the vicinity of the church. Up through the village I drove like a rampaging bull. Across the bridge. Then I took a lunging sharp left towards the sea. I was frantic. It was the only thing I could think of doing. Driving out into the sea, to end it all. End the pain. It was an overwhelming urge. But not a surprising one. Many times in my life I had contemplated such an end. Contemplated following my father's footsteps.

This was a by-road, narrow, bumpy. I had the accelerator pedal jammed to the floor. The old van was lurching and heaving. Eventually it hit a hump on the road and gave an almighty bounce, banging my head off the roof. Only then did I release the pedal, slacken the pace. Approaching the shore I was dismayed, frustrated, to be confronted by the wide band of dark exposed rock. Typical of my luck. The frigging tide was out.

I wheeled around to the right just before the shoreline and slowed down to a crawl. It was difficult to

10

take my eyes off the road and continue steering the van, so I cast quick glances along the dark rocks and at the tide sulking in the distance. Bitch. There was deep water nowhere, not even at the tip of the pier. There was so much bare rock it must have been a spring tide, and fully out at that. I followed this thin ribbon of a road that wound around the shore, up and down, over and back, as if it had been worn from a cow-path. But nowhere, nowhere did the tide offer me even the hint of an invitation. Finally the shore road entered the Cimin, an expanse of commonage that was pock-marked with little sand-pits. I drove up on the grass, steering my way carefully between two of the sand-pits and halted. I needed time. To think. To work out a strategy. To decide.

"Let me out of here you half-wit." His Reverence in the back of the van, banging on the side, on the roof, thumping with his fists. Half-wit. What the world called me, but never His Reverence. Not until now. Always polite as mince pie was His Reverence. "Stop this immediately, you fool. Let me out of here at once, or I'll have your soul roasted on the hottest spit in hell."

I laughed at that. My kind of laugh. A grunt of a laugh. Out loud. But there was no mirth in it. What a threat. If his Hell existed, then we were all on our way to it. Myself. The French whore. But the hottest spit would be reserved specially for His Reverence. And well he deserved it.

I could not understand her. I could not understand. A priest. Especially His Reverence. He who sat with my pious mother and my pious aunt in the parlour, making conversation about religion, and the church, and the conversion of Russia. Night after night. Sipping tea out of china cups. Nibbling sweet cake, bought specially, kept jealously, for such entertainment. A priest, for frig's sake. And here I was once more, looking at the world from the outside. Looking at it in total bewilderment.

11

That morning His Reverence had halted me on the road, had slowed down in his black Audi as he approached, had waved his black arm up and down, up and down, until the van and the Audi had come to a stop alongside one another on the road. Windows rolled down. He was speaking up at me.

"The mission has started, Tommy. Aren't you going to service it this year? "

I was looking down into the plush interior of the Audi. His question seemed simple enough. Innocent enough. But it was the leer on his face that unnerved me. The leer on his face. And the way his eyes settled on the back of the van. As if he knew. But how could he know? Who would have gone telling him? Confused, as always in such situations, I could think of nothing to say. Frigging nothing. So I just continued staring like an idiot at that leering face in the shiny black car.

"Two evenings into the mission, and no stall outside the church. We're falling down. What?"

Under pressure. I went on staring, conscious of my jaw adrift, conscious of my face reddening.

"I'll expect to see you parked outside this evening then. The mission wouldn't be the same without the stall outside. Never break a custom. That's an old saying. Did you ever hear it? It's a good motto. A good motto."

With a smooth confident acceleration he was gone, leaving me staring at the place where his leering face had been.

This was the kind of situation I hated. The kind of situation that had always been my undoing. I was no use under pressure. I could not think clearly. My brain went to pieces. Became hopelessly muddled. Useless. Commanded by His Reverence to be outside the church, I could not think of any sensible ploy. Any plausible excuse. I had nothing to sell. Not so much as a string of rosary beads. I was bringing Michelle around and she was in the back. No stock whatsoever. And there wasn't enough time to bring Michelle back to Sligo, return home, load the stock, and get to the church in time for the mission. Not enough time by a long shot.

It would have been a relief to talk to her about it. But how could I? She would not understand. Anyway, my stuttering efforts at talk were awkward at the best of times, in situations like this I clammed up into total silence. No, I was on my own. As always. And, as always, I made a horse's collar of it.

The missions had been the main-stay of my business. I could not afford to dump them. Could not afford to snub His slick Reverence. So I decided the best thing to do was to put in a token appearance, to park the van outside the church while the parishioners were inside at the service, and then to strike off before they emerged. People would have noticed my movements. The publican, for example, loitering outside the door of his empty premises. The men huddled inside the porch of the church. Someone would have noticed me. Of that I could be certain. And when the faithful came out, clamouring for scapulars, and miraculous medals, and holy water bottles, the word would go round that, yes, I had been there, but had driven off suddenly. That way I would have shown my continued interest in the mission. And by the time I had to explain myself the following day, I would have thought up a good excuse for my abrupt departure. That had been my plan.

But the sheer stupidity of the plan was quickly exposed. Even though the service was still on, His Reverence emerged from the church door brisk as a spring calf. Evidently he was surplus to requirements on the altar, the missioners having assumed responsibility.

"Ah Tommy, you came. All ready for business. " His leer was more than disconcerting now; it was downright alarming, as he strode towards the back door of the van. Panic-stricken, almost paralysed by terror, I tried to think of some way of distracting him. I managed to struggle out of the cab and lumbered leaden-footed towards the back.

"I suppose we should inspect the goods. Give them the old imprimatur. Before you start distributing them to the faithful, you know. What do you say, Tommy? Eh?"

He opened the door and hopped nimbly into the back of the van before I could intercept him. The door swung shut behind him.

I was left riveted to the ground, staring at the back door of the van, not knowing what to do, my jaw, no doubt, hanging down to my knees. There was a black spot just under the handle, kidney-shaped, where a tiny bit of the red paint had been chipped off. Normally I would not have noticed if all the paint had disappeared off the van overnight, but there I was, my eyes glued to this little spot, examining it as if it foreshadowed the imminent disintegration of the whole vehicle. It had been there so frigging long there was rust beginning to ooze through the black undercoat.

I don't know how long I was standing there like a fool studying this scab on the back door of the van, but it seemed an eternity. If time stands still when you're enjoying yourself, it must go backwards when you're sweating acid.

I was expecting His Reverence to burst forth from the van doors, irate, triumphant, threatening damnation, or, worst of all, threatening to tell my mother. But there was no sign of him. I was puzzled. Perhaps he was going to take a softer line. Talk to Michelle about the wickedness of her ways. Convert her. Save her soul. But no, he was from the side of the Creator. More likely to be chastising her, indulging his righteousness, wreaking his anger, subjecting her to abysmal humiliation.

This image of Michelle being brow-beaten by the man in cloth eventually began to loosen me up. The terror began to melt. My mind began to clear. Anger and indignation welled up in me, flushed away the dregs of my terror. I reached up, opened the van door, and, holding it slightly ajar, I peered inside.

The gasp that erupted from the pit of my stomach, the weird guttural ejaculation that escaped from my vocal chords, brought the priest's head around with a jerk. Our eyes met. The expression on the priest's face was one of intense petulance, annoyance at the intrusion, as if I had no right to be there. I could not see Michelle's face, but it was evident that she was party to what was going on.

Then that feeling once again. That sensation that you are a blow-in from another frigging planet. That it is you who is utterly defective. That you haven't even the vaguest understanding of the simplest principles governing life on earth, life as it is being lived by other human beings. There he is, this lap-dog of the Creator, this arch gob-shite, doing unspeakable things in the back of my van, and he looks at me as if I should know better than to go key-holing on him.

Of one thing I was now absolutely sure - how he had found out about Michelle. It explained the leer on his face. The timing was too significant to be coincidental. And I, of all people, should have anticipated it. There was no excuse. More than anyone, I knew what happened every time the mission came around. I knew how the black hounds of the Creator were unleashed on the innocent sinners, how they went sniffing and sniffing around the parish, until all strays were rounded up and delivered to the pens for purging and for reinstalling among the flocks of the compliant. Yes they were all lined up for confession. And what would they do but trot out the story of their misdemeanours, revealing all, about Michelle, about the van, about me? It had been as inevitable as night follows day, yet I had not anticipated it.

I cursed myself. Cursed the cringing penitents in the confessional boxes thrashing their chests, begging for forgiveness. They might get forgiveness from the Creator. No doubt they would. They had turned over to him. Traitors all. Sheep was what they aspired to be. Sheep they would be. With the black hounds of the Creator squatting outside the pens to make sure no one made a bolt for freedom. Did they give even a thought to the fact that they were betraying me? Maybe they did. And maybe they were all now having a great long laugh at my expense. Maybe so. Maybe so indeed.

2

THE BANGING CONTINUED ON THE BACK of the van, but the Cimin was remote. Not a house around. And no one could approach within earshot without my seeing them. So His Reverence could thump all he liked, could thump until his fist was worn to the bone. No one would hear him. Still, his noise was unnerving me. And I needed calm. Peace. In order to think clearly. Funny the way you need peace to think clearly, and the very time you need to think clearly is when you have no peace at all. Frigging ironic, isn't it?

I tried breathing deeply. It didn't work. I closed my eyes tightly. Concentrated. Tiny little globules floated around aimlessly like frog-spawn on the red pond inside my eyelids. I didn't like that. I have always hated that. And my mind was still seized. And when I opened my eyes the sea was still blue, and hard, and far away.

I lit a cigarette. Fire. I could burn the van. With the three of us inside. That would be good. Appropriate. His Reverence would get a roasting before he reached Hell at all. Very appropriate. How to carry it out was the problem. How to achieve it with myself in the van. Disastrous if I survived having torched the other two. More disastrous still if I managed to incinerate myself in the cab and allow the two in the back to escape.

No, the sea was best on every count. The most attractive. And it was a guarantee that we would all sink together. In front of me was the brooding old cliff called the Alt. Facing north, it always presented a dark face to the world, and the black shadows of caves and crevices made it appear even more sombre and more ominous. If only I could drive the

17

van to the top of that cliff, I would be sure of deep water when I hurtled over, sure of a quick snuff at the end of the plunge. But there was no road to the top of the Alt. Boulders and bare rock marked the conclusion of the shore road just beyond the stretch of commonage.

But there were other cliffs. The whole coast was lined with frigging cliffs. I could surely find one with a causeway. Specially made for tipping vans full of whores, priests, and idiots. And if anyone could find it, it should be me. I knew the roads and the by-roads of Tireragh as well as I knew my own garden. Every lane and every boreen in the countryside. I'd been over them often enough.

My mind was still not very clear, but at least that much was decided. That much was resolved. I was becoming calmer. Lit another cigarette. Looking out at the Cimin through the haze of tobacco smoke, a chill of loneliness passed over me. It wasn't caused solely by my plight; the place had always affected me like that. The sea, stretching to the north, always appeared steel cold, never tempered by an overseeing sun. Pale on the horizon was a braid of mountains. Knocknarea. Ben Bulben. Farther off, the Donegal Mountains. So far-off, so pale, they could be shoring back the ice-floes of the Arctic.

Beside me, all around me, were the little stretches of low stone wall the local men used for drying the slatamaras. Sheegans, they were called. They plucked another memory, those stone walls, causing another surge of loneliness. As if I wasn't bad enough.

The memory was of my father. I pulled deeply on the cigarette. Pulled so deeply I might have been dragging up smoke from the very ground beneath me. What I would have given for my father's hand on my shoulder. Even a reassuring wink from him in that oblique impish manner of his. My recollections of my father were scant and faint. But I remembered his wink. When he was all intent on something he was doing, and I was watching him like a hawk, that's when he would glance at me, sideways, and give his little wink, conspiratorially, his face otherwise dead-pan.

My father died before I was five years old. But he was a presence in my mind every day of my life since then. His physical features I kept in sharp focus by browsing whenever I got a chance through the few old photographs that were stored in a biscuit tin at home. Little events, things he said, things he did, I recalled clearly myself. Like frying chops on a Sunday morning before going to mass. Much to my mother's irritation. To her mind everyone should be fasting from the previous midnight in order to be in a proper state to receive communion. My father was like that. Quiet, but persistent. With little winning ways. Everyone seemed to like him. Except my mother. Which had always appeared odd to me, considering that she had married him.

I recalled him on the Cimin. Sitting on one of those low stone walls. Among the sand-pits and the patches of hungry grass. I was nestling in the hollow of his lap. He was describing how the shore road had been built. Back in his grandfather's time. Maybe his great-grandfather's. A relief project. Hundreds of men, women, children. Working in teams. The men and boys doing the heavy work. Probably. The women and girls doing the lighter work, or bringing the meals. Stirabout mostly. That was porridge, he explained. Each family with a stretch of road to finish. So many people in those days. So many people. The shore road must have looked like a wheat-field on the day of harvesting. Paid enough to keep starvation at bay. Just enough. And the road was still there. Their legacy. Even though it had to be repaired frequently when it was battered by winter storms. And I snuggled closer into my father's lap, as though to shelter from those imagined storms. The pictures that he created, the cadence of his voice, even his very words, sinking into my child's mind. There to remain. To grow. So that whenever I saw the shore road afterwards, I saw it from the time of its making, down through its frequent repairing, to the day my father sat with me on his lap on the low stone wall. Down to the present day.

My father's death did not impact on me as a single event. He seemed to disappear from my life. I heard the words "dead" and "drowned", but I was not involved, and the words meant nothing to me at the time. People looked at me in a strange way for a while afterwards, but they never mentioned my father. My mother never mentioned him either. So, as I have said, he just disappeared without trace out of my life. And I copied everyone else and also stopped mentioning his name. But I remembered him. Day in, day out. There were times I wanted to scream out his name, to call him back, to tell him I needed him. And how I needed him. But then that's the story of my frigging life. Isn't it?

How I needed him now! Have you ever ached for someone? I mean really ached. Felt a gaping pain deep inside you – a chasm which that person only can fill. I'm sure you have. And so have I. Many times. Many times. What advice would he give me if he were here? Well, he would certainly be able to give me plenty of advice shortly, because I would be joining him, wouldn't I? Out there in the depths. Yes, that was definitely the way. No other way to silence the pounding in the back of the van, no other way to shake the agony that was eating me to the very marrow. Betrayal. I thought I had friends. Thought I had done some good for them. Relieved some of their pain. And they had betrayed me. I thought I had known them. Felt that I could have trusted them with my life. Now I questioned whether I had known them at all. Questioned whether I could ever know anybody. And Michelle. She was more of a mystery than ever. Yes, the sea, the sea it had to be, and the sooner I found a congenial cliff the better.

The cliff I would most like to drive over was Aughris Head. Plenty of deep water there. Even the fleeting thought of it made me giddy. Now that was a cliff. The highest I had ever seen. Its dizzy, dizzy height induced vertigo at the merest thinking of it. I had walked along the top of it as a child. My mother was showing a visiting nun the great cleft called Cor a d'Tonn. I was there as an appendage. Tagging along. The nun holding me by the hand. My proximity to the edge had terrified me. Then and ever afterwards. Had disturbed my sleep with the sensation of falling, falling, depth beyond depths.

Standing over the gigantic cleft in the rock-face, the nun seemed stunned to silence. I was listening while my mother explained to the occasionally nodding nun all about the Cor a d'Tonn, the choir of the waves, how the waves in storm rush into this cleft and on into a huge sea-cavern that extends the cleft deep underground, compressing the air within, then withdrawing, releasing the air, like a slow powerful note exhaled from a gigantic bag-pipes. On the day of a heavy swell the extraordinary lament could be heard on the other side of the Ox Mountains.

Some people, my mother was expounding, maintained that the lament was for the plight of Ireland. But she had it on good authority that the waves were lamenting the wickedness and depravity of mankind. And she could prove it. She brought us around to the other side of the gorge and pointed out the imprint of horse's hooves. There they were, clear as daylight, in the solid rock, as if the rock had been as impressionable as kneaded clay. A priest, in Penal Times, had to jump his horse across the gorge to escape from his persecutors. And that was where he had landed. Wasn't that evidence of ingrained wickedness that a priest should be hunted like a wild animal? Prevented from saying mass, from visiting the sick, from anointing the dying. What else would the waves be lamenting but that such wickedness should exist in the very garden of the saints?

That brave tormented priest, the sheer drop beneath the flight of his horse, made as powerful an impression on my mind as he did on the rock. I thought about him by day, dreamt about him by night. I wanted to become a priest.

On Sundays, kneeling in the front pew of the church, I watched every move of the priest as he celebrated mass on the raised altar, listened to every syllable he uttered. And when he lifted the bread in the hushed awe of consecration, I was breathless with wonder. Saw myself in his robes effecting that same miracle, the miracle of transforming bread into the body of Jesus. And I saw myself descending to the rails below with the body of Jesus, distributing it to the people so that they too could share in this sacrifice. Yes, I wanted to be a priest.

Of course I realised that I had to wait to grow up before I could become a priest, a wait that seemed interminable. The hours were long in our house, and the days were like boring visitors who just wouldn't go away. Waiting to grow up was therefore harrowing. But wait I did. Patiently. And I relished the thought of how proud my mother would be when I told her I was going to be a priest. In the mean time it was a secret, my secret. There were times when I was tempted to reveal my secret, times when she was in such a dark mood, and not talking to me for days on end, that I thought of lightening her life by announcing that I was going to be a priest. However, I refrained, and kept my mouth shut, something which had always come natural to me anyway. It was a great comfort to me, all the same, to have this trump card in reserve for when I needed it most. And the older I grew the more I realised I would need such a trump card because of my inadequacies.

Yes. My frigging inadequacies. That is the real story of my life. Obviously I was wanting from the day I was born, but I suppose my intense awareness of being inadequate began the day I started school. I was the new boy that morning, the only one starting. It was not the school my mother taught in, so she dropped me off on the way to her own school, in the black Morris Minor. She brought me into the school yard and called one of the older girls to mind me until Mrs Murnane arrived. I was petrified. Already the other children were eyeing me with smirks on their faces. Well, why wouldn't they? I could see immediately that I stood out like a goose in a duck pond. I was dressed in a black suit with long trousers, for frig's sake. All the other boys in their coarse short trousers and frayed jumpers.

Mrs Murnane arrived and they all ran to line up immediately. The older girl into whose care I had been given held me firmly, self-importantly, by the hand and marched me up to the teacher. She nodded coldly, as if she had been expecting me, and pointed to the line of Junior Infants. We filed in to the school. All went well for a while. The teacher busied herself calling the roll, checking copybooks, setting classes work to do. I began to feel easy, no longer the focus of attention. Until Mrs. Murnane asked me a question. The class of Junior Infants was standing in a semi-circle around the teacher. She was holding up charts on each of which was a single letter. Suddenly she turned to me, and she asked, " What is your name?"

That floored me. I did not understand. What did she mean? She knew my name. Everyone knew my name. I was Tommy Loftus. So that could not be what she was asking me. It had to be more complicated than that. I was still trying to unravel what exactly she was trying to find out when she barked again, " What is your name?"

I was utterly confused. How could she be asking what my name was when she knew what my name was? I was also unnerved by her tone. I looked into her hard sharp face but found no clue there. I felt my neck getting sweaty under my tight shirt-collar. My face burning like a coal. I did not want to make a fool of myself. Confusion. Anxiety. Embarrassment. All swirling around in my brain. And my mind went blank.

Then it happened. A warm sensation flowing gently down my leg. I knew what it was and hoped and hoped, prayed, that the long trouser legs would soak it, that no one would notice. But the warm sensation reached my ankles, and when I glanced down I was dismayed to see the trickle worm its way across the floor, etching a stark trail over the dusty floor-boards. An eruption of jeering laughter from the other children had, at least, the saving grace of dissipating the tension. Even the teacher's hard features softened into a slight supercilious sneer. The older children rising from their desks. Look. Did you see what he did? Pandemonium. And the teacher seemed in no hurry to restore order.

She asked me no more questions that day. But when people came in there was much whispering. Much nodding in my direction. I caught the whiff of conversations. Why did she not bring him to her own school? Ashamed? Do-do. And that evening Mrs Murnane clearly took a satisfying pleasure in relating the incident back to my mother when she came to collect me. Again I heard the word 'do-do' used to describe me.

Thus my school career started, and thus it was to continue. But no matter how woefully I floundered, no matter how pitiably I froze in the face of the barbed ice that was directed at me by the teacher, I did not despair in those early days at school. I still had my dream. Still stood on a rock of hope. My secret. A heroic future. I was going to be a priest. I would command their respect, even against their will. Might gain even their approval.

Even their affection. But definitely their respect. It would be a different story then with those who mocked me and jeered me. It would be a different story with the hard-faced bitch of a teacher, with her questions that I could not answer. With her smirk of satisfaction when she saw my terror and my confusion. The smirk would be on the other side of her razor-bill then. It would be a different story too with my mother.

The suspicion frequently crossed my mind that Mrs Murnane was right, that my mother was ashamed to bring me to her own school. She never explained her decision to me, and whenever I raised the question she brushed me off with declarations that I would be closer to home in that school, that I would make friends with local children. These didn't seem very good reasons to me, as I experienced nothing but ridicule from my fellow pupils in those early days. Her moods grew darker and she was always short-tempered with me when we returned home in the evening. No doubt the result of the stories she was being told about me. On such evenings I was tempted to cheer her up by breaking the news of my glorious future. But I held back, vaguely conscious that, though those days might be bleak, there could be bleaker days to follow.

Finally, I could hold out no longer. It was a dark wet evening, I remember well, one of those evenings when the rain seems to hang suspended in the air, and the clouds seem to be pressing down on the very chimney pots of the houses. Mrs Murnane had engaged my mother in a long peevish conversation, so we were late reaching home. The dinner that Aunt Brigid had cooked tasted cold and stale. Not only did my mother freeze me out, she also blacked out my aunt. No conversation. Dark looks. Movements tense. The usual, but worse. Much worse. When she had eaten her dinner, she went down to her room and banged the door shut.

After a while I timidly opened the door. She was lying on the bed staring at the ceiling. She didn't break the stare even to acknowledge my entry. I went over to the side of the bed and hesitantly called her. She didn't move. I took a gulp of breath, stuck out my chest and announced, with as much panache as I could muster, that I was going to be a priest when I grew up.

She revolved her head slowly on the pillow until she was looking at me straight in the face. I was waiting for the joy to well up in her eyes. The pride. The exultation. Instead, her upper lip curled into a sneer. The same dark expression. Cold. Her words like an icy wind. She said you need brains to be a priest, that the Creator hadn't seen fit to bless me with brains, and if the Creator hadn't given me brains then he certainly didn't want me to be a priest. She revolved her head back on the pillow and resumed staring at the ceiling.

I was demolished. All my ideals, all my hopes, all my dreams, squashed. As when someone brings down a heavy boot upon a snail, a snail that has its own shape and size, its own pace and sense of purpose, and reduces it to a shapeless inanimate blob of slime and grit. That's how I felt. I knew I was defective, inadequate. I had accepted that. But I had no idea that that defect, that inadequacy, could stand between me and my dream of becoming a priest. No idea at all.

Can you imagine my frigging desolation? My inadequacy was a bar to the priesthood. I had no hope. An idiot. Couldn't answer a simple question like what is your name. Or, how much is two and two. Wet my trousers, I did, instead of answering a question. And there was no place for such a person in the Church. No vacancy. I could frig off, myself and my handicaps. I wasn't needed. The Creator had something else in mind when he put me together.

I had been able to bear the shame of my inadequacy while I had my dream. Now, there was nothing. I was the school idiot, and there was no salvation. No escape. And the legend of my stupidity was travelling far and wide. A teacher's son. How they marvelled, and laughed. Children from my school would point me out to children from other schools. The wonder of the seven parishes. Can't read. Can't write. Turns scarlet when asked a question. And from behind my back, the taunts: how much is two and two? what is your name? Now, no longer, could I find solace in dreams of an heroic future.

I brooded on the sense of justice of a God who had left me a couple of cards short when he was dealing out the hands to potential priests. Brooded on this perverse Creator with deep resentment.

Up until now I had listened intently to every word spoken during Sunday mass, the Epistle and the Gospel, the reading from the Old Testament, the reading from the New Testament. All in the line of business, as it were. If I was going to be a priest, then I needed to know as much as possible about religion. And when I went home I tested myself on how much I remembered. I could recall almost everything. Could probably have repeated it to myself word for word. Now I listened just as intently to the readings, but with resentment, trying to unravel the logic of this being who had discarded me even as he had created me. And the more I listened, the less I liked this Creator. Jesus was alright, but I couldn't understand what Jesus saw in the God who, for example, tortured and killed the poor Egyptians when he could just as easily have whisked the Jews back to Israel.

From then on a nun or a priest coming to the house was as welcome as a lone magpie. I resented them. Every frigging one of them. I resented the constant reminder that God had eliminated me from his calculations. I resented the attention that my mother lavished on these scavenging magpies. But the more resentful I became, the more pious my mother and my aunt seemed to become. They dedicated more and more of their time, and their energy, and their money, to the church and to the clergy. It was always they who organised the Women's Sodality, and the meetings of the Pioneer Total Abstinence Association. It was they who decked the altar with flowers for the Feast Days. It was they who cooked dinner for the priests whenever their housekeepers were absent. While my wounds were festering away underneath my own silence.

3

WHAT PEACE. THIS PEACE BEFORE THE impact of the wall. What light in the deep shadow of death. Am I careering towards the wall, or is the wall careering towards me? Right now it's a stand-off. Peace. Calm. Maybe my days have gone careering on without me and I am already outside. An observer? Anyway, the depth of this peace I have never experienced before. Ironic. My problem always has been that I have buckled, collapsed, disintegrated, in moments of the slightest intensity. And here I am in the most enormous crisis, poised between life and death, and all I feel is utter calm. Total clarity. Frigging ironic alright. If I could bottle some of this peace like oasis water and go back to cross the same desert again, how different it would be. How frigging different.

I tried everything over the years to eliminate the fluster, the confusion. Like smoking. It didn't help either, but I enjoyed it, and when I was under stress I smoked like a clapped-out engine. Sitting in the van on the Cimin, I was going through the packet of Sweet Afton one by one in rapid succession. The cab was filling up with a haze of blue smoke, its opaqueness contrasting with the clear bright evening outside. His Reverence was managing to keep up the racket in the back of the van, but for a change there was no one to listen to his thundering. Not what he was used to. Not what he was used to at all. Through the mirror I kept an eye on the winding road from Easkey. The road I had just come. Deserted. With the dark silhouette of the castle standing guard over the coast. In front of me no one could approach unless he came down the Wrack Road, a by-road from Killeenduff. I was secure for the moment. I could think. If I could manage to ignore the thumping of His Reverence.

My tongue was beginning to parch and burn from the continuous smoking. But, frig it, there was no point in worrying about a sore tongue when you were planning to drive over a cliff. One way of curing it. Not much point either in having fags left in your pocket when you took the plunge.

She it was who introduced me to smoking. On those late evenings out by the lake. French cigarettes she used to smoke at first. The way she held them, delicately, fingers straight. The way she put them to her puckered lips as if she were kissing the tips of her fingers. And the exhaled smoke like blown kisses, spreading its aroma out on the evening air. Across the dark waters of the lake. Up the craggy mountain slopes. Into my mind. No wonder I associated cigarette smoke with tranquillity.

No wonder I started puffing them myself. Sweet Afton I chose. Because I liked the packet. Even when I was a child I loved to see men pulling out those yellow packets. The picture of the Scottish poet, Robert Burns. The incomprehensible squiggles underneath, which I knew, nevertheless, to be the lines of a poem. I knew them by heart, had got someone to read them to me one time. Had never forgotten them. Flow gently, sweet Afton, among thy green braes, Flow gently, I'll sing thee a song in thy praise.

Through the haze of tobacco smoke I was looking at the cattle grazing in the sloping fields of Lower Killeen. Realised that I was seeing this landscape for the last time. The last time. What feelings that unleashed. What varied feelings. Love and hate. Yes to the very extremes. And many others. Even nostalgia. Even frigging nostalgia. Even the Cimin was steeped in association, quite apart from the memory of my father that I have told you about, quite apart from the ghosts of those hungry people who built the shore

30

road. I recalled going winkle-picking among the rocks, waiting for the fisherman's boat to return from the sea laden to the gunwale with pollock and mackerel, playing in the sand bunkers when I was a child. But the associations were not limited to my own memories. From my listening to old men and old women ruminating down through the years I had developed a sense of the past of things. The castle, for, instance. When I looked at its familiar outline now in the wing mirror I saw a derelict in grey stone, as anyone else might have seen it. I loved it even as it was. Even as a grey derelict. But it was never as simple as that with me. There was the other dimension. The past. The old people had recounted how the castle had once spanned the river. When the O'Dowds were chieftains. And the bountiful river that flowed through the courtyard brought fish to the very door of the kitchen where the cook had a device for hauling one in whenever he required some for the table. Wasn't that clever? Convenient? It was probably in the castle also that Dubhaltach, the last of the McFirbis clan of scholars and historians, ended his days, writing and recording the history of the whole country. Yes, when I looked on the castle I saw these things too. I saw it as a hub of activity for the whole of Tireragh. And because I saw these things, it was to me much more than a pile of grey stones perched on a headland with only the seabirds left to provide the sound of living.

I had been staring too long at the image of the castle in the wing mirror, had forgotten to keep an eye to the front, had failed to notice the elderly couple strolling down the road towards me from that direction. They had emerged from the bottom of the Wrack Road and were now within a hundred yards of me. I recognised them. Retired teachers. Not mine. Not mine. A nice couple. They walked the Shore Road interminably .

Quickly I revved the engine to a roar, and threw it into gear. Tossed the butt of my cigarette out the window. I pulled off the grass and back on to the road. I accelerated as rapidly as I could. And when they saw me coming they stepped up on the verge to let me by. I gave a long blare on the horn as I passed them in order to smother any noise His Reverence might be making. My animated salute was greeted with a polite smile, a nod, a restrained finger-wave. I watched them through the wing-mirror. They had turned to continue their stroll. Relief. Evidently their suspicions had not been aroused.

Climbing away from the sea, up the slopes of the Wrack Road, the engine roaring away, I began to feel more secure. Even the thumping and shouting had ceased. Presumably he was getting tired. Or his fists were sore. Good enough for him. He would be worse, a lot worse, by the time I had finished with him.

I tried to put him out of my mind and concentrate on the road. The roads that I had loved. The roads that had become my element. The roads that I was now travelling for the last time. This reflection caused me to slow down automatically. If it was the last time, then I wanted to have a good gaze at them. I wanted to bid my farewell. I knew the roads of Tireragh intimately. Oh, how intimately I knew them. Every rise and dip. Every jagged pothole. Every gap in the hedge alongside. I slowed down more. To look closer. To concentrate. To re-create the emotion that I had always experienced every time I began to move through the open countryside. The exhilaration. The sheer joy of it.

How different this journey had been in those days after I was presented with the freedom of the road. The delight I took in the van. Every bump and every hollow, every cluster of nettles, every rusting bedstead masquerading as a gate, all belonged to an astonishing new world, and I gazed at them then, as I gazed at them now, in wonder.

At the top of the Wrack Road there was a junction, the Forge Corner. Not much trace of the forges left, where generations of blacksmiths had smitten metal over anvils inside their dark dens. Only the crumbling walls of the last forge. That and the lingering wisps in the memories of the old people, the enduring reputations of the blacksmiths in the rambling narratives or the concise anecdotes that I had listened to with such relish.

To my left, the road to Sligo town. Ballina to my right. This road had been the artery of all my journeying. I turned left, still going slowly, passing the front gates to cottages that no longer existed. Just stones in a field. Like Munns's house. I remembered an old man, Tom Mannion, refer casually to Munns's house in the company of much younger people. They were mystified. Thought he had lost the thread of his own conversation and called him to account. He was equally mystified to find that they did not know where Munns's house was, and referred them to this heap of stones in the field to my left.

The Split Rock was coming up on my right, and I slowed down even more. For a last glimpse. One of my favourite landmarks. The story was that Fionn Mac Cumhaill and a rival were standing on the distant Ox Mountains. Challenged each other to a stone-throwing contest. Fionn took up this boulder and cast it as far as this spot. His rival took up the other stone and hurled it all the way to the sea-shore about a mile further on. Fionn was so angry at losing the contest that he demonstrated his strength by slicing his stone with his little finger. Some wallop. I paused to look over the wall. But the squat bulk of the giant rock appeared broken to me now. Broken rather than split. Why all so bleak? My final tour of paradise before the plunge into hell, all should be coloured with nostalgia. But no. Bleak and cold. Yes, this was my paradise, alright, and my hell; hell was nothing more than paradise without the glow.

How different it was in those heady days when I first took the freedom of the road in the van. Those were days of unqualified bliss. The glow was in the landscape then alright. Every twist of the road was a brush of warm familiarity. Lumbering along, unhurried because I was still mastering the skill of driving, I was singing. Not aloud. That would not be me. But inside. In my mind. In my heart. In the furthest reaches of my soul. How I was singing. How I loved the ancient stone walls that accompanied the road wherever it went, like two tipsy companions escorting a drunken friend, staggering, falling, standing, as I passed by. I loved the hedgerows, the lush growth of weeds, so verdant, especially during the summer when they threatened to smother the delicate stretch of tar altogether and make people forget the very thought of travelling.

It was the lure of travelling and exploring that brought me out as far as the Split Rock in the beginning. When I was a child. That, and an ever-present urge to get away from my own house. To get away from the constant visitation by the magpies. To get away from my mother's coldness. I had come to the conclusion that I would never be a credit to my mother, no matter how hard I tried. And I did try. Even after all ambition had been quashed. I tried to please. I wanted to be liked. Even to be accepted. But the harder I tried, the more ludicrous my efforts seemed, the more of an embarrassment to her I became. My stupidity was becoming legendary. The unending cycle of stories was told over and over to illustrate how unbelievably obtuse I really was. Told for unending entertainment. Told right in front of my own face, for frig's sake. On the assumption that I was too thick to understand, or that my ability to feel pain was diminished in proportion to my ability at answering questions in school. Perhaps they thought that I was amused by the stories, that I enjoyed hearing them repeated as much as they did. Like the one about the long hairy line. Did you hear the one about the long hairy line? No? Go on, you must have. Everyone has heard about the long hairy line. Not you? I don't believe it. Alright. I'll tell you. If I don't, someone else surely will.

You remember how I kept getting caught out because I thought the answer to a question must be much more complex and obscure than it really was. Like, 'what is your name?' All I had to answer was, 'my name is Tommy Loftus', and I was safe. On the pig's back. But under the pressure of the moment I didn't realise that, did I? No, instead, I wet my trousers trying to unravel the tangled threads of meaning in the question. It was afterwards, when given time to reflect, and I was given plenty of time to reflect in between my debacles, I realised there was no complexity in the question at all, that the simple answer was the correct frigging answer. Anyway. This day Mrs Murnane was teaching us Geography. A map of Ireland drawn on the blackboard. All kinds of lines and squiggles all over the map. Most of the time she left me alone, and I was happy to be dreaming away. But then sometimes she would suddenly pounce on me. Just to show that everyone was entitled to a share of the caning, I suppose. She turned to me. Pointed to the blackboard. Rasping voice. "What is that?" I looked at the tip of her cane which had come to rest inside the map of Ireland. Consternation. As frigging always. I could feel the beetroot boiling in my cheeks. Total confusion. Sweating. Under my collar. In my armpits. Every frigging where. "What-is-that?" rasped the emphatic but trembling voice again. I saw the point of the cane was beginning to spread like a hen's foot, she was jamming it so hard into the map of Ireland. Her bile was rising. I was terrified. Had to say something. The flaking would be worse if I said nothing. I looked at the board. I was always getting caught out by not recognising the simplicity of a question. So this time I decided to try the obvious. As it happened, she was pointing to the Ox Mountain range, which was signified by the usual symbol. I looked hard, and told her what it was: "a long hairy line, Miss."

There were repressed explosions of laughter all over the class. Repressed, because they knew Mrs Murnane was not in an indulgent mood. Not by a long shot. Her face had tightened. Whatever little red had been in her lips had turned to fine strokes of lime whiteness. As a tense hush fell, she walked down to me. With the tip of her cane she raised my right hand into the receiving position. Quick swishes. She delivered five powerful slaps on that hand. Then the other hand. Same procedure. The cane had totally disintegrated from the impact of the slaps. She threw it in the bin. Went to the press, and from a large paper-wrapped parcel she drew another one. Fresh. Hard. Imbued with latent pain. It held the gaze of the scholars. And they were silent. She proceeded with her lesson, and I followed every move and twitch of the new cane with fascination. Was there a factory for producing these canes? Were people employed putting the curls on the handles? Testing them for sting? And did these people ever think of the children who would be at the receiving end of the punishment? My classmates may have had similar thoughts, but they maintained total concentration until break-time.

Then the explosions. Uninhibited. Everyone contorted in spasms of laughter. Children from other classes running over to hear the story. They in turn falling into convulsions. "Did you hear about Lofty?" "A long hairy line, Miss." There was so much laughing in the school that day, they should have called a holiday. A frigging carnival. At least the mortification I was suffering in my mind distracted from the aching of my two hands. For months afterwards I had to endure the cat-calls, 'a long hairy line, Miss.' Until some fresh story replaced it. Capped it.

No doubt these stories all made their way back to my mother, and she distanced herself from me more and more. Not that she had ever been close, for frig's sake. But you know what I mean. Cold. She got colder. And when she was in the house I was tense and sweating for fear I would do anything to annoy her. The relief when I stepped outside the door was amazing. It was instant. It was physical. Like an electric switch turning off the power.

The shed was my first retreat. And I could spend the whole day there if I wanted to. No call for meals. No anxious mother or aunt peering in to make sure I was alright. Just as well. In the shed there was no tension. I could escape. Relax. Dream. And it was no inconvenience to me to spend my whole day dreaming.

It was a wonderful place, the shed. Built with large stones lightly cemented together, it squatted in among the fuschia and the boundary walls, its back to the wind that blew constantly off the sea. It always felt snug inside. The crude wooden door had a bolt on the outside, with a pad-lock which was never used. No one stole things in our locality. Anyway there was nothing in the shed worth stealing. Bits of old bicycles. Boxes of rags. A few tools that must have belonged to my father. There was a small window, green, caked with dust and old cob-webs. Underneath it a tea-chest turned upside down provided me with a place to sit. And there I sat and dreamed. Not of being a priest anymore. But vague engrossing dreams. You know the kind. Sometimes playing as well. Gathering up pebbles and pretending they were cattle. The top of the tea-chest was my farm. And I put out my cattle to graze. All I had to do was watch them graze. Occasionally I would move them to ensure they grazed the fields evenly. Apart from that I sat and watched. Happy, and free from pressure. You know the feeling. But then maybe you don't. Maybe no one else has spent the most enjoyable part of his childhood gazing at a little cluster of pebbles on top of a tea-chest.

Yes, the shed was my first place of refuge. From my mother. From the black tension that she radiated. From the world outside the garden gate where children jeered and laughed at me, where adults even smiled when they looked at me, as if they were remembering the last joke they had heard about me or all the stories that had given them so much frigging amusement in the past. That's what I saw behind their smiles.

At school my torture continued through the year of Low Infants, through High Infants, into First Class. I was left behind while my class-mates learned to read and write, to do arithmetic and geography. Therefore there were more and more opportunities to play tricks on me, to make fun of me. And they grasped every opportunity, relished every little satisfaction in demonstrating their superiority.

Until a single event changed everything. I was in the corner of the school yard with a crowd of my class-mates around me. Asking me things. Prodding me. Trying to make me say something silly. So they could jeer and laugh and tell everyone the latest Lofty story. Then a boy who was in the class immediately above ours broke off kicking a tin can around in a football game with his friends. He came over and roughly cut his way through the baying crowd. They stood back silently looking at him.

"I want to let you know that he's my cousin, and the next person who says a word to him or about him will get my fist rammed down his throat." And he held up a clenched fist with bone-white knuckles.

The silenced crowd drifted backwards in awe.

"But he's my cousin too," said one of the boys who had been tormenting me.

"And mine," said another.

"And mine."

"Then why don't you leave him alone?" asked the older boy. It was an order as well as a question.

38

There was no answer. A few shrugs. Uncomfortable looks on their faces. That was all.

And that took the wind from the sails of my persecutors. The beginning of a new era opened up dramatically for me by the incantation of that single magical word, 'cousin'.

I recited the word over and over. It had no meaning for me. When I asked at the dinner table what the word meant, all I got was a derisive snort from my mother, a contemptuous roll of the eyes to heaven.

Of course I had heard the word before and had built up a vague understanding of the term as meaning some kind of bond. But what this bond was I did not understand, and was curious to find out.

Unencumbered now at break-time in school I followed Jimmy Scott around like a sheep-dog. But he didn't seem to mind. He was my 'cousin'.

Jimmy's house was not far out the road, about half way between my house and the school. I took to walking home in the afternoons now that I was not being taunted and jeered. One such afternoon, as we reached his gate, Jimmy invited me in. The kind of invitation that is neither question not command. You know the kind. And I ended up following him into his house.

His mother was in the kitchen slicing up bread. There was a pot of tea in the middle of the table. Jimmy's two older sisters were already sitting down and buttering slices of the bread. They glanced at me as I stood inside the door, feeling like an intruder, about to retreat. But they passed no more heed, as if it was normal for someone to wander into their house. His mother greeted me very warmly and placed another chair at the table for me to sit on. She put a slice of the soda cake in front of me and handed me a knife to do my own buttering.

To this day I can still taste that soda bread. The fresh smell of it. The hard crispy crust. The butter lumps refusing to spread or melt. And there was an atmosphere in that kitchen that I had never experienced before. Peace. Relaxation. As if it was tuned in to some kind of natural harmony. Do you know what I mean? A peace and harmony that was not just of the moment - that was permanent and pervasive. At least that's what I felt while I ate my slice of bread and drank my mug of tea, as if I belonged in this house.

Afterwards, outside, I asked Jimmy what a cousin was.

"Your father and my mother were first cousins. Right? That means that you and I are second cousins."

I was obviously looking perplexed, so he brought me back in to his mother.

"Will you tell him what a cousin is?"

"Your father's father, your grandfather in other words, and my father were brothers. So your father and I were first cousins. In other words we had the same grandfather and grandmother. Do you understand?"

Of course I could follow that. And I loved the way they explained it to me in a normal way. You know. As if I wasn't a half-wit.

I was late home from school that evening. But apart from a casual question from my aunt as to what kept me, there was no fuss. And that was my cue to start rambling, as it was called.

Rambling became my passion and my chief preoccupation. At first it was out to Scotts I went. Every chance I got. It was the warmth in the house that drew me. No frigging wonder, coming from the freezing wastes of my own house. There was an ease in the way they talked to one another, parents and children. There was a natural wholesome quality even about the way they shouted at each other when they were fighting and arguing. Yes, it was a change from the frigid restraint which was the way we conducted our relationships at home.

40

Cousins. I discovered them everywhere. Everything that moved I seemed to be related to it. And these cousins seemed to think it natural for me to hover about their houses until I was invited in. And once I gained admission I came back again and again. Just to sit in the corner. Just to watch. To listen.

They were so different. These people. These cousins. It was as if some warm spring of human nature bubbled to the surface from their midst. They were poor. They had troubles and anxieties like everyone else. More than everyone else, for frig's sake. They were rearing their children for the boat. No prospects of work or comfort. Their future was loneliness for the parents, England or America for the children. They knew that. Were aware of that. Spoke about it. Cursed it, even. And yet they took each day as if it was a gift of incredible riches.

Yes, they were special. These cousins. Far removed from the dry and lifeless conversations that were taking place in our front parlour between my mother, my aunt, and their clerical callers.

Still I had to be grateful for small indulgences. And I found it hard to believe I was being given so much freedom. Even when I was away from morning until night there was no fuss, nothing more that the polite enquiry as to whether I had eaten or not. And I always had. Whatever house I rambled into I was fed there. So I didn't have to return home for dinner or for tea. Sometimes I even came home after the family rosary was recited, but there was still no reprimand.

The one family engagement which I was not allowed to renege on was mass on Sunday. I was dressed up by my aunt in a suit and a white shirt with a tie. The three of us always marched up to the front seat. I found it exceedingly dull. What the magpies had to say was always banal. And it was frustrating not being able to examine the congregation. Whenever I turned around to have a peek, my mother would jerk her bony elbow into my shoulder. That wasn't pleasant, so I concentrated on the altar instead.

Anyway, I was still very interested in the Creator and I paid the utmost attention whenever he was mentioned. I loved the readings from the Old Testament, especially whenever the priest announced 'from the Book of Exodus'. It was reassuring to find that he was no great shakes himself. The Creator. I had it in for him since the day my mother revealed that he had left me short-changed at birth. It didn't surprise me, therefore when I found him ordering Abraham to kill his own son. As a sacrifice. To him. To honour him. What kind of a pervert was he? And look at all he did to the poor Egyptians. He hardened their hearts so that they wouldn't let his chosen people go, and that gave him the excuse to send plagues and to slaughter them. A nice way to behave, when he was responsible for the Egyptians as well as the Israelites. There were plenty of readings like that from the Bible, and they did me the world of good. The Gospel was interesting too, because Jesus seemed to have his doubts about the Creator as well. He told the people to put aside the Ten Commandments, that there were only two commandments: love God and love your neighbour. There wasn't much love of your neighbour going on in the Old Testament, I'll tell you that, and I had listened closely. An eye for an eye and a tooth for a tooth. And it was this God of the Old Testament, the Creator, that I blamed for my deficiency. It helped to be able to identify him, to picture him in my mind's eye, to lay responsibility for my disappointment squarely at his feet.

So, at least, I did get some satisfaction out of going to mass. And apart from mass-time, I was allowed to wander as I wished. When other children were ordered home to do their housework or to do their exercises for school, I was free to roam the neighbourhood. My mother was a teacher, so there was no farm work to be

42

done, like feeding the pigs, milking cows, or forking out dung from stables. Those were the kind of chores other boys had waiting for them when they went home. And as for school exercises, what could an idiot do in the line of exercises when he thought a mountain range was a long hairy line? Instead I visited my cousins and my neighbours, working from house to house until I had got to know everybody from the village out to the Split Rock.

The old people were the most interesting of all. And many of the houses had only old people in them. Old people living alone. Old people in pairs. Sometimes a house-full of them, all growing old together. And they talked to me. Talked to me endlessly. Talked to me about everything. Even though I never talked back. And they were all different. Tom Connor always managed to have a bar of chocolate for me every time I called, even though he lived like a hermit and was never to be seen in the shops. Lily and Lolly, two old ladies who had spent time in America when they were young, kept peacocks and guinea fowl as pets and had a huge grandfather clock inside their front door.

Now you know why the Split Rock was special. It was the boundary mark of a very particular territory, a territory that was closest of all to my heart. Difficult to say goodbye. It was with great reluctance that I began to move past it, that I began to accelerate again up Kilcullen's hill.

4

YES, IT WAS THIS VAN THAT OPENED UP the roads of Tireragh to me. Giddy with excitement, I must have been a danger to myself and to everyone else in those early days. Not just because of my inexperienced driving. Sometimes my eyes were not even on the road, so fascinated was I by the knobs and dials and buttons that bejewelled the inside of the cab. I drove along with one eye on the road, the other on the dazzling array of dials. Long after I had learned to use them properly, I still played with the knobs and switches, flashing the headlights in the middle of the day, just for the fun of it, beeping the horn to salute a cow with its serious face gaping through the rungs of a gate, switching the crackling radio on and off for the sheer thrill of operating the knob.

It was my mother bought me the van. With the little business thrown in. For that I must be grateful to her. She attributed that particular piece of inspiration to the Holy Spirit. Whoever inspired her deserved a medal. If they could do with another medal. Probably not. Probably blue in the face looking at medals, even if it is their own pictures that are on them. Anyway. It solved my mother's problem about me. Her many problems, more likely. Above all, her frigging anxiety that I would bring even more disgrace on her. Up until then she showed nothing but distaste for anything to do with me, so she was obviously motivated by a desire to have me off her hands. That's what I felt anyway. Nevertheless, the outcome couldn't have suited me better.

By this time I was eighteen and becoming even more estranged from my mother. Not that we had ever been close. No. She had been ashamed of me from the day I was born. Without doubt. Ashamed because of

44

my handicap. My stupidity. Even my frigging appearance, I imagine. I suppose it was no wonder when you consider it. After all didn't I share her opinion? Didn't I despise myself? Wasn't I repulsed when I looked in the mirror and saw this round face with small round pig's eyes in round glasses staring back at me? A mouth hanging permanently open, no matter how much I tried to remember to keep it closed. Yes, it turned my own frigging stomach to look at myself in the mirror, so, in a way, why should I blame my mother for feeling as she did about me.

Even the glasses didn't change my appearance. When I was getting the glasses, I hoped I would look a bit more intelligent. But instead they seemed to emphasise the vacancy of my staring eyes. Anyway, the humiliation I associated with the event itself left me with a very negative disposition towards the same frigging glasses. Did I tell you that story? About the testing? No? Well you can imagine the problem. The optician came to the school and set up her gear to test all the children one after the other. When she put me sitting down and asked me to read off the letters on the test card, she was clearly puzzled.

"Can you read none of those letters?" she asked me in a slightly bewildered tone, "Your sight is quite bad so."

She put a frame over my eyes and slotted in two lenses which brought up the letters so clear and so stark they were almost prodding the eyes out of me. Yet I could not read them. For the obvious reason. And of course the usual panic and paralysis had set in anyway, so that my eyes were watering, and my face was burning, and drops of sweat were running into rivulets down my forehead and in behind the frame.

The optician detected my distress and began to fluster. "It's all right. Those are the strongest lenses I brought with me. But I can get stronger. I'll bring stronger ones when I come back next time. Or perhaps your parents might bring you to my shop in Sligo, and we will fix you up, don't worry."

She went to consult with the teacher. I could see the two huddled heads talking intently and throwing glances in my direction. Eventually the optician returned. She started talking to me in this weird tone, pronouncing each syllable slowly, as if she thought I was deaf as well as blind. As if she was talking to a baby in a pram who couldn't understand what she was saying.

"Now, litt - le - boy. Take - this - chart. It - has all - the - same - lett - ers - that - are - on - the - screen, and - when - I - point - out - a - lett - er - on - the - screen, see - if - you - can - pick - it - out -on - your - chart. Do you understand? Good. Now - we - will - start."

The procedure was simple. And it worked. I was able to match the letters without difficulty. Pointing them out with my finger. And I got a pair of glasses that helped me to see things in the distance. Things I was not able to see before. Innnishmurray swelling from the sea on a clear calm day. The white specks of houses on the side of the Ox Mountains. And I was delighted. Yet the humiliation of being treated like a total moron was a feeling I always associated with my glasses. So, no, they did not make me look or feel more intelligent.

My mother's way of coping with my disability, I think, was to disown me. You are your father's son, she hissed at me under her teeth one day when the black mood was upon her. The remark cut deep at the time because I knew it was not meant as a compliment. I was also amazed because she never referred to my father unless she had to. But when the hurt had eased, the remark had another effect on me. It made me curious. More than curious. If I were like him I wanted to know more about him. However, the mention of his name at home was akin to opening a door on a wintry night and letting in an icy draught. How dare

I? Had I no feelings? No sense of decency? In other words, what kind of a monster was I to even whisper his name?

My aunt Brigid was a little more forthcoming when my mother was not around. He had been a great athlete, she said. There was no one in the seven parishes could beat him at running or jumping. A great swimmer too. There she stopped. As if she had already gone too far. Aunt Brigid was one of those quiet self-effacing people, who was defined, and probably defined herself, in relation to my mother. She was the sister of Mrs Loftus. Mrs Loftus, the teacher. She was a kind of shadow to my mother. Did the housework while my mother was out teaching, but apart from that she accompanied my mother everywhere, did everything my mother did. So I knew she would not wander far beyond the limits that had been set down.

In order to find out more about my father, I began to quiz the cousins, who were all his relations. His brothers and sisters had emigrated to America when they were young, and needless to say they did not communicate with my mother. I doubt if she was sending them Christmas cards either. But he had cousins around. Lots of them. All over the place. On every side. A whole cluster of them lived in a row of cottages just outside the village. They were wild and rough, infamous for drinking and fighting, and I liked them a lot. And they seemed to like me. Always greeted me and spoke to me warmly and naturally. As if they never even noticed I was different. Just accepted me as another person. Never mocked me. I was a normal human being to them. I also liked the way they talked freely, without inhibition, about everyone. It was sheer entertainment to sit back and listen while they tore strips off those who draped themselves in pretension. Even my mother. Especially my mother. She walks so straight and haughty, you'd think she had a ram-rod up her arse. The airs of her as if her piss was Eau-de-Cologne.

You'd think she didn't have to fart like the rest of us. Such comments. And I took no offence.

About my father, on the other hand, they had never a bad word. He was different. Nice to everyone. Not rough like them, they said. Should have gone to school. Should have gone to college. He would have done well. He was that type. But he didn't. Go to school or college. Didn't leave either. He stayed, and married the school teacher. Worse thing that ever happened to him. Cold bitch. A wonder she married at all. A wonder she didn't keep her legs crossed for Jesus. No surprise that the poor man did himself in. Yes, that's what they said. As bluntly as that. Just as if I was one of them. The poor man did himself in.

That was the unofficial version. But probably true. The official version was different. He had gone swimming and was swept away by a powerful tidal wave. Not true, said the cousins, the tidal wave came afterwards, the normal angry reaction of the sea to a drowning. He had declared his intention of swimming across the mouth of Cuangearr, from one headland to the other, not a great distance for a powerful swimmer like himself. Yes, said the cousins, but even the tinker's ass knows that at the mouth of Cuangearr is a huge submerged rock called Temple Rock which causes such currents and swirls that the fishermen steer well clear of it when they are putting out to sea, and if the fishermen give it a wide berth for fear it will suck down a boat, what chance had a swimmer? No, he was not a fool. He knew what he was doing. Sure, he put a face on it. Bragged about swimming across the mouth of the bay. But he knew he would never reach the further shore. And sure enough his body was never found.

Yes, I became very attached to my clan of cousins. No matter which road I took out of the village of Easkey I had cousins on every side. They had the smallest farms, and many of them had no land at all. They had the biggest families, and were no doubt the poorest, but on the other hand they had personality and exuberance which I could never find among wealthier neighbours.

My favourite family among all the cousins was, of course, the Scotts. From the day Jimmy took my part in school we became friends, and I tended to visit his house more often than the other people's houses.

In the evenings, after school, Jimmy would bring me up through the fields, hunting rabbits. There were wonderful fields up behind his house, belonging to a neglectful farmer called Walter Tuffy who spent most of his life in the pubs arguing about politics and criticising the government for the way they were running the country. Everyone joked about him. They said, there he is spouting out of him as to how the country should be run, and the thistles and the buachallans are growing so tall in his fields that they're looking out at you over the walls. Anyway, we loved his fields. A wilderness. Clumps of furze bushes. Old ditches that were porous with rabbit burrows. Thistles, with purple burrs on the top of them and little patches of grass around their stems where the sheep nibbled fastidiously at a safe distance. And Walter was never around to bother us.

Jimmy had a mangy little dog called Bran, which had the temperament of a terrier and behaved like a terrier, but had the outward appearance of a dwarf greyhound. He looked the business alright even if he wasn't quite Fionn Mac Cumhaill's wolfhound, from whom he had acquired the name. Jimmy and I beat the whin bushes to flush out any rabbit or hare that might be having an afternoon nap. And as soon as it hit the open ground, Bran was after it like a flash. Well that was the way it was supposed to be, and we did catch the odd one. But Bran was an unfocused bugger. Easily distracted. Full of energy, he would chase around sniffing and smelling every tuft and every rabbit hole, as if he meant serious business; but, more

49

often than not, he went on energetically sniffing and smelling even after the hare or rabbit had started from under his nose and chased off across the open field with us gazing helplessly after it.

Anyway, we had good fun. And whenever we caught a rabbit or a hare, Jimmy's mother would cook it for the dinner. We felt like lords tucking into the delicious tender meat, knowing that it was we who had put it on the table. One evening we caught three rabbits and Jimmy urged me to bring one of them home. Reluctantly I agreed. He selected a big plump healthy-looking one, the finest we had ever caught. My mother was correcting copies and drinking a cup of tea beside the range when I went in with the rabbit. She reacted with alarmed disgust, as if the rabbit had died of some disease, and ordered me to throw it in the garbage bin immediately. No cooking there. I wouldn't mind, but she went out and bought one from the butcher's van the following day. Is there any explaining that?

When we finished in the primary school Jimmy and I went our different ways. Like many of the other boys and girls, Jimmy took the boat to England. Over to his older brothers and sisters who had settled in London. Nothing like that for me. So, I just hung around, rambling from one house to another, getting my dinner here, my tea there, making myself inconspicuous while people talked.

And how they talked. Especially the old people. They talked freely. Never looking for a response. As if I wasn't there. Yet it was my being there which stimulated them to talk. They went on about the old days, spinning yarns about characters who had lived before their fathers' fathers. They confided personal problems and disappointments. They imparted scurrilous information about their neighbours. Perhaps they assumed that I could not understand a word they said. Just because I was silent. Just because I was the half-wit. But I understood alright, and remembered.

Remembered everything. Often I could have corrected them on something factual that they had got wrong. But the sound of my own voice would have been enough to strike me with paralysis. Probably would have struck anyone else with frigging paralysis as well, they had become so accustomed to the easy silence I had cultivated and practised. It suited me. People accepted me as the half-wit, so why should I disturb our relationship by correcting them, or pointing out that they were contradicting today what they had said in my presence no more than a year earlier. No, it was better to let things be and not distress myself by getting into an argument for which I was ill equipped with my stuttering monosyllables and my embarrassed red face. It was better to maintain silence. And listen.

As I have told you, my mother had a peculiarly ambiguous attitude to my constant rambling from house to house. On the one hand she never prevented me from wandering, never enquired as to where I'd been, never complained no matter how late in the evening I returned. On the other hand, she was in a continuous state of umbrage that I should want to spend my time with those people, as she called them. However, she did start objecting when she began to spot me regularly loitering on the street corners in the village. Corner boys, was what she called those who congregated at the Post Office or on the bridge every evening for a chat. What she found objectionable in that I could never fathom, since they were the same boys and men I met in my rambles around the countryside.

When I turned eighteen and tentatively mentioned that I was thinking of collecting the dole like everyone else, she became agitated, to put it frigging mildly. Talked about jobs immediately. My going away to some place where I would be looked after. I didn't like the sound of that option. Anyway, as I have said, inspiration struck. Lucky for me. She fell into conversation with Stephen Hanlon one day. She had been rummaging through his stall searching among the array of religious objects for a medal of St Christopher. Ever since the Pope had abolished himself and St Philomena, my mother had increased her devotion to them. Refused to believe that they never existed. Saints, who had looked down so benignly on the human race for centuries, had carried the burden of its supplication, the weight of its great need, how could anyone turn around just like that and say that they never existed? Even the Pope. Especially the Pope.

Having failed to unearth a medal of St Christopher, she had browsed through the rest of the stall and eventually settled on a statue of Blessed Martin de Porres. Why she needed another statue was a puzzle, because the house was filled with statues of every saint and martyr known to man. It was probably because this fellow wasn't a saint yet, and might be pushier than the rest, seeing that he was in the shake-up for promotion. Stephen Hanlon was a trader in religious goods, whose van and canvas-covered stall had been a feature of religious events and fair-days for almost half-a-century.

My mother was lamenting the decline of piety, exemplified by the abolition of saints. More saints we needed, not fewer. Stephen concurred, pointing out that the abolition of saints had a detrimental effect on his business. St Christopher medals had been a steady line. A bread-and-butter line. Did the Pope realise that when he was abolishing him? Business was scant enough without the Pope cutting swaths out of it by abolishing saints. It wasn't like the old days when the business was lucrative and such losses could have been shrugged off. Then there had been a demand for objects of piety. But not any more. Not any more. Now it barely sustained him. Anyway, he was getting too old. It was time for him to retire. He had four sons, all set up in good professions. So there was no further need for him to endure the rigours of weather and travel. It wasn't like the old days when there were half-a-dozen stalls outside a church the week of a mission, and all doing well. There was banter and bustle, and camaraderie. Now that was gone. No fun. Only himself left. And scarcely the turn-over to justify his continuing on the road.

According to my mother, she couldn't sleep that night, pondering the conversation. In school the next day she set the students working by themselves, doing revision, while her mind continued to be pre-occupied. As soon as the bell rang at three o'clock she sat into her car and drove the twenty miles to Stephen Hanlon's house. There she was greeted with surprise, but much civility, and was brought into the parlour, in deference to her position as a school-teacher. There over tea and home-made soda bread, she hammered out a deal with Stephen Hanlon. All this she recounted more to my aunt than to me when she returned.

She never said how much she had paid. Money was not regarded as a suitable subject for conversation. She agreed to buy the business from Stephen at the end of the season, when he had planned to retire. The deal included the van, the stall, the stock, the goodwill. In addition, he agreed to take me on straight away, as an unpaid apprentice, and teach me everything I would need to know about the business. And he would teach me to drive the van.

My mother was overjoyed. Well, 'overjoyed' might not be the right word. It might give the wrong impression of my mother. Let's say she was pleased. She smiled. And she even talked to me. Well, a little anyway, and in an indirect kind of fahion. It would suit me down to the ground. A small business. And in the religious line too. Yes, divine inspiration. No doubt with the help of St Philomena or St Christopher, just to show that they were still around. Just to show they still had influence. Yes, St Christopher it had to be. Patron saint of travel. And he would continue to look after me, my mother said.

I had no objection to St Christopher looking after me, especially as he no longer existed. But the very thought of this venture left me petrified. Frigging petrified. Such was its enormity. How could I? I who could neither read nor write. Could neither add nor subtract. I was the half-wit. How could I run a business? And how could I drive a van? A van? For frig's sake! Whenever I was a passenger in my mother's car, she still made me sit in the back seat, even when the front seat was vacant. So I had never so much as watched how a car was driven. A van. It was impossible.

Slowly the possibility of it began to penetrate to my imagination. Wild fantasies of worth and importance. They were shut down abruptly at first. Only to return. Appearing more reasonable and logical and familiar every time. Stirring up dreams of independence, and purpose, and standing. My peers, those I met on the bridge or at the Post Office corner, were all from farming backgrounds or labouring backgrounds. Nearly all of them drew the dole, but they also worked on the family farm, or had little side-lines which earned them a few bob to jingle in their pockets. I had nothing. My mother gave me the money if I wanted to go to the cinema, or if I wanted to buy an ice-cream. But always the exact amount. Not a penny more. She could hardly be described as mean or miserly. No, she was generous, considering all she spent on the church. But that was the kind she was. Measured. Precise. She gave you what you asked. If she approved, of course. Not a penny less. Not a penny more. Therefore the prospect of having my own income with the freedom to do what I liked with it was more than exciting. It was exhilarating. It was awesome. And the prospect of having a van, and driving it - it took many days before I managed to get that into my head.

5

THE PRESENT MOMENT IS THE MOST important moment in your life. Especially if it's your last frigging moment. Then it is your frigging life. Laden with the past, pregnant with the future. It is eternal and infinite. Time is not like a river, no matter what anyone says. It is more of a lake, or a puddle, a scoop of water trapped in the bottom of a tar-barrel. Your birth is an event, like a pebble falling on the surface of the pool, and it sets up a sequence of ripples circling outwards and outwards. Looking down on the ripples you can observe the whole pattern at once, from the centre to the outer circle. Have you ever noticed that?

This idea does not come to me now, spontaneously, at this highly significant moment of my frigging life. Not at all. It was an idea that came to me many years ago. I was about sixteen, when William Flately committed suicide by ducking himself head first into a rain-water barrel. A converted tar-barrel, you know the type. I knew Billy Flately. He was a quiet man who went about his business and was polite to everyone, and apart from being polite to everyone, he kept himself to himself, as everyone said and repeated afterwards.

I was shocked. My father's death had cast a shadow about me, of course, and I had brooded on it ceaselessly, but the event itself had happened totally unknown to me. Understanding its significance was something that came to me only afterwards and gradually. It was different with Billy Flately. He was the first person that I was aware of actually committing suicide.

I was also fascinated. How could a grown man manage to drown himself in a water barrel? Of course officially, it was an accident: the poor man slipped while he was retrieving something from the bottom of the barrel. Therefore he could be buried in the cemetery beside his mother and father.

And so began my interest in tar-barrels. There was always one or two outside every house, catching the rain, or more often the drizzle, that was forever condensing on the roof, that trickled into the gutters, and dribbled through the downpipe. Some people had timber barrels, but it was mostly old tar-barrels that were used to catch the rain-water. They were in plentiful supply, as the tar for road-repairing was delivered in these metal barrels and, more often than not, they were left thrown in ditches after the road-workers had moved on. When the residue of tar hardened and dried it sealed the inside of the metal barrels against rust so that they lasted for years. Even after people had the spring water piped into their houses, they kept the barrels for rain-water. Better for washing they said, and the tar was good for the complexion.

For a long time after Billy Flately's suicide, I could not resist looking into any barrel I came across. Have you ever done that? Looked into a tarbarrel? Jet black. It's difficult to detect where the surface of the water is. The first thing you see is the big disk reflecting the sky. Very blue on a good day. But then of course you see your own grotesque face staring blankly back at you as if it is wondering what the hell you are doing looking down into a barrel. But forget about your ugly face. Ignore it if you can for a moment. Concentrate on the disk of still water. Now drop a pebble into the centre of the disk and watch the magic of the ripples working their way out in perfect circles until they reach the rim. Then, wham, they turn back again, and you have two movements of circles, one moving from the centre out and one moving from the outside in. And if you could follow the movements you should be able to see the first circle return to the single point it started from.

I was mesmerised by this exercise of dropping pebbles into tar-barrels. Then one day I was looking down into a barrel, far down, as there was only a small amount of water in the bottom. I started looking at my own dark shadow blotting out the blue sky. And I thought, I'm just like him, like the Creator, looking down on the earth. On the whole frigging universe. Everything and everyone within his power. And he sets off ripples by dropping his own pebbles. But he has us all in his barrel and no matter how far the circles expand, it's eventually, wham, and back they go again. Always in his power. Always trapped.

Why did Billy Flately pitch himself into the centre of that pool? Why was his pain so great? He had no illness, no worries, no responsibilities. Just an ordinary man who was polite to everyone. Yet carrying around a pain so intense he had to snuff it out, as a blacksmith would snuff out a piece of red-hot steel. Who reddened that pain in Billy Flately? And why?

Well, it was obvious who was frigging responsible. Wouldn't you agree? The one who made Billy Flately. Who else? The same one that made me and put the idea in my mind of becoming a priest, while at the same time making sure that I couldn't by leaving me a mite short in the mental department. Did he enjoy this kind of mockery? And if he did, why? I listened more closely to the readings at mass. All I could figure out was that he was an insecure bugger, always getting worked up if he wasn't given the kind of respect that he demanded. Yes, there was something strange about the Creator, and I went on looking into barrels and trying to figure out what it was. Until people began to notice, and make jokes about it. Like a wet bag hanging over the side of the barrel. That's what they said I looked like. And so I had to do it privately, more surreptitiously. But that was no bother because I had my very own tar-barrel at the corner of the shed. Catching the sweating mist from the galvanised roof.

Now, here I am, about to experience the full impact of the Creator's wall. My particular ripple has reached its limit. What happens after that - who knows?

Are you familiar with the roads of Tireragh? With how wonderful they are. Every turn brings a new marvel. Driving up Kilcullen's hill, how I wished I had a different cargo. How I wished I could just dump His Reverence. Just take him to the sea and dump him. Get rid of him. The way a farmer gets rid of an unwanted dog by putting him in a bag with a stone inside and flinging him into the tide. That would be appropriate alright. Then there would be only Michelle and me. Once more. The way it had been. And even if she was in the back and couldn't see how Sligo Bay suddenly opened up before me when I crossed the brow of the hill, at least I could feel I was sharing the experience with her because she was so close. Now it was he who was close to her. And I resented that. But I also resented the quenching of the glow of paradise. The glow that had been there when I was travelling these same roads with Michelle. The glow that had been there long before that when I travelled the road with the van full to the brim with my wares. That had been there the day I set out with Stephen Hanlon to learn the business of the trader in religious goods. Now, the very same landscape, no glow. Not a glimmer. All cold and lifeless. Like the frigging corpse of someone you knew and loved. I'm sure you know what I'm talking about.

The sooner I found my cliff the better. So I turned down the by-road to the sea at Doonalton. On my left was the wooded river valley called Alternan. In the middle of it, the shrine called the Kieve. A place of pilgrimage for thousands of years. Before the Christians arrived, the people celebrated the feast of Lughnasa here. Worshipping the clear water that sprang from the rocks. Worshipping the green hazels laden with the bounty of the land. Celebrating the harvest. Celebrating life. Then St Farnan came and turned it into his own personal shrine. But the celebrations continued. Now in honour of the patron saint. The Pattern, they called it. Garland Sunday to the feast of the Assumption. The festival of Lughnasa, but in honour of the Saint. Marvellous place. Not much festivities any more. The clergy put an end to them. Dismal people. A tacky statue of St Patrick down there. For some reason. Probably came cheap. Italian job. Probably supplied indeed by Stephen Hanlon. He would have made a few bob on that deal alright.

Yes, it was probably Stephen who supplied it, without doubt. Knew his job inside out. Had a quiet way of talking with people, so that he found out what was happening. And when it was something in his line, people came automatically to him. As if it was natural. To ask his advice. In the end to give him the business.

There was nothing false in his dealings with people. Even where business was concerned. He never appeared to be grubbing for sales, he just let them fall his way. Naturally. People came up to talk to him. He was helpful. Reassuring. And he took pride in his knowledge and experience. If he made a sale, good and well, if he didn't, there was nothing lost.

And he seemed to be content to be passing on that knowledge and experience to me. Strange really. On the other hand, maybe not. I was the only one he had to take over from him at the end of his days. But, I suppose, the way he looked at it, better a half-wit than nobody. Better that than having to drive the van into a ditch and leave it there to rust into the earth.

It must have seemed a daunting task when he saw my first efforts. But he was so cool-headed. So totally relaxed. Whenever I expected him to get frustrated, or excited, or annoyed, it never happened. He would take out his pipe and slowly light it. By the time he had completed that operation he would be ready to re-focus his attention and deal with the crisis.

He tried to teach me the same technique. Keeping cool, that is.

"Listen, son," he said to me after he had been observing me for a few days. "Anyone can see you have a problem. There's no denying you have a problem. But it's only a problem. It's not the end of the world. What we've got to do is identify what the problem is and then find a way of solving it or else a way of getting around it. My opinion is that you are far too excitable. You get worked up about everything. If an old lady comes up to the stall to buy a statue of the Sacred Heart from you, that is a transaction, not a blooming crisis. So there is no need to get excited. No need to pump every ounce of blood from your toes up into your face. No need to blow fuses all over the place. The old lady is a customer, that's all. She does not see you as a person. She doesn't think of you as a person. She is not wondering whether you are happy or sad, whether you are carefree or laden down with the worries of the world. She wants a statue of the Sacred Heart, and she wants to give you the money. That's the height of it. So you've got to detach yourself. You've got to find the switches inside you and learn to switch on the brain and switch off the feelings. Then you'll be able to think with your brain alone, and not with your belly or your heart."

You know, that made sense to me. It was the first time in my life I got a bit of advice that actually made sense. And I began to work on it. I began to develop little techniques for staying cool. Detached. I would say, over and over, to myself : these are customers, not people. All they want from me is to be served. They don't know me. I don't know them. They are not interested in me, and I don't give a fiddler's curse about them. And it slowly began to have an effect. Whenever there was a problem, or

60

someone asked me a question I could not answer immediately, I tried to use his trick of taking a couple of steps back in rapt concentration, working out the response, and then turning back to the customer. But I couldn't manage it. I was too static. Like it or not, I was rooted to the ground, staring at the customer, mouth open no doubt. However, in my mind I followed his procedure. Switched off, thought about the problem, worked out the answer, then came back to the customer, so to speak.

He should have been a teacher. Stephen Hanlon. He had that kind of way with him. He would show me how to do something. Demonstrate it. Then invite me to have a go. Say, erecting the bars for the stall and pinning the canvas around it. When I got stuck, as I always did in the early days, he would step in. First of all he would point out how much I had got right. Focus on that first. Then, with my confidence boosted, he would show me where I had gone astray, and how to proceed. All of this in his calm and calming manner. Yes, Stephen should have been a teacher. He was great.

Soon I was harder to overawe. Guided by his gentle nudges, grunts, and nods, I began to learn the business. How to pack and unpack the stock. How to set up the stall from the back of the van. How to lay out the display of items so that people would see each one clearly.

"That's good, son, but do you think the rosary beads would look better hanging up somewhere?" he would ask in slow earnestness. And of course when I searched, I would discover there was a hook attached to an overhead bar perfectly placed for the hanging of rosary beads.

I loved the way he called me 'son'. It wasn't exactly a term of affection with him, but it wasn't patronising either. And it sounded so appropriate from him because of his age. He must have been seventy, but he was a very fresh seventy. Slight of build. Clear skin. White hair, but no sign of balding. He wore clothes more appropriate to a younger man. A short tweed overcoat, navy blue. Trousers that were cut slim on the legs. A soft hat, tweed, with a little feather in the band of it. And of course the pipe. Always there or thereabouts. If he wasn't smoking it, he was cleaning it out, or priming it with fresh tobacco. He used a brand called Clan, already flaked, which came in a green packet with a tartan design.

He called me 'son' and it seemed genuine, seemed to signify a bond between us. Which astonished me. I'm not saying I felt disowned by everyone else in the whole world. Not altogether disowned. The range of people's attitudes would have gone from cold contempt, in my mother's case, to indifference, in the case of most people, to a kind of warm acceptance by my cousins and all the old people I visited. The only person I ever felt really close to was my father. At least that's my memory of our brief relationship. But I was a child then, his child, so that was different. Now, here I was at eighteen, awkward and ugly, couldn't read nor write, couldn't put two words together towards a conversation, and yet this old man seemed to like me, seemed to have adopted me.

It was just as well he felt positive towards me, because he had to teach me the business one way or the other. My lack of the skills I should have picked up in school were the next obstacle.

"I've been watching you, son, and you get into a hell of a fluster whenever a person wants to buy more than one thing. You mustn't be too good at the old addition."

"No," I grunted.

"Yet, you know the price of everything. I'm amazed how smartly you picked up the prices."

"I'm good at remembering."

"Are you now?" he laughed. "Why don't we try you out then? We'll change the prices on a dozen items. I'll write them down as I call them out, and we'll see how many you can remember."

He took out his notebook and the little pencil that was sheathed in the spine. "Now," he said, and began to rattle off items from the stall, putting new prices on each one.

I concentrated, because I liked to impress him, and this was child's play to me. Concentrated on his voice. Registered it on my ear.

When he had finished, he paused. "Now, are you ready?"

I nodded. He called out items at random and I put a price on them. I could see him ticking them off as he called them out. When he called out the last one he lowered the notebook and looked at me. I gave him my answer.

"Bloody amazing," he said. "Every single one right. There's no one else that I know of who could do that. That's brilliant. Now, will we try out the additions?"

"Alright." I was delighted he had been impressed with my feat of memory, but I braced myself for the imminent fall.

"A customer buys two items costing seventeen pence and twenty eight pence. How much does he owe you?"

I struggled hard with the sum but could make no headway.

"How much is eight and seven?" he prompted me.

"Fifteen."

"How do you know that?"

"I learned my tables in school." Yes, learning tables had never been a problem. I learned then to the point of boredom, while listening to other children reciting theirs.

"If you know your tables, you should be able to add. Try this out. Make a picture in your head of a sheet of white paper. Right? Now put down twenty eight on that piece of paper. Right? Underneath that put seventeen. Right? Draw a line. Now add it up the way you would on a real sheet of paper."

I tried. Tried hard. But the figures on the piece of paper kept floating around and fading away. Like those magic notepads from Woolworth's from which the writing disappears as soon as you bend it. I wrote down the figures again, tried to concentrate more intensely on them, twenty eight, seventeen, but, as soon as I went to write an answer down, the original figures floated off the page.

Not that I would have been any better with an actual sheet of paper. Moments like these I grew impatient with him. Wanted to shout, look, I'm thick, can you not see that? Ask anyone. They'll tell you how thick I am. Frigging quick they'll tell you, with a hundred stories to prove the point.

But Stephen Hanlon was not one who let other people do his thinking for him. A problem was a problem until a solution was found. Or a way around the problem. A few days later he turned up with a calculator, the first I had ever seen.

"I think this might be the answer, son. You're a wizard at remembering prices. So all you have to do is clock them in here like this. Press the button here to add them up. Now if somebody gives you a bigger amount, and you have to subtract what he owes you, clock this in as well. Press this subtract button, and would you believe, there's the change you have to give him."

I couldn't believe it. A gadget to do all the things I could never manage. I took it from him as if it was gold, as if it was so fragile it might disintegrate in my hands. I felt like kneeling before the ingenuity of it. No mirage either. There it was. In my hands. A gadget. To add and subtract. Nothing could get the better of me anymore. With this gadget I could conquer the world.

I loved the business. I loved those plaster statues, those crucifixes, those rosary beads and scapulars. I loved them all. Laid them out with loving care. Took pride in knowing where to buy them wholesale, at what price. Knowing where they were manufactured. Italy mostly.

But the real ecstasy was in learning to drive the van. It was bliss even to sit in the cab. The upholstery worn away. Coming apart at the seams. The stuffed fibre peeping out. When my Aunt Brigid looked inside one day and noticed this, she threatened to crochet a set of seat covers. I hoped fervently she would forget about this. I preferred it the way it was. More manly. Coarse. In keeping with the used appearance of the van itself. Definitely no crocheted coverings. Yes, the rest of the cab was in character with the tattered upholstery. The paint on the dash was chipped off on protruding surfaces. The glass lens of the fuel gauge was cracked. Far from being blemishes, these were beauty spots to me. I could scarcely wait until the van was mine. Totally mine.

Driving along to a fair or a mission, Stephen used the time to train me. Always used the time.

"Now, son, get out the calculator. Mrs Murphy has come into some money, twenty pounds that her sister sent her from the States for her birthday. She is a very religious woman, Mrs Murphy, and she comes to your stall to buy presents for the whole family."

"Good old Mrs Murphy," I chirped in approval, as I set up the calculator on my knees.

"Now, she buys two miraculous medals on silver chains for Molly and Mary, the twins, at seventy five pence each, a new rosary beads for himself at one twenty five - he has the old one worn down to the chain praying for whatever nag he puts a few bob on out of his pension money every Friday, a mass card at sixty pence to send back to her sister, Dolly, in the States, after she has it signed by Father Dempsey himself, of course, a statue of the Child of Prague for the sitting-room to replace the one with the broken head that himself knocked down last Patrick's Day when he came staggering home, that's a big investment at four seventy five, and she almost forgot, another mass card for her cousin's anniversary that's coming up in a fortnight's time."

"Nothing like buying in time," I chirped.

"You pack that lot into the big shopping bag that she brought with her. She hands you her twenty quid. How much change will you give her?"

Tapping away on the calculator ignoring his deliberate rambling distractions, I reply confidently: " Her bill is eight seventy. She gives me twenty, so I give her back eleven thirty."

"Correct."

"Yahoo." I yelled in triumph.

"You'll have no bother," said Stephen. "No bother at all. If you can get that brain of yours working, there will be no stopping you. You remind me of one time I called to a house of certain friends of mine. When I sat down, the woman of the house put on the kettle, and asked me would I have an egg. I said I would. Over she went to this sparkling new washing machine that was standing in the corner, opened the lid, and took out an egg. I started laughing and said it was a strange place to keep her eggs. 'I might as well make some use of it,' says she. 'John in America sent over the money for it to Murrays' shop and they landed it up, as a surprise. John remembered how much scrubbing I did on the clothes every Monday and he thought that this machine would do the scrubbing for me. But I have been trying to figure out how it works, and the devil damn me, but I can't make head nor tail of it.' 'Did they give you a manual, a book of instructions?' said I. 'They did,' said she, taking it down from the dresser and putting it on the table in front of me. 'See if you can figure it out.' I started reading the manual and went over to look at the machine. There was something odd about it alright. Then I twigged it. It was the wrong manual. They had given her the instructions for a different model altogether. And do you know what I think? I think schools are a bit like that. They have one manual, one set of instructions, and a whole range of different models in front of them. And I'll tell you what, son, you were one of the models that didn't match their set of instructions. That's the only reason you got left behind. That's why you can't read or write. So if you'll take my advice, you'll search for the right set of instructions and start all over again trying to get that old washing machine of yours working. In the mean time every night you should kneel down beside your bed and say three times, 'I am not thick, just different.' Will you do that, son? And now it's time you took a little turn at the wheel."

And he halted on a stretch of open road. He got out slowly, walked around to the passenger door, while I clambered into the driving seat, my head full of wild possibilities, pincered between ecstatic excitement and terrified trepidation.

6

HAVE YOU EVER NOTICED HOW SCARCE something becomes when you discover you really need it? Even though your impression had been that there was an abundance. As with cliffs on the coast of Tireragh. Curious, isn't it? Ironic. The shore at Doonalton wasn't any more generous with its services. The road came to a full stop. Tantalising cliffs on either side, but not so much as a frigging goat-path leading up to them. Was there no consideration for people in my situation? I halted. I had no choice but to halt.

I had travelled these roads with Stephen, and later by myself, later again with Michelle, and had never taken note of such things as access to cliff-tops. Funny isn't it? It's only when your needs demand it that you really notice particular things or learn particular things.

That's the way it was, learning the business from Stephen. I had to, and I wanted to, so I did. But it was easy learning from Stephen. Long before, he had scaled down his operation; now, for my benefit, he began to take in all the old stands again. He wanted to show me the full extent of the business, as it was when it was at its peak, and therefore the full extent of its possibilities.

"Soon you'll be taking over yourself, son, and it's important that you realise all the options. It's better to know too much, and scrap what you don't need, than to be short of ideas. By the time we're finished, anything I know, you'll know."

So we set up in villages for the Fair Day, when the only livestock on offer might be a litter of pigs that a farmer was selling from the back of a car trailer. On

68

the Market Day in another village there might be a single youth tending a display of vegetables spread out on a low wall. Nevertheless, as soon as we set up, a trickle of people would approach, mainly older women.

"Stephen, how are you? We haven't seen you here in donkeys' years." And they would browse among the artefacts, probably out of nostalgia, but occasionally buying something.

"You see what I mean, son. You'll always sell something. Whether it's worth your time, and whether it pays for your petrol, is another matter. You'll have to work that one out for yourself. I knew the time when a village like this would be packed for the Fair Day. All kinds of animals, and all kinds of men trying to sell them. And hawkers like myself - there might be a half-dozen of us. All jostling and jockeying for the best positions in order to make the most money. Often the jostling would flare up into a fight. A fair day was never complete without two farmers skelping the daylight out of each other with their cattle-sticks or two hawkers kicking each other's stalls until they toppled. Where are they all now? Plenty of place for them now, but where are they? Probably over in England selling second-hand cars. No, son, there's no point in getting too worked-up. Don't compete. There's too much competition and aggression in the world as it is. And at the end of the day it comes to nothing. Look at this empty street where men drew blood from one another competing for the best pitch. They could have the whole street now. It's all a game, son, and someone else is always making up the rules. So don't play. You'll only encourage them if you do, because the rules will always suit them. Always. Stand back, and let them at it if they want to."

Stephen was treated like an old friend at the wholesalers, and we always made a day of it when we went in to town to order our stock. There was a season for many things, and the knack of buying at the wholesalers was

69

to take enough of the stock that was in season. Too much, and you might have the left-over on your hands until the following year. Too little, and the wholesaler might be cleaned out when you came back for more, so you would lose out on sales. Spring and early summer was the time for children's First Communion and Confirmation gear – prayer books, rosettes, white rosary beads. High summer there was great demand for Knock holy water bottles and statues of Our Lady of Lourdes. From Easter until Halloween there was a run of weddings, and so a demand for blank picture frames for the Papal Blessing – there was no demand for those during Lent or Advent.

During a mission, of course, you could sell almost anything. That was the best stand of all – outside the church gate the week of the mission. Yes. The missions were the spuds and cabbage of the business; the fairs and markets were only the gravy. The mission was a special week in every parish when the big guns were brought in to blast everyone out of the trenches of their worldliness. Sometimes a parish priest who was easy-going might short-change his congregation by bringing in a colleague from a neighbouring parish to conduct the ceremonies and give the talks. But it never worked, Stephen explained. He knew, because the failure of the mission was always reflected in the takings on the stall outside. Too watery. Too mediocre. No, you needed the men from the religious orders, fierce-looking men with tonsures and bare feet, who rolled up their sleeves and ranted from the altar. Best of all were the Redemptorists. They were the men who could conjure up hell-fire, who could direct fingers of hell-flame to singe the backsides of the most hardened sinners. Who could put the fear of God into the most cynical boyos and send them out after the service, panting for holy-water bottles, scapulars, missals, statues, pictures of Our Lady of Perpetual Succour.

70

Yes, the Redemptorists were the men. And you could see it in the sales from the stall.

"If ever you hear of Redemptorists giving a mission," continued Stephen, "be sure to be parked outside that church. One time I hit upon a pair of Redemptorists, from Limerick, who were booked to do a whole series of missions all over the province of Connaught. They were so good that I followed them around week after week. Slept in the van, I did. And boy could they drink whiskey and polish off their T Bone steaks. But the harder they drank, the more hell-fire they gave the congregation next day. Unbelievable. They had the congregation steamed-up, terrified out of their wits, evening after evening, men and women, even children, so that when they came out of the church they descended on the stall like locusts. Cleaned it out. I followed them all over Connaught for ten weeks, and, at the end of that time, I was able to go home and buy a new van, this one in fact."

One day I observed to him that I had never seen him go into a church, in spite of the fact that we were permanently parked outside. He smiled wryly and gave me a sharp glance.

"Well, the way I look at it, son, there has to be some perk going with this job."

Learning to drive the van I found most difficult. I was terrified at the beginning. Petrified. Because I wanted it so much. And the enormity of being able to drive the van was utterly daunting. Stephen was patient. Whenever we had time on the road, or a free day, he would put me practising. The clutch. The brakes. The throttle. The gear-lever. And of course the steering wheel. At first I was afraid of the controls. Until one day, Stephen hardened his voice.

"Listen, son, you've got to relax, and get it into your head that nothing is that difficult. If it was hard to drive a car every yob in the country wouldn't be tearing around on four wheels. Relax, man. Keep cool. And

71

remember to let your head do the thinking. Stop feeling that you can't do it, and let your head tell you that you can.

His words helped, but the terror was still there. However, it became a delicious terror. Eyes fixed on the road, the steering wheel in a stiff clasp, foot poised over the clutch pedal, I careered along the road at twenty miles an hour. Wheee. And the hedges and ditches flying past. Blackthorn and elder bushes whizzing past. Wheee. Gates and grazing cows mere flashing images in the corners of my eyes. Wheee. And Stephen smiling, nervously no doubt, in the passenger seat.

My apprenticeship with Stephen was coming to an end. He had taught me to drive. Taught me the intricacies of the trade. Taught me to engage with the world. But the more he taught me, the more I wanted to learn from him. The more I wanted to rely on him. I knew that that couldn't continue forever, so it was with mixed feelings of excitement and dread that I looked forward to my independence.

The inevitable happened one Saturday evening at the end of October, the day before Hallowe'en, when Stephen drove the van to my house, and parked it in the yard. I went out to greet him, and he handed the keys to me ceremoniously.

"It's all yours, son. And the best of luck to you. The left-over stock is in the back, and it's all listed here." He handed me a sheaf of stock-lists, noted in his neat hand-writing, all with wholesale prices and totals. It was useless to me, of course, but I took it anyway. And my stomach began to murmur doubts about my ability to carry on alone when I couldn't even read a stock-list. But I marshalled my mind, and concentrated on my new responsibilities. Whatever I needed to do, I would do. I couldn't read a stock-list, but I could keep the lists in my own way - in my head. And when I had to make up their value, I had the calculator. That's what Stephen taught me - that there is a way of doing everything.

My mother and my aunt were in the parlour waiting to receive Stephen. A pot of tea was ready for pouring into the china cups. For the first time I felt I was in this room by right and not on sufferance.

"Thank you for everything, Mr Hanlon. You're a gentleman." My mother handed Stephen a cup of tea and moved a plate of scones over beside him on the table. "And what do we owe you altogether?"

Stephen put sugar and milk in his tea, sipped a little, then took the sheaf of dockets which I was still holding in my hand. He turned to the final page and pointed out where he had the total figure for stock, the van, and the business, all added up. My mother looked at it and nodded, then rummaged in her handbag for her cheque-book.

"You might like to go through the stock and do your own count before you fix up with me."

"Not at all, Mr Hanlon. We trust you entirely." She handed over the cheque, and tucked the docket with the final tot into her handbag. Probably didn't want me to know how much the business had cost.

Stephen finished his cup of tea in a few quick mouthfuls. It was obvious that he was not at ease in parlours.

"Now, you must have a drink to celebrate with us."

I was amused. It must indeed have been a momentous occasion for my mother to take out the bottle of sherry from the locked cabinet in the sideboard. Christmas in October. She ran her hand over the top of the bottle to wipe away the dust, uncorked it and poured a measured drop into a small glass for Stephen. But it was lemonade for the rest of us. At least she had prepared for the celebration by buying a large bottle. Yes, sherry for the visitor, lemonade for the Loftus family. A royal celebration. No question of alcohol for me of course. Until the age of twenty one. The Confirmation pledge. After that who knows? Maybe the Pioneers. Total abstinence. My mother expected no less. You could see that. But she filled my glass to the brim with lemonade, and I was happy. They toasted my health and the success of my new career.

7

THERE I WAS ONCE MORE, GAZING AT THE sea. From the shore at Doonaltan. I spent most of my frigging life gazing at something. Even as I am now gazing at death. Maybe that's why it's so slow in hitting me. Kept at bay by my gaze. Like a tiger in a circus cage.

The waves were certainly keeping their distance from me. Shunning me. Like girls at a dance. There was silence from the back of the van. I wondered about Michelle. Hadn't stopped wondering about her, for frig's sake. Was she worried? Was she crying? What was she saying to His Reverence in her curious accent? What was the gobshite saying to her? He could hardly be reprimanding her for her sinful ways, could he? I suppose it wouldn't be beyond him. Comforting her? A twinge of jealousy cut through me with that thought. Abruptly I started turning the van.

Climbing back along the Kieve Road, I now had Alternan down to my right. Tried to occupy my mind by remembering all I had ever heard about the Kieve. The patterns. Garland Sunday to the Feast of the Assumption. Thousands of people. Maybe. Certainly hundreds. In honour of the saint. Festivities. Drinking. Singing. Praying. Carousing. Faction fights. Parish against parish. Or townland against townland. Or family against family. Men with ash plants. Walloping each other. In honour of the Saint. Women who came barren and went home with child. Miracles. The power of the Saint. The effects of the water springing from the cliff face. The Kieve. The well of the Saint. And old Frank Kivlehan sitting in a corner of his kitchen, near the fire, rambling on and on about what it was like. While I listened attentively. Listened to every word. Registered every word. Even though it was obvious from his tone that he was not telling these things to me; he was merely using my presence as an excuse to talk. I was only a half-wit who would not understand what he was saying, would not remember a word of it, was no more interested in it than was his own clan who preferred to watch blinking television pictures or go to the pub. So he rambled on. And I sat in the chair opposite, giving him the excuse to talk.

Back on the main road, I turned left up Borua hill. A long slow climb until I reached the summit at Ballykillcash. Here I turned off the main road once more. The by-road went closer to the sea. I halted the van. I had never once passed this spot without halting the van. Laid out in front of me, the most beautiful landscape in the world. Had to be. The whole ring of Sligo Bay. The mountain wall on the horizon, the Ox Mountains, Knocknarea, Ben Bulben, the Donegal Mountains. Down below me, the Long Rock prodding into the sea. Over on my left, capping the brow of the hill, the watch tower. Stone built. In the time of Napoleon. To guard the sea-coast and watch for an invasion.

That tower was what brought my father's ancestors into Tireragh. From Carbury, the other side of Sligo town. Stone-masons they were. Came for the work. And stayed. The job itself hadn't been finished when it was abandoned. I could see, even from where I sat, that the pointing on the stones reached only two thirds of the way up. But not a stone had been dislodged by wind or rain in the mean time. Well built. Built to last. Even though it didn't need to be. Napoleon's fleet of ships had been destroyed in a sea battle somewhere, and that was the end of the threat. So they abandoned the towers. Told the men to go home. But my fathers' ancestors didn't want to go home. They liked the place. Liked the people. And so they stayed. That was why they were land-less. Then and ever after. Drifted in.

76

No foothold. But they could build. Got more work. Building houses, walls, eventually churches - they built most of the churches in Tireragh. Not that that made them rich. Not by a long shot. Not dealing with the clergy. Those boys were able to squeeze the money out of the people alright, but do you think they paid the builders. Not on your life. They pocketed the money. And let the builders starve. And they did. Starve. Generation after generation. At home in poverty. Or in the Workhouse. That's what the clergy were like, even in those days. So nothing changes.

Thinking about the clergy vexed me. And reminded me of the specimen in the back. The maker's sample. A cliff. A cliff. But now, I was looking at it. Right in front of me. The most magnificent cliff in Tireragh. Aughris Head. Centre-piece of this landscape. This paradise without the glow. All of Dromard, and Skreen, and Templeboy, spread out under the arm of the Ox Mountains. And then, in the centre, this head-land sweeping magnificently out into the bay, rising as it went so that the tip had a sheer drop to the water's edge. And set into that cliff-face, somewhere, was the Cor a d'Tonn. Where the dream began. If only I could find it.

If only I had someone to talk to. Anyone. "Whenever you need advice, just give me a shout" Stephen had said to me that Saturday night he left me the van. The invitation would hardly have covered this situation. Not likely. Stephen was an understanding man, a broad-minded man, but he would surely be perplexed if he knew the situation I was in now. A whore and a priest in the back of the van, and myself looking for a cliff to drive over. After he set me up in a respectable business selling holy pictures, and statues, and rosary beads. Oh Stephen, Stephen. Had I let him down? I had inherited more than the van, more than the business from him. I had inherited a whole tradition, a way of life, an outlook on the world and beyond. Was I responsible for continuing all that? Had I taken on such a responsibility? If so, I had failed him, failed him badly. He had given me confidence and freedom. But I had been found wanting. As frigging usual.

Still, I had not betrayed my responsibilities as badly as His Reverence had betrayed his. And Michelle, what had she betrayed?

And yet, I was conscious that I had never made a decision to forsake anything, to betray anything. No, I had been following a light and, with darkness falling, this was where I found myself. It was something like that.

Yes, this was where I was, and there could be no frigging regrets.

The task now was to finish off the journey as quickly as possible. In every sense. Aughris Head. Like a sleek sea monster now. It would be worth it if I could get that far. The Cor a d'Tonn. Where it all began. To finish it there. Very appropriate. Into the depths. Into the vaults of the deep, where my father was being held, perhaps. As punishment for his sin. The ultimate sin. Punished by the Creator, the jealous God. For not having turned to him. Despair is the loss of confidence in God – the pupils in the Confirmation class had chanted their catechism out loud. Left no hope of redemption, the teacher explained, and that was why suicide was the one sin that could never be forgiven, the one sin that guaranteed damnation. And I could see the glances of the other children flickering in my direction.

I often wondered if that was why my mother never mentioned his name. Because he had committed suicide. Never permitted discussion of him in the house. According to my cousins, her antipathy towards my father was there long before he disappeared into the sea. The chill had set in as soon as the wedding celebrations were over. And by the time I was born, it was the north wind that was blowing relentlessly through their lives. And it continued blowing after he had gone. I felt it, for example, every time there was a mention of my father's relatives, felt the contempt, the antagonism. As I have said, she hated to hear of me fraternising with them, yet she never forbade it. Never even discouraged it. I suppose I was more of an embarrassment to her than they were. As a half-wit I was never going to count for anything anyway, so it made frig all difference who I fraternised with or how I spent my time. She let me grow like a weed. Yet I could always sense the constant tension, the constant anxiety, for fear I would disgrace her in the future even more than I had disgraced her in the past. And that continued until the big change. Until that moment of blessed inspiration when she talked with Stephen Hanlon.

Yes, I was fascinated by my father. And my mother's silence, the embargo on any talk of him, far from banishing his ghost, served only to ensure that he remained an emotionally charged presence in our lives. It was as if he might walk in the door, return from the deep, so strong was that presence in our house. Maybe that was what my mother feared. Who knows? Who knows? She certainly didn't confide in me, and I doubt if she ever confided in anyone.

I liked him. Liked what I remembered of him from my own scant memories. I liked him even more from all the little accounts I gleaned among his relations. Nora, his first cousin, mother of my friend, Jimmy, had grown up with him and gone to school with him. She was an endless source of little anecdotes. Like the time he organised a tug-of-war team for the Sports Day at Easkey. Highly partisan, always. Sending out the challenge to other parishes. Pride and glory were the stake. Training every evening at the Seafield Hotel. And the challenge brought the teams from the other parishes, and the crowds as well. Excitement on the day. He was the anchorman. The rope wrapped around him, his heels dug into the ground, shouting instructions, 'heave, lads, heave, heave'. Getting the rhythm going. 'Now.' Allowing quick slack to knock the other team off balance. Then off again, 'heave, heave, heave.' Did they win the competition? Well of course they did. They must have won, they were so good. Especially my father. She was nothing if not biased. "You know," she said, "of all of us growing up together your father was the one who stood out as special, the one who was the light for the rest of us. It was as if he was marked out for great things, but the great things never happened."

And Frank, her husband, joining in. He had recollections of him as well. The two of them with another companion, Paddy, lying in the little wood called the Rosan, on the bank of the river. Hiding. Watching out for the water bailiff. Satisfied that he was not in the vicinity, they emerged from the cluster of hazel and crept down to the water's edge. An extensive deep pool sunken down-stream of a flat reef was their target. Elsewhere the water was flowing thinly over stones and shallows. My father had a canvas bag hung over his shoulder. Out of it he took a glass bottle which was packed with quick-lime. The three of them scanned the pool avidly. This was where the salmon rested on its journey upstream. This was the haunt of brown trout grown fat on the richness of the river. Paddy had the eye of a hawk, and picked out the spot. 'There.' He pointed. And my father lobbed the bottle into the pool. The three of them dived to the ground covering their faces against possible flying glass. A loud puff of an explosion as the bottle of quick-lime blew up. They waited a few seconds. Then up like hares. Waded into the river. Two large salmon floated silver-bellied on the stream. Snatched them. Dozens of brown trout similarly floating, drifting off. Tried to snatch up every one. Didn't want the evidence wiggling its way down to the village where the water-bailiff would surely spot it. Packed them into the bag. Then scuttled back into the wood to find a secure hiding place in which to stash the fish until they could reclaim them under cover of darkness.

Yes, nobody spoke ill of my father. So what went wrong between himself and my mother? He was certainly unhappy, according to Nora. Was drinking more and more. Becoming withdrawn. Losing interest in all his former passions. Perhaps he had a glimpse of the future and did not like the prospect. Preferred to go out as he was then. Have people remember him as he was then. Perhaps.

Anyway, he disappeared from my life, leaving only a clutch of images and a great dark shadow.

Stephen Hanlon was the only real father-figure in my life. I never did go back to him for advice or help after he handed over the van to me. On the business front I didn't have to, so thorough was my training. Even though I was terrified at the beginning, I fell into the ways of the business with little difficulty and grew in confidence slowly. There was very little to do at that time of the year anyway. An odd fair. An odd market. Sales were slow. I had plenty of time and no pressure. It was the ideal season to be going out on my own.

Coming up to Christmas there was an upsurge in demand. People buying presents. Mainly the bigger items. Statues. Framed pictures. Such like. In January and February everything fell slack again.

Even though it was the low season in terms of sales, I was enthusiastically active. Visiting the wholesalers regularly to scrutinise their stock. Practising my driving in the van. Rummaging in the backs of churches to see what they were selling. They seemed to have a good line going in pamphlets. With my handicap, I could make very little of them, however.

I picked up samples of these pamphlets and brought them home to my mother and my aunt. To find out what was in them. To assess their potential for my market. My mother seemed even happy to help. I suppose she thought I was developing an interest in religion, not just researching the market. She read out bits from the pamphlets. They were mainly published by a company called the Catholic Truth Society. Many of them were dull and I couldn't imagine anyone buying them to read. However I enjoyed a series called Lives of the Saints. They were interesting enough buggers in their own way. The saints. Take St Augustine. He was some get. Committed every sin he could think of, while his mother, St Monica, prayed for his conversion. Eventually he gave up sinning and took to religion in a big way. The one I liked best though was 'St Jude Thaddeus - the Forgotten Apostle'. He was one of the twelve apostles, but, because his name sounded so similar to Judas, people confused them, and poor old Jude was ignored. He was given the job of patron of hopeless cases. Very appropriate. Yes he was my kind of man. On the back cover there was a picture of him in flowing green robes, so I tore out that picture and stuck it on the dashboard of the van.

Not being able to read or write was something I had always accepted with resignation, despite the sheer frigging embarrassment I suffered whenever my handicap was exposed. But now I was becoming more and more annoyed with myself when I realised the drawback it was in conducting my business. I thought back to Stephen Hanlon and his outlook, that there was always a solution to a problem. Heard his voice in my ear, saying 'if five year old children can do it, why can't you?'

Surreptitiously I began to examine the reading books belonging to my mother that were lying around. The simplest ones. One picture on each page and one word underneath : DOG, HOUSE, PETER, MARY. I began to study the letters and to spell out the words to myself. I had no difficulty remembering the spelling once I said them to myself; many of the spellings were still ringing in my ears from my earliest days at school. Matching the spellings with the pictures, there was where my problem lay. When I took a sheet of paper and tried to put down the letters, I had difficulty. The shapes of the letters would not stay in my mind, kept dissolving, one into the other, no matter how hard I concentrated. I was depressed and frustrated. But Stephen was still whispering in my ear relentlessly, 'if there is a problem, there is a solution. Keep trying.' And I did keep trying. But it was no good. I could not remember things from looking at them, I had to hear them.

One night it came to me. Accidentally. I said to myself, 'H - goal-posts', and I never forgot H again. So I tried, another one, 'M is like a mountain.' And M was copper-fastened. 'B - fat Billy'. 'Y a diviner's rod'. 'S - hook'. In no time I had the whole alphabet committed to memory. In my own fashion.

If only I had managed to do this while at school. But that was a different story. When I failed to master the letters, I was left behind. The class moved on. And Mrs Murnane moved with them. Seldom she asked me a question. Only when she felt I was due a caning, as I have said. I was retarded. Questions were an embarrassment to me and to her. Immediate confusion and terror was my response. Always. And so she left me alone to day-dream in the back of her class. By the time I moved to the senior classes and her husband's half of the school, I was a lost cause. He just glowered at me. The only time I raised my voice was to say, 'Present', when the roll was being called in the morning.

I would have been mortified, had my mother or my aunt caught me with the infants' reading books, so I waited every night until they were in bed and asleep before I started. Their night-time routine was simple. They got into their two single beds. Said the Rosary. Within minutes they were fast asleep. I, on the other hand, stayed up into the early hours. I had always liked this time of the day best, and my business did not impose any change on my sleeping pattern, as I did not have to stir out in the morning until the rest of the world was fully awake.

Going through those reading books, I had to whisper the words to myself before I could understand them. So that I could memorise them. 'PETER IS PLAYING WITH THE DOG.' Times I got so carried away with the adventures of Peter and Mary and the Dog that I found myself reciting the words out loud, and in consternation I would stop and listen for the even breathing from the bedroom. In this manner I worked my way through the children's reading books until I had reached those of Sixth Class. I was proud, so proud of myself.

Confidence is a marvellous thing. When you gain confidence, you begin to believe that you can move mountains. Driving along in the van, I saluted people, the way an adult would, and they saluted back. As if I too were an adult. Normal. And I took delight in wandering in to the village in the evenings. To hang around the bridge or the Post Office corner. To hang on the edge of conversations, about the weather, about work. To feel that I belonged to the same world as these men and these youths masquerading as men. To jingle money in my pocket knowing it was my own. Earned. And when the talk became animated, with the youths bragging about the work they had done or the money they had earned, and the men poking fun at them, in such moments I was often on the point of tossing in a comment about my own business, but I could not find the voice. Or dreaded to hear the sound of that voice. Feared that the world would stand in silence if I opened my mouth, and then would collapse in derisive laughter. So I stayed silent, on the edge of conversations, happy in the knowledge that I was part of this adult world, and that my status was being acknowledged especially in so far as I was not being taunted anymore, nor ridiculed, nor patronised.

It was bliss also to go around puzzling out words wherever I saw them. On signposts. On bill-boards advertising dances and show-bands. On shop-fronts. That was something that fascinated me, the names on shop-fronts. I had never realised it before, of course: the fact that it was always the man's name that was written in bold letters on every premises. Never the woman's. Even though it was nearly always the woman who ran the shop and did all the work. Daughters too were excluded. John Murphy and Son. Even though it was Mrs Murphy and their four daughters who ran that hardware and drapery, while John Murphy was scratching himself at fairs and marts buying and selling a few cattle, posing as a dealer. As for their son. He was away in college somewhere. Not only that, but the business had belonged to Mrs Murphy and her family. Clarke was her maiden name. An only daughter. And John Murphy married in to the place. First thing he did, apparently, was stick his name up over the shop. As if he had built it. He added 'and Son' when that particular addition arrived at the end of a line of daughters. Strange.

Strange also the covers of books. After the title of the book the first thing you read is the name of the person who wrote it. Even the reading books that I had been borrowing from my mother's bag, with nothing more difficult in them than PETER RUNS TO THE SHOP, carried the name of the man who wrote them, Charles Mc Ginley, B.A. As if we should all stand back and admire him.

Maybe that was what they were all about. Demanding homage. Just like the Creator. Wanting people to recognise their importance. John Murphy more than anyone wanted recognition. His were the biggest boldest letters of all. For fear anyone might attempt to refer to the shop as his wife's. And the

Creator's first demand: 'I am the Lord, thy God. Thou shalt not have strange gods before me. Yes, it figured.

Now and again I worried that I was mellowing in my feud with him, with the Creator. That I too had been bought over. Now that I was happier. Now that religion seemed to be conferring some benefits on me. Worried that I was even becoming like him, for frig's sake. You know. With my own business that I was so proud of. The shed now totally appropriated and secured with a new pad-lock. It wasn't that I had become concerned about the danger of theft. Who would go stealing a picture of the Sacred Heart, for frig's sake? No, I was enjoying the sense of control. Revelling in the feeling of possession. Absolutely indulging in the pleasure of pottering about in the shed all by myself late into the evenings.

I put up shelves to store the goods in such a way that every item was visible and I could check the stock at a glance. The shelves were make-shift. Boards resting on concrete blocks. But I was pleased with my improvisation, and was forever arranging and re-arranging the items on these shelves.

I became enterprising too. I had nothing on St Farnan. And he was our local saint. No leaflet. No medal. No statue. I had never seen an image of him. The statue at the Kieve was of St Patrick. With his bishop's hat, his crosier resting on the head of a snake, his foot trampling another, his robe a deep green, he fooled nobody. It was St Patrick without question. So what about St Farnan? I asked the man at the whole-salers. He shook his head pensively, produced a large bound catalogue from under the counter, and the two of us began to scour the pages in search of some representation of St Farnan. There were dozens and dozens of statues pictured in the catalogue with exotic names underneath them which I could not decipher. But the salesman called out the name of any statue I pointed to. We did not find St Farnan. In the end I picked out a very simple statue of a monkish figure in a brown habit. There was no name written on the actual statue, and even the salesman could not pronounce the foreign name of the saint from the catalogue. So I settled on that. Decided it was closer to St Farnan than the frigging statue of St Patrick anyway. I ordered half-a-dozen. And sure enough, when I displayed them on the stall with the notice St FARNAN beside them, they sold like ice-cream on a hot summer's Sunday.

Yes, I was becoming enterprising alright. Another day I had taken the van out for a drive. Nowhere in particular to go that day, nothing in particular to do. Just driving along. For the practice. For the enjoyment. Below Dromore West I turned up the Stirabout Road, a narrow by-road leading towards the mountains. A short distance up the road, I found myself tailing Culkin's grocery van. On the back was written in big letters 'Mobile Shop – Home Deliveries.' The road was so narrow that I was afraid to pass him out, even when he stopped outside a house to drop off a delivery. At the next house he pulled right up on the verge and waved me on. But I was still afraid to attempt the narrow passage, and indicated to him that I would wait.

I sat there and watched. The woman of the house came out carrying a tray of eggs. She went to the back of the van and Culkin opened the doors. Lowered a set of steps. The woman climbed the steps and handed over her eggs. Then she browsed through the array of goods and picked out her groceries. Culkin took the money from her, obviously allowing credit for the eggs. The woman descended with her armful of purchases, and returned into her house. Culkin folded up the steps, closed the back doors of the van, waved at me to acknowledge my patience, and moved on. A little further up the road was a junction, and I took the opportunity of turning the van and coming back.

But it set me thinking. There were days upon days when I had nothing to do, when I drove the van around empty roads, just to be out and about. The fairs and markets took up only a handful of days in the month. Special events, like parish fetes were once-off affairs. The season for the missions was a long way off. So why could I not call around to the houses the same way as Culkin did in his mobile shop? Make a few sales? Pay for the petrol I was using up driving around the roads?

The next day I loaded up the van with a selection of stock, pictures, statues, prayer-books, rosary beads. The full range. Even one of the water-filled jars with the model of Knock Chapel inside. You know the one. When you shake it, or turn it upside down, white snow floats down over the chapel. I always had it on display, even when the season for Knock was a long time away. Because it was my favourite. In idle moments I loved shaking it up and watching those snowflakes slowly drift down over the roof and gable of the chapel, settling on the figures in the apparition. It was so peaceful, that scene.

And so I set forth, taking the same route up the Stirabout Road that I had seen Culkin working the day before.

I stopped at the first house. Knocked on the door. Waited. Petrified. Heard the steps coming to the door. It opened. An old woman stood there. A look of friendly curiosity on her face. That look softened my terror a little. I knew I was red-faced, and staring. Tried to loosen my tongue.

"Would you like to buy something from the van?" I mumbled.

"What is it?" she asked, cocking her head sideways, as if that might help her make out what I was saying.

I cleared my throat. Braced myself. "Would you like to buy something from the van?" I managed to repeat in a clearer voice.

She stared at me. I stared at her.

"And what have you in the van?" she asked, after what seemed a life-time.

"Religious things."

She stared at me again. I stared back at her.

"Ah, now I know who you are. You're the young fellow from Easkey who took over the stall from Stephen Hanlon. Am I right?"

"Yeah." I felt relieved. Reassured by her tone. Pleased that she had not identified me as Tommy Loftus, the half-wit son of the teacher. Surprised that she hadn't so identified me.

"Come in, come in for a minute. Would you like a cup of tea."

"No thanks. I'm alright."

"Well, wait now for a minute, and I'll go out and see what you have in the van."

She ambled back into the house, taking off her apron as she went. When she returned she had her purse in her hand. It looked hopeful.

I opened the back of the van, took out a timber box and fixed it on the ground so she could step up into the van. It would have been easier if I had steps like Culkin, but my van was smaller than his, and older. However, I supported her arm, and she managed the step.

She browsed through the selection of goods with what appeared some enjoyment. Eventually she surprised me, delighted me, by fixing on a big picture of St Francis. She held it up, and looked at it, front and back. It had quite a heavy ornamental frame. She stood back to admire it. There were plenty of little details, little animals and birds scattered all over the place, but all listening attentively to the saint.

"That's a fine picture. That picture would look good in the spare bedroom. Yes, I'll take that. How much is that?"

"Five pounds fifty." I held my breath, fearing she would be put off by the price.

But she didn't flinch. She opened up her purse and counted out five pounds fifty into my hand. I could scarcely believe it. I had often stood on a windy street for the whole of a fair day and sold less.

I thanked her. Mrs Keaveney was her name, I found out afterwards. And moved on.

Further delight at almost every house. People came out to the van curious, and rummaged until they found something to buy, a rosary beads, a crucifix, even a small statue.

After that, I went out every day. It took me a full week to cover the parish of Kilmacshalgan. And there were seven parishes in Tireragh. I was skipping. Selling stock at a time of year when there was otherwise very little moving. Making money. Advancing my business.

Occasionally I was earthed by a run of houses where no door was opened. Despite that sense of their being someone at home. Some frigger behind the curtain. You know what I mean. It was difficult to be even-minded about such slights. Difficult to avoid dark confidence-sapping thoughts. That they saw me approach. And because it was me, they would not afford me the courtesy of answering the knock on the door. But such thoughts were scattered when I made a sale at another house. Yes, life was good. Couldn't be better.

8

THIS LANDSCAPE LAID OUT BEFORE ME from the brow of Ballykillcash had always reminded me of that reading from the Gospel where the Devil brings Jesus up to the top of a mountain and shows him the beautiful landscapes of the world. You know the reading. He offers them to him, as a present, if Jesus will kneel down and adore him. And I always wondered how could the Devil have the giving of the world, if he didn't own it. Did he own it? Or was it the Creator himself, so paranoid about getting homage, who was was asking Jesus to do something unacceptable. To pay him a reverence that was not his due. It puzzled me.

Anyway. Myself - I would have been bought off if someone offered me this sweep of countryside in front of me. And every time I stopped the van to admire it, I wished someone would turn up to make me an offer.

Aughris Head. My final destination. Far away, and beginning to fade into the twilight. Time to be moving if I was going to reach it before the darkness did. That was an anxiety. It was a journey. And another anxiety struck me too, that they might come looking for His Reverence. If they had noticed his absence. If they had noticed him getting into my van. Still, they would hardly imagine he had been kidnapped. By me. No. They would probably speculate that he had gone off on a sudden sick call. Still it must have been a surprise to the congregation to find him gone. Not there smiling and nodding to all as they made their way out.

Down the steep hill. At the bottom, the turn for Colleary's Shore, for Pullarone, the great sea cave that had been home to a colony of seals since life began. The next boreen, the Weasel Road. Why was

91

it called that? Nobody could ever tell me, and I had asked.

That had been one of the delights of pursuing my business through the travelling shop. I got to know people. People all over the Barony of Tireragh. People I had never met before. And we became friendly, very friendly. The friendship began in earnest only when I started on my second round of the parishes. When they didn't want more objects of piety, but bought a medal or a scapular, something cheap, out of generosity. And invited me in for a cup of tea. Decent people who were reluctant to turn me away empty-handed. I sensed that. Besides most of them had time on their hands, a lot of time. And were hungry for company. Any company. Even the company of a retard.

But, as I have mentioned, I was always a good listener, even if I had nothing to say. It was no inconvenience to me to sit at a table sipping a cup of tea and listen to a rambling monologue for a couple of hours. No bother at all. In that way I became as knowledgeable about the other parishes of Tireragh as I already was about my own. I listened to their genealogies and to the registers of their scattered families. I listened to the travails of their lives, and to the stories of their joys as well. They talked out of their need to talk, imagining, if they reflected on it at all, that they were pouring water into a sieve. They did not realise that every word of it was etched forever on my memory. How could they have realised? I never told them.

The ones I probably enjoyed listening to most of all were the single farmers, middle-aged or old, who lived in little cottages in far-flung places. Up the sides of mountains. Down long boreens. In the middle of bogs. Their solitary condition, their total isolation, made their loneliness more intense than that of others. And I could identify with that. Their stories too had an edge to them, full of longing and regret. You know the style. How everything went wrong. The chances they missed. Yes, they were my kind of people. But, even though their lives contained more disappointment than satisfaction, they were not sour. They complained, and questioned their fate, to the point of bitterness, but the bitterness did not sour their nature. They were among the warmest, most generous people I had met. And there were so many of them. Hundreds. Living alone. And frigging delighted with a visit from me. Could you believe it?

People like John Cawley. One evening I called on him and he invited me in for a cup of tea. The kitchen of his two-roomed house was jammed with bags of potatoes, sacks of meal, even a sheaf of hay. And the hens kept wandering in and out scuttering all over the floor as they went. He was telling me how he produced his own milk and eggs, made his own butter, grew his own spuds and cabbage. All he needed, he said, were the few chops, and a little woman to fry them. And he chuckled at the good of that joke, and I chuckled too while I lashed into his home-made bread and his home-made butter and the tea that had rich globules of cream floating on the surface. The next thing the cow came as far as the door and stuck its head around the door-post. "Ah, begobs, poor Pruggy." That was the way he spoke. "It's time to milk her." He fetched a galvanized bucket from the corner, and a low stool. As soon as the cow heard the clink of the bucket she surged through the door and took up a position right in the middle of the kitchen. John placed the bucket under her udder, sat down on the stool, and started to milk her. It was obviously their evening routine. And I was fascinated. The next thing the cow started arching her back and spreading her hind legs. "Quick, give me the basin," John shouted to me. I handed him the tin basin that was beside me on the table. He deftly emptied the milk into the basin and positioned the empty bucket strategically behind the legs of the cow. A powerful gush of piss flowed straight into the bucket. "That was close," he said with a note of satisfaction in his voice. When the last dribble had fallen he took up the bucket, walked as far as the door, and with a clean sweep he emptied the contents of the bucket out into the yard. Holding the bucket upside down, he drained the last few drops out of it. Then back he went to the stool, placed the bucket under the cow once more, and resumed milking her. I looked at my milky tea, and the home-made butter on the home-made bread. It was with great difficulty that I repressed the surge of my stomach as I made a hurried retreat from John's homely kitchen.

Or like Tom MacSharry. He lived up near the foot of the mountains at the top of Dunowla, and must have been a hundred years old, he was so wizened. But tough. Tough as the gnarled old bushes that clung to the earth here and there around his cottage. It was long past his time to die. But he declared he could not die. He was the last of his tribe and, if he died, his whole tribe died with him. I suggested that, if his tribe had passed on, it would be a consolation for himself to join them. He fixed me with a dart of his eye, then mellowed to pity as he seemed to realise who he was talking to. No, he said, it wasn't like that. While he was alive, they were alive. They were in his head and in his heart. He could name them and relate the life story of each and every one. Back for generations. Back to the time of Cromwell, when they came walking from the rich land of Co. Meath. To hell or to Connaught was the choice they had been given. And they chose Connaught. But family legend had it that when they passed through Jamestown Gate into Co. Leitrim, and got their first glimpse of Connaught they wondered if they had made the right choice.

But they brought their fiddles and their music and their songs. They earned a livelihood by growing and compounding herbs for healing. Therefore they were a threat to no one's existence, and were made welcome wherever they went. Eventually they settled in Tireragh. On land that they wrested from the mountain. They married into local families, and yet they retained their separateness. Practised their ancient ways in music and healing.

Right down to Tom. Tom had it all inside him. He had the music. The healing. People came to him when they had lost faith in the doctors. And he mixed the cures for them. He had the genealogy of his tribe in his head. Personal recollection of his grandparents and their generation who were born before the Great Famine. He couldn't die because all of that would die with him. As long as he lived, they lived.

I told him that he could relate it to me. All of it. And that I would commit it to memory. Then he could die content knowing that the story of his tribe and the knowledge of his people would live on.

He looked at me in amazement. Then burst out laughing. He laughed hard and long.

"You're surely one of God's people," he said. "You surely are." And I knew what he meant. The futility of entrusting his knowledge to a half-wit as a way of avoiding obliteration. No, he had no choice but to go on living. He did not realise that I could have relieved him of his burden. And I did not have the way of convincing him.

I was continually arranging and re-arranging the display inside the van. Trying to make it look more attractive. More impressive. Wet days were plentiful in Tireragh, ideal for staying at home and pottering around in the shed and in the van. On such a day, when the wind off the sea was driving the rain horizontal, like gunshot, I acted on a whimsical idea. I cleared out the van entirely and painted the inside sky-blue. When that coat was dry I got some white paint and, on the panel behind the cab, I daubed in a few puffy little white clouds floating around at the top. They were not very well drawn - I was no good at this sort of thing - but, when I stood back, the white blotches on the blue background were unmistakably suggestive of clouds.

Then I got some chicken wire and rolled it into an arch. I set it against the back panel, stretching it from the floor on one side, up more than half way to the roof, and then down to the floor on the other side. Having secured it to the panel, I covered it with grey crepe paper. Then I got the biggest statue of the Virgin that I had and placed it within the arch. I stood back to admire it. Delighted. I had managed to simulate a grotto. Using the technique that my mother used to create the Crib in the Church, Christmas after Christmas. Using the same chicken wire as well.

It looked good. The Virgin's hands were joined and her eyes were cast upwards. At my puffy white clouds. I got out of the van and looked at it from the back door. Still looked good, but the blue appeared darker in the shadow of the interior than I had hoped it would be. A few steps backwards and I was sheltering under the gable end of the house, still looking directly into the back of the van. The grotto was swallowed up in the interior darkness. What I needed was light.

I secured the statue by tying it to the back panel with nylon fishing line. Invisible. Just the job. Then I drove the van down to Philip Morrow, the electrician. I took Philip into the back of the van and while the two of us squatted studying the grotto, I explained what I needed. Light.

Philip suggested a circuit with five bulbs. The flex could be tucked into the chicken wire and the bulbs shaded so that the light would be directed down on to the statue. He could run the circuit off a special twelve-volt battery which would be wired to the engine and therefore re-charged while the engine was running. There would then be plenty of power in the battery to feed the lights while the engine was off. It was exactly what I needed, and I asked him to go ahead and do it. He was clever Philip Morrow. You could talk to him. He understood you. And decent. He didn't rob you when it came to charging for his work.

I was delighted with the result. It exceeded my expectation totally. I studied it from different distances. The further I stood back the more magical it appeared. It looked like a real shrine. Even Philip Morrow was impressed. And he never went to church, chapel, nor meeting house. He was smiling. I paid him and drove home to load up.

It did wonders for the display of goods as well. Lit up the whole back of the van. Balanced the light coming from the open door. The innermost area had always been waste space, because of the pocket of darkness, suitable only for large items or storage. Now, thanks to the illuminated grotto, it was the most attractive area and I was able to re-organise my display of small items, deploying some at the back some at the front.

I resisted the temptation to call my mother and my aunt. They would see it whenever they bothered to look. After the initial excitement about my business their interest had begun to wane. And in a way I was happier to be working things out on my own. Just, sometimes, I felt the urge to call someone, anyone, to share my satisfaction in some achievement. You know the feeling. Anyway. It wasn't to be. Not with them anyway.

The following day the weather had improved. The rain had eased into mist, and the cloudbank was beginning to lift out to the west over Mayo. I set off in that direction. Hoping for clearer weather. Hoping to impress my customers. If they were impressed with my new display they might be more inclined to buy goods. When I reached Kilglass I started working the cluster of houses around the village. I can't say I was disappointed. The people who came aboard were oohing and aahing at the grotto. They thought it was lovely. As good as they'd seen. Knock at home, they joked. I can't say I was satisfied either. It seemed to increase my turnover, but not by a dramatic amount. Little by little, I counselled myself.

The next day I took the Glen Easkey road, starting from the High Road and working towards the mountain. It was the same story. Everybody impressed. Everybody buying a little more. But not that much more.

Up at the furthest end of Glen Easkey, up where the river comes tumbling from the hills, one of the last houses was the home of a widow, Mrs Callaghan. Religious. A regular customer. I never failed to call on her when I was working the area, and she never failed to purchase something. I was keen to see how she would react to my grotto.

As soon as I halted the van, she came trudging through the muck of her stable yard.

"Oh, it's you, Lofty. When I heard the sound of the engine I thought it was the vet. I've been expecting him for the last two hours, whatever is keeping him. Up all night I've been, with a sick cow. She's been trying to calve. But getting nowhere. Now she's at death's door. And still not a sign of that bugger of a vet. I'm worn out."

She certainly had all the signs of being worn out. Drawn and haggard across the face, she stepped towards the van as if she could barely lift her wellington boots.

"Sorry about the cow," I said. "Hope she comes through."

"Hope she does. But hope can break your heart. Have you got any Brigid's Cross? I was thinking last night, while I was minding the cow, that I should have a Brigid's Cross hanging up in the stable."

As usual, put on the spot to recall whether I had any in stock, my mind went blank. I went quickly to search for one in the back of the van. When I opened the door,

98

of course, the lights came on around the grotto, but I was so preoccupied with the search for the Brigid's Cross that all thoughts of showing-off to Mrs Callaghan had gone from my mind. I had even forgotten about her momentarily in the intensity of the search, until I heard a little gasp of surprise behind me. She had followed me up into the back of the van and was standing, awe-struck, gazing at the illuminated statue of the Virgin.

"Wonderful. It's like an apparition," she whispered as if she were in church,

"Oh, yeah, do you like it?" I asked as I unearthed a Brigid's Cross from a cardboard box full of odds and ends. I turned around to hand it to her.

But she had dropped to her knees in an involuntary action, still gazing at the statue, and was blessing herself. I could sense the burden of fatigue and anxiety which she was placing at the foot of the Virgin in the course of the little prayer she was muttering.

Nevertheless, I was alarmed. Shocked. But I didn't interrupt. This was a plaster statue in the back of a van. Nothing more. Nothing that one should kneel before. But she was so wrapped up in her thoughts that she did not detect my alarm. So I stood there. The Brigid's Cross held limply in my hand. She made the sign of the cross to finish her prayer and got up off her knees.

I was trying to find the words to point out to her how inappropriate it was to treat my sales display as a religious shrine, to treat my van as a place of worship. But I could see that the great weight of her distress had been lightened, and consequently there seemed little point to my scruples.

She took the Brigid's Cross from me, and touched it reverently off the statue.

"It's all up to her now," she murmured. "It's all up to the Mother of God. Anything short of a miracle will be no good to me."

I followed her down. Tried to refuse the few pence for the Brigid's Cross. But had to accept them. Thanked her.

I was still disturbed by the incident as I turned the van around in the yard and drove back down the narrow boreen. Disturbed enough to call it a day, even though there were still a few hours of light remaining. I drove home, parked the van, and spent the rest of the evening lying on my bed. Thinking.

The following morning I was eating my breakfast, still thinking, thinking of dismantling the grotto. There was a knock on the door, which my aunt answered. Who was ushered in to the kitchen but Mrs Callaghan, dressed in her Sunday finery? Only for she was on my mind I probably wouldn't have recognised her, she looked so different out of her wellingtons.

As soon as she came in she gazed at me with the weirdest expression. A bit like the way she was gazing at the statue the previous day, except with joy. There was no trace of the worry and exhaustion she had been wrestling with on that occasion. My aunt was standing by, bewildered.

"You saved the cow," she eventually intoned. "You remember how I knelt down before the statue of Our Lady in your van, and said a prayer. You gave me a Brigid's Cross. I touched the Cross on the statue and asked Our Lady to save the cow. To save her because if she died I would not have the money to buy another. And where would I be then? I was looking for a miracle. I think I told you that. And a miracle I got. I went back to the stable after you left. The cow was still lying on the ground. Almost lifeless. Making no effort to give birth. I touched her brow with the Brigid's Cross. She looked up at me for a little while, and the next thing she shook herself, struggled to her feet, and began to deliver the calf."

Mrs Callaghan was almost choking with emotion. I didn't know what to say or do. My aunt came forward and invited her to take off her coat and sit down. Which she did. Then my aunt filled the kettle with water and began to prepare tea.

Settled in at the table, Mrs Callaghan continued. "A lovely little bull calf she had. And as soon as the birth was over, the cow was as right as rain. She started eating hay. Ravenous she was. I brought her a bucket of water and she drank it back without lifting her head. When the vet arrived a few minutes later he took one look and said there was nothing the matter with the cow. If he had come when he was called, he would have found plenty the matter with her. But he didn't come. Instead you came. And you brought help from the Mother of God."

I was confused. Flattered that she was giving me credit for saving her cow, and in such a respectful tone. Delighted that she had been saved from ruin. She was a woman I liked. And a very good customer. On the other hand, I was disturbed by her ascribing the cure to the statue in my van and to the Brigid's Cross I sold her. I saw these as nothing but artefacts, goods, objects, like the sugar and the butter that Culkin sold from his van. To attribute supernatural powers to them I found unsettling.

"I'd like to see the statue of Our Lady again, if it's alright with you. To say thanks. You know."

I couldn't even start to argue with her, she was so sincere, so totally convinced in what she was saying and what she was doing. There was a certainty there, against which I was powerless.

So, when she had finished her tea, I brought her out to the van and opened up the back. She watched, rapt, as the lights came on. I put down the crate, and she stepped up as if she were in a daze, her eyes fixed on the statue of the Virgin. She knelt down and prayed as reverently as she had on the first occasion.

As I watched her my scruples dissolved. The statue might be a lump of clay lit up by a string of lights, but it

101

was clearly doing some good for Mrs Callaghan. And she was a decent woman who surely deserved a favour. If the grotto in my van was helping to lighten the weight of her anxieties, then it had value of some kind. And if it did her good, then who was I to question it? Who indeed?

As she descended from the van, I reached up my hand to give her balance while she was stretching her foot towards the crate.

"Thanks, Lofty," she said. "You're one of the chosen ones. You have the gift. Don't be afraid to use it. Don't be afraid. You can lift the burden from people. You have been chosen for a role in life, believe me."

Flattered. Terrified. Confused, as frigging always. I had nothing to say. Only blush and smile.

She went over to her bicycle, which was propped against the gable, and took from the handlebars a shopping bag which was packed full.

"For you," she said, handing me the bag. "A little token of gratitude. A token from the plentiness of the farm, which has not been diminished, thanks to yourself."

I opened the bag and examined the contents. Eggs, butter, milk, vegetables, lovingly packed. I turned back to her in a gesture which conveyed my surprise, my gratitude, but also my response that this was too much, totally out of proportion with any favour she believed I had done her.

"Now, say nothing, but accept the gift. It is a token, no more than that."

Again her earnestness disarmed me. I felt it would be ungracious not to accept. So, in the end, all I said was, "Thanks."

I took out all the items she had so meticulously packed, and put them on the floor of the van so that I could give her back her bag. There were so many things packed in there that, by the time I had taken them all out and spread them on the floor of the van, they reached right up to the feet of the Virgin.

I was still admiring the array of food she had given me long after she had gone, until my aunt came out to find me. She was as excited as a fox in a chicken coop, when she saw the ingredients for several meals, and began to gather them up.

That night I found it impossible to sleep, I was so agitated by the incident. By the time morning came, I had decided that the only way to banish these disturbing thoughts was to go back to Mrs Callaghan's farm yard, and visit the stable, and see the cow, so that I could convince myself that there was nothing out of the ordinary in what had happened. Just pure coincidence. Nature taking its course without intervention from outside or above or anywhere else.

Mrs Callaghan was surprised to see me. But pleased. And she brought me to the stable where she was holding the cow and calf inside for a while.

It was a small stable with a galvanised iron roof. In two parts. One part was for storing hay. Separated by a dividing wall about four foot high from the other part, which had byres for about four cattle.

An air of peace struck me as soon as I entered. Warmth. The cow and calf were lying down, but when Mrs Callaghan prodded her with her toe, the cow rose smartly to her feet. The calf followed suit.

We stood there looking at the cow and calf. Enveloped in the wonder of it all. It was hard to imagine they had been nosing into the darkness only two days before. Now they were vibrant. With life. Light. Health.

"It's all thanks to you and to the Mother of God," she said, so softly she seemed to be sensitive to the tenderness of the moment. Anxious not to dispel it.

"No thanks to me," I mumbled back. "It's only a statue. There is nothing in the van but goods for sale."

"The Mother of God is there. And she is here. She is everywhere."

I had no inclination to contradict her. Especially as there was a warmth in the stable which had nothing to do with the weather outside. There was a cold north wind blowing from the sea, and occasional squalls of rain combed across the plain beneath us. But here in the stable was a cosiness which was unnatural in such weather.

After a while Mrs Callaghan began to fidget. No doubt she had much to do, chores to look after. I understood that. But I didn't want to leave.

"Is it alright if I stay here a while?" I asked her.

"Of course, Lofty, of course. You stay here as long as you like. Who is more entitled to be here than yourself?"

She went off and pulled the improvised door behind her. Three upright boards, two horizontal, hinged with wire to the doorframe. Daylight teeming through the gaps. Teeming through gaps in the walls too. Leaving the stable bright despite the absence of windows.

The calf was sucking the cow. The cow licked her calf. Adding to the flood of warmth that saturated the stable. Maternal warmth. The Mother of God was everywhere, as Mrs Callaghan said. No denying her presence here.

There was a low wall to contain the manger and I sat down on it close to the cow's head, to watch her. Leaned my back against the side wall. I was happy here. In a place like this I could find peace, peace such as I could never find at home. There was an atmosphere. A sense of some overwhelming spirit of love penetrating even into this most forsaken corner. The Mother of God.

I began to ponder that one. The Creator having a mother. It would explain a few things alright. Why he was so worked up about recognition. Why he demanded obedience and reverence. It had always struck me that he seemed insecure. Maybe that was why. Before him and above him was his mother. The Mother of God. Her love penetrating everywhere. From her, life. That was it. It had to be. From her, a son, the Creator. This compulsive craftsman. Builder. Hungry for recog-

104

nition, and honour, and respect. Jealous, even of his own mother. Shielding the truth of her existence from man. Man. His creation. Yes, his creation, but from material supplied by her.

From her another son, Jesus. Whom she sends into the Creator's world with the message of love. To liberate his creatures from bondage, from pain. To tell them love is more important than worship. Yes, it all made sense now. And her other son, the Holy Spirit. Three divine persons in one God. But that God was above them all. Mother of God. It all made sense now.

I must have been there for hours, blissfully re-working the creation of the world, looking at the cow and calf, absorbing the peace that flowed through the stable like a warm breeze in summer. Unawares.

When Mrs Callaghan opened the door and spoke to me through the darkness, only then did I realise how long I had spent in the stable.

"I was working down in the lower field, setting cabbage. I didn't realise you were still here, or I would have came back sooner to make the tea."

I followed her back to her kitchen and sat down at the table while she put the kettle on the gas cooker to boil.

9

IS THE MOMENT OF DEATH WHEN THE RIPPLE hits the outer wall? What is death, anyway? Maybe it is not the point of annihilation at all. Maybe the annihilation happens when the ripple converges on the centre again? Do we live our lives twice, once in reverse? For frig's sake. Maybe many times. Going out and coming back over the pool of water trapped in the bottom of the Creator's tar-barrel? Maybe he has us trapped forever.

That time I visited Mrs Callaghan's stable gave me a new insight into an awful lot of things. I was now certain the Creator had us trapped alright within this frigging construction of his. Certainly he had made us for his own purpose, to worship him. And that, no doubt, was why he had probably made us all, every one of us, with some deficiency or other, so that we could never be happy in this Garden of Eden he had set us in. Yes, he had probably left everyone short in one way or another. Even where he bestowed the riches of the earth on someone, he no doubt deprived him of the health or the peace of mind to enjoy it. And where he put health in his path, he made sure to combine it with poverty and misfortune for fear he would become too content. It was a neat nasty game. A neat nasty frigging trick, that's what it was. Heaven and Hell, all wrapped up in the one parcel. Making us turn to him in our misery. Making us kow-tow to him. Gutting each other in our attempts to make the most favourable impression.

But his mother obviously did not approve of all of this. Sent her other son to liberate us. With the message of love. Yes, it all made sense. The only way he could infiltrate and get his message, her message, through to us was by being born himself into the Creator's world. It explained that problem that had interested me for so long, the tempting of Jesus on the mountain. It wasn't Satan at all. It was his own renegade brother, the Creator and proprietor of this world, who offered it to Jesus if he would kneel down and adore him. It was a power game. That's how desperate he was for recognition and homage. There would have been greater satisfaction of his pride if he had got Jesus, his own brother, to acknowledge his superiority. One up on his mother. Well worth trading the world for that. Well worth bartering the human race for a pledge of worship from his own brother. That would have been some frigging notch on his stick. That would have made him top dog in heaven. If he could have swung it. But Jesus wasn't having any of it. Knew it was a trick. If he was stupid enough to try and save the world that way, then he would be a renegade too. And the world would be lost anyway. He wasn't going to betray his mother. Not like that. Told the Creator to frig off.

Yes, it was all falling into place for me. Now I could see why I was born with the inclination to be a priest, but deprived of the frigging brains, as my mother put it. And I felt better about it all now that I understood what was going on. Not that I wanted to be a priest anymore. I had long since come to reject the whole race of them. They were in league with the Creator. They had received the message from Jesus but they had distorted it until it was unrecognisable. Yes, they had taken upon themselves to twist the words of Jesus around until the same words appeared to be endorsing the Creator. Might even have stuck in the word "father" wherever Jesus said "mother". Wouldn't put it past them. Certainly they had cultivated hatred with the fervour they should have used to promote love, as Jesus would have had them do. But they were just like their frigging boss, all for power, and control, and recognition.

And they were all men. From the Pope down. Every one of them. That made sense too. Busily disguising the truth, that love flowed from the Mother of God, and that love was without limits. Yes, the truth was the very opposite of what all busy-body men tried to pretend, with their churches, and their governments, and their armies, and their businesses, and their balance sheets, and their frigging self-importance. They were probably all in league with the Creator, trying to convince us that it was their aggression, and activity, and endless competition, that mattered. Maybe Stephen Hanlon had come to the same conclusion that time he was warning me about competition. Maybe that was why he never went inside the churches he serviced for fifty years. Maybe he had come to the conclusion too that it was the Mother of God who gave love without condition, gave it with total generosity. No strings attached. No fishing for recognition. No adoration required. With just the advice to spread it around. The love. The message. And she was more likely to be found outside the front gate than inside the church. It was a relief to me to have it all worked out at last. It was also a relief to think that maybe there were other people who had worked it out in the same way.

There were other consequences too of my encounter with Mrs Callaghan. She was spreading her own message around about the miraculous curing of her cow. After three days the whole parish seemed to know about her recovery. After a week the seven parishes of Tireragh were abuzz with the story. Embellished for dramatic effect. No credit given to the poor old cow for pulling herself through. No credit given to Mrs Callaghan for nursing her through the night. No allowance for the possibility that it was a pure coincidence I was there at the time of recovery. No. The cow was cured through the statue of Our Lady in my van. And, by association, she was cured by me.

It's amazing how changeable people are. I mean people in general. Okay, there are individuals who never change. The old people, for example. They are like the boulders that squat in their hungry fields outside, never changing. But the rest. A different frigging story altogether. At one stage they treated me like an idiot. Later they afforded me a grudging respect because of my business. Now, because of Mrs Callaghan and her cow, they were looking at me as if I was a frigging saint or something. Looking at me with awe. Even though I was the same person. Even though I had done nothing to change their outlook. As I have said, people were always a mystery to me. I never understood them and, of course, now, I never will.

Yes, I was a frigging celebrity. Suddenly the appearance of the red van on the road was no longer a nuisance to be tolerated at the minimum cost. No longer a signal for the miserly to go lurking behind curtains. It was a visitation.

Everywhere I went there were people. Waiting to pray at the shrine. Waiting to see the statue of the Virgin. Waiting to buy some token from the van. Waiting with their requests, their arms laden with offerings from the fruit of their labour. Sometimes the offerings were placed in anticipation of a favour, sometimes in thanksgiving for a favour granted. Always the offerings were generous in scale. Farm produce generally, but also turf, hand-crafted furniture. Even money, even money, for frig's sake.

People knelt before the shrine and prayed. For all kinds of things. They prayed for the recovery of sick animals, as Mrs Callaghan had done, and they rejoiced when the animals did not die. They prayed for the safety of their crops in the face of some spreading disease, and when the threat passed and their crops survived they showed their gratitude by loading my van from the weight of their abundance. Above all they prayed for delivery from the weather, that most precarious and unpredictable factor in farm life. They prayed for sun when the rain dribbled down from an overcast sky for forty days without pause. They prayed for rain when drought was shrivelling the grass out of reach of the searching teeth of their sheep. And always they seemed to think their prayers had been answered. Strange.

And it was always the cream of their produce that they loaded on to the floor of my van. Eggs, milk, potatoes, vegetables. Someone tethered a lamb to the bumper of the van once. Would you believe that? Someone also dumped a load of the best peat turf at the gable of my house in thanksgiving for the good weather that enabled him to save it. And when they received a good price for their livestock at the fair or the mart, they pressed money surreptitiously into my fist. As if I had been their jobber.

At first I was embarrassed by this excess of generosity. And I was at a loss as to what I should do with these gifts. The way they were left before the grotto, I felt they really didn't belong to me at all. A feeling that was re-inforced when I reflected on the fact that I had done nothing, absolutely nothing, to earn them. In the past I had experienced guilt when I knew somebody was buying a medal or a picture that he didn't really want. But at least that was a transaction. He had the medal and could do what he wished with it. But there was no transaction here. And it worried me.

But then I was thinking, and thinking, what if I had been chosen by the Mother of God, as Mrs Callaghan had suggested. What if I was chosen as some kind of agent? It was not my choice. I could not help it. I had to accept my fate. At one time, fate had made me the butt of every joke and jibe, had treated me worse than any tinker's ass, and I had put up with it. Had no choice. Now it was showering me with these gifts, so why should I not put up with that too? Anyway, it would be an insult to the Mother of God to let them rot, or to be churlish in accepting generosity if it came from her. So my aunt and my mother were provided with all the food they could cook and eat. When there was a surplus, my aunt proposed that she take it to the grocer's shop and exchange it for items that she needed. But I would not hear of this and insisted that they give it to the St Vincent de Paul people for the needy.

In this way we became very comfortable indeed. I was earning stacks of money. Several times a week I had to go to the wholesalers and load the van. I expected that the wave of enthusiasm for my statue and my goods would pass soon enough. That the charm of my grotto would soon fade. I was well enough versed in business to understand the vagaries of demand in the market. But, you know, the charm didn't fade. Demand kept growing.

Although I believed more and more every day in my speculation regarding the Mother of God, my previous experience of life was such that I was nevertheless waiting each day for the big disappointment. You will understand my state of mind. I was bracing myself for disillusion. But nothing happened to undermine my belief. Quite the contrary. The more I thought about the world, the more convinced I was that I had stumbled into the truth. Day after day reports were coming in on the radio of Catholics killing Protestants and Protestants killing Catholics in Northern Ireland. And I thought, yes, this is his work. The Creator keeps planting different images of himself in people's minds, so they will fight each other, slaughter each other, to prove their devotion to him. It was the same all over the world. People killing each other to push their image of the Creator as the proper one, the only acceptable one. And all the time this same jealous God was looking down and demanding more and more fervour. Yes, it made frigging sense alright.

But despite all that, flowing on relentlessly, were life and love, which went back to a source above and beyond the Creator. Yes, and they would continue to flow, continue to resist his efforts to suppress or to mould them. And wasn't it ironic that here were people waiting at every cross-roads, totally without knowing, to pay homage to the Mother of God? To ask her for life and love. Without ever understanding the significance of their own words, 'Mother of God'.

I could not drive with ease along the roads anymore with people popping out from gateways to wave me down. People waiting at cross-roads for me to come. People converging on the van wherever I stopped. To say a prayer before the statue. To buy a medal. To press five times the value of the medal into my reluctant fist.

They prayed for the fertility of their land, and saw the visit of the red Ford van and the shrine as an opportunity to underline the sincerity of their prayer. And when the first shoots of the spring appeared, green and eager, they credited the miraculous statue and the Mother of God more than the natural turn of the seasons, more than their own careful nurturing.

Once I got over my initial scruples I started to enjoy being a sort of agricultural charm. And I was also getting satisfaction from the feeling that I was promoting the Mother of God in opposition to my old enemy, the Creator. It was a life with no disadvantages. People did not seem to blame me, or the statue, or the Mother of God, if an animal died, or a crop failed. They resigned themselves to such reverses. I was caught up in a spiral of advantage. And the satisfaction of the people seemed genuine. They calculated the yield of their crops and declared it to be far ahead of previous years. They could not recall when they lost so few lambs at birth. And despite this abundance, they got better prices for their produce than ever before.

To avoid the tedium of stopping at every house and every cross-roads, I decided to adopt a pattern of making prolonged stops at holy places, such as wells, trees, standing stones and the like. I felt that such places were more in tune with the deeper devotion to the Mother of God than were churches and chapels. Besides I liked the atmosphere in these places. And, of course, dozens of people converged as soon as they saw the red van parked there.

I was very happy doing that. Providing the mobile shrine, stopping at my favourite land-marks. But, after a while, I found that people were expecting more and more from me personally, in a way that was disconcerting. The limits which I felt comfortable within were being pushed and breached continually.

People started to regard me personally as a healer. And that disturbed me. That was a change from regarding the shrine or the Mother of God as the source of the healing. One day I was parked beside the Holy Well in Dromard. Quite a cluster of people around, as usual. Saying prayers at the Well and taking its water, queuing up for a turn at the shrine in the back of the van, buying objects from the stall I had set up. The usual requests, farmers concerned about the weather, housewives with their hopes for the flocks of geese and turkeys they were rearing. The usual.

But then this woman approached me. She was tugging a girl of about sixteen behind her. The woman asked me to pray over the girl to cure her. I stared at her in amazement.

"I have no cure," I managed to stammer in indignation.

She stared back at me. "Of course you have the cure. Haven't you cured half the animals from here to the Moy, and saved half the crops as well. Haven't you increased the yield from the land three-fold. Of course you have the cure. Haven't you brought rain when the grass was scorched to the roots? Haven't you given us the sun when we were lost in an eternal cloud? And if you have done all these things, then you can cure my Maura, if you want to."

Yes, I was amazed at the words I was hearing. Despite all that had happened, despite the fact that it was happening day in day out, I myself felt distanced from it. You know what I mean. As if it had little or nothing to do with me personally. As if I were outside looking on. Now this woman was making it personal, demanding my involvement. And my immediate instinct was to look over my shoulder to establish if it was really me she was talking to. I was at a loss. Continued staring at her. But wondering what the girl's problem was.

The domineering mother started up again. "Maura is late, if you get my meaning. Late. You know . She hasn't started her bleeding yet."

I hadn't a notion of what she was talking about, but noticed that this mention of her problem caused Maura to go crimson in the face, to retreat even closer behind her mother, and inspect more intently the ground beneath her feet. Whatever her 'bleeding' problem was, it was obviously very embarrassing for her.

"She will be sixteen in a month's time. So she's very late. I brought her to the doctor, but he said to leave it be, that it would all happen in its own good time. But it can't be good. There was always a cure for it in the old days. A remedy. But damned if I can find a single person alive who can make it up. So I thought you might have the cure. Your type of cure."

I still did not know what the woman was talking about. Still kept staring at the attractive little girl who was being skewered in front of me. I blurted out the only thing that came into my blank void of a frigging mind. To free myself from this situation. This embarrassment.

"Why don't you say a prayer at the statue?"

The mother stood silently, absorbing this pronouncement. Looking at me with reverence. And relief. As if that was it. The problem solved.

"Okay, Maura," she said with hushed voice. "Do as he says. Up with you."

The girl appeared as relieved as I was that the interview had come to an end. She hopped up eagerly on the back of the van to join the queue and say her prayer before the shrine. The mother paused, still looking at me. Then she reached out and touched my arm, ever so gently, ever so respectfully, as if she were testing to see if she would get an electric shock. Then she turned and followed her daughter up into the back of the van.

Apparently, poor Maura's bleeding started within a few days. I'm not surprised. The encounter would have set a frigging stone bleeding, not to mind a little girl. I heard that bit of news in the usual way. Rumours of another miracle. Eventually reaching my mother's ears. And my mother, screened behind the newspaper she was reading, rounded off: "She was a few years behind alright. But apparently she's okay now."

I was glad poor Maura was okay, and that her body was now functioning like a woman, but, as I have said, being drawn personally into the business of curing was certainly a development that made me feel extremely uncomfortable. It was one thing having the hopes for an ailing cow vested in my statue, or someone buying a medal to protect himself on a journey, it was a different matter myself being loaded with the responsibility for a sick child.

Night after night, I couldn't sleep after that encounter with Maura and her mother. Tossing and turning. Wracked by scruples.

Until the anxiety eased. And I could think again. In the dead of night. What if? What if I really were being used by the Mother of God? Her grace, her love, held at bay by the hard crust of the Creator's dike. Could penetrate, could filter through only where it found chink or fault. Like spring water oozing through a crack in the earth's rock floor. Maybe that was it. Maybe it was the very flaws in his creation which provided the best openings for his mother.

Nice one. To punish this consummate craftsman through the flaws he had deliberately created. Good enough for him. He created this world, this universe of extra-ordinary beauty and complexity, wove the fabric from the threads of life and love. But made it imperfect. Deliberately. To divert attention from where he had stolen the threads in the first place. Injected hatred and aggression, fear, violence, death, confusion. To keep us occupied. To keep us insecure. Persuaded us that we were responsible for our own imperfection, responsible for the evil that he had injected into his creation. Made us feel like miserable shits. And when he had us thoroughly confused, he flashed images of himself before our slavish eyes, and demanded recognition as the sole creator of all that was good in the world, all that was good for us. Demanded respect and adulation from us poor trembling sods who knew no better. Who feared to trust our ingrained instinct that love and life flowed free and deep, felt more natural than his unnatural surface storm of hatred and aggression.

Oh, yes. He had a million ways to confuse us, to manipulate us. He dazzled us. Dangled the satisfactions of the world before us. If. If we were prepared to bow down before him. As the almighty. As the creator of the heavens and the earth. If we were prepared to put no other gods before him. Not even his mother. And unlike Jesus, we were terrified to tell him to frig off.

But the ocean of her love was pressing at his ramparts. Was spouting and spurting through faults and cracks. And if I was one of the flaws through which she poured her sympathy for the suffering of the Creator's world, then so be it. So be frigging it. Who was I to contest her will?

116

10

YES. THE TAR-BARREL SEEMS LESS OF A black hole, don't you think, when you realise that the face looking down at you from on high, the face of your gaoler, is not that of the ultimate power. Not by a long shot. And you realise that the time will come when the tar-barrel will be awash in the final overwhelming surge of her compassion and indignation. Putting an end to time. Putting an end to all physical limitation. Calling a halt to the Creator's wilful games. And all the puny dregs in which he has had us locked will run free down into the ocean. And he will be looking on like a naughty child who has had his toys confiscated.

Indeed.

Anyway. It was the real ocean I was glancing at and thinking about while I drove down the shore road heading for Aughris. Heading for the big plunge.

Have you ever watched a blacksmith plunge a piece of red-hot metal into a water trough? Watched the seething and sizzling until the heat is quenched. That's how I visualised the plunge of the van. Seething and sizzling until the last spark of pain is extinguished. But never mind. I was torn between the urgency to beat the darkness to Aughris, and the need to bid farewell to this countryside as I was passing through it for the last time. Darkness. Many of my favourite landmarks flashing past. Place-names I could recite now when probably no one else could. Cuanawad. Cuanariadaigh. Uachwore. Donagh. Names I had heard recited in the litanies of the old people. And the names of the families who had lived here for generations I had also heard recited. And they too were engraved in my memory. Wonderful, strange sounding names, like Killawee, Lavelle, Kilrehill. Families who had been turning sods in these fields for thousands of years, others who had come with the Normans or the English or the Spanish or the French. Giving the place a character, a spirit. Lifting it out of the realm of mere matter, mere rock, mere water and vegetation.

Across the fields, on the main road, looking down over Farranaharpy, was the grey chair erected as a memorial to the great historian Dubhaltach Mac Firbis. Last of a line of hereditary historians. Ended up in Easkey, as I mentioned. After his castle at Lacken was confiscated by the Cromwellians. Last of a whole tribe, who for hundreds and hundreds of years recorded the history and the genealogy, the poems and the stories of Ireland. They recorded so that the people who walked the land for thousands and thousands of years would not be forgotten, would not cease to exist, as Tom Mac Sharry feared would happen to his tribe if he were to die. Dubhaltach, the last of his tribe. Still working, still recording at Easkey, even after he had lost his castle, lost his land. Even after his old patrons the O'Dowds had been uprooted and driven into the mountains, and the whole of Tireragh confiscated by the plundering English.

He was murdered in Farranaharpy. Just across the fields. Where his monument stands today. The chair of learning. Murdered by the buck, Thomas Crofton. From the ranks of the new English rulers and land-lords. Mac Firbis, an old man, going to the assistance of a young woman in a tavern who was being molested by Crofton. Thomas Crofton, local toff. Mac Firbis, the last of his tribe of hereditary scribes and historians, poets and scholars, law men. The very last. Not a man, nor a woman, nor a child carrying his name in Tireragh from that day to this. Mac Firbis. The name I heard over and over from the old people. A name that stirred the blood.

118

Yes, my mind was filled with the people who had lived in Tireragh generations ago. Listening to the old people, I had picked up a vast knowledge of families. I knew who their fathers and mothers were, their grandfathers and grandmothers. And therefore I knew which family was related to which. First Cousins. Second Cousins. Third. Even more. And I could picture them too, those ghostly ancestors of the living generations. In my mind's eye. Picture them more clearly, more defined in feature and character, than I could their living descendants. If the truth were told.

That was one of my failings. Remembering the frigging faces of the living. Do you have difficulty remembering faces? It's fine if the people are dead. If they remain in your head. You can put a face on them and it stays there. But if the people are alive, they keep undermining the picture you have of them. Travelling around the countryside, I knew most people in their own plots. Knew to expect them there when I drove up in the van. Recognised them a mile off. But when they were dressed differently, and I met them in another place, I was lost. In town on a Saturday. Outside the church on a Sunday when they were spruced up and dressed in their finery. I wouldn't recognise them from Adam.

Looking at them filing past on a busy shopping street, they all looked so similar to me. I was always getting myself in trouble. First of all, I had the habit of staring at people. And that was unsettling for them. Then, when I thought I recognised someone I would make friendly gestures in his direction, only to be greeted by a blank face. Or a puzzled expression.

The worst was when I was parked outside the church, say, on the day of a mission or a special event. I watched the file of parishioners going by. As they passed, each and every one of them would greet me by my name. I should know them. I would have known them if I had encountered them on their own patch.

But here I could not recognise any of them. Their features went into a state of flux before my eyes, and I mistook one for the other. I failed to recognise even someone who gave me a generous donation the day before.

I developed my own way of coping, though. Half-baked. I never called someone by his name when I met him on alien territory. Just mumbled a greeting in an embarrassed sort of way. And I addressed them all as 'Boss'. It was a little trick of Stephen Hanlon's. He called everyone 'Boss' to make him feel good. Important. Superior. More inclined to buy something. I could not command the same easy manner, but it served a purpose, nevertheless. To hide the fact that I could not recognise these people. A vital purpose.

I curbed my inclination to greet people in the street whom I thought I recognised. But I could never eliminate my habit of staring. It was the fascination. The wonder at the unknown. People were infinitely interesting in so far as everything that happened under that exterior was a mystery. Even their faces were a frigging mystery to me. You'd think with all that staring that I'd register some of their physical characteristics. Even their clothes. That used to drive my mother into a frenzy of frustration.

"Did you meet anyone today?" she would ask over the dinner table by way of an effort at conversation.

"Mrs Walsh."

"Did you, really? And how was she looking? The poor woman hasn't been well lately."

"She looked okay."

"But was she yellowish in the face? It was a touch of jaundice she had."

"I didn't notice"

"She might have been on her way to the hospital. Was she dressed up?"

" I don't remember."

"Well, did she have a coat, or a hat?"

"I can't remember."

"Well, she must have been wearing some kind of clothes. She was hardly naked. Do you remember anything she was wearing?"

"No."

Aside from my tendency to seize up under such interrogation by my mother, it was true. I could not recollect anything of what the woman was wearing. She was not naked. Of that much I could be certain. That I would have noticed. Would have remembered. My mother thought it extraordinary that I could recall nothing, ever, of what a person was wearing. And I suppose it was unusual. If it was my aunt she was talking to, the two of them would be down to describing the shade and shape of the buttons on the woman's dress.

In order to know people, I had to keep them in my head. And if they existed in the physical world, as I have said, I was left floundering whenever I encountered them in unusual surroundings. I suppose that is why I was so fond of the dead. They stayed in my head. Fixed. I knew them. They did not come to my stall, in disguise as it were, and say something to perplex me. To make me question myself whether I knew them at all. Whether I knew anything. For frig's sake, if I couldn't recognise someone's face how could I presume to know what was happening behind the face. It kept bringing me back to myself, to my own defectiveness.

Still. I had my strengths. I could remember what I heard even if I could remember nothing of what I saw. I had even taught myself to read using my talent for such remembering. And sometimes when I wanted to record something for relating back to my mother, I would use the same technique. If I met Mrs Walsh at the Agricultural Show in Skreen, and I wanted to ensure that I was able to describe her clothes in detail to my mother, I would whisper to myself, "Mrs Walsh is wearing a green two-piece suit, a black hat that has a little bit of net hanging down from it, black high-heel shoes, and nylon stockings." That account was then lodged in my mind and I had not the slightest difficulty in reciting it for my mother when I went home. Or six months later, if the need arose. Frigging weird, isn't it?

Maybe it was this uneasiness with ordinary people that made me seek out the older people and their talk of the past. Their narratives I could grasp and know and inhabit in my imagination. Even when people were clamouring for me at a cross-roads or waiting patiently at an ancient mass-rock, I would often take a detour and pay a visit to John Robertson, or Peter Kilduff, or Maggy Brett. Into their kitchens I would go, and sit down, and happily listen to them talking, for hours on end.

Peter Kilduff was one of my favourites. Like a friend. A real friend. Spoke to me in a normal sort of way. Quite religious too. He would go into the back of the van as soon as I arrived and kneel down before the statue.

Having said his few prayers he would come out and declare in his tough unsentimental way, "That's good. It might help. Those whores of spuds over there could do with a bit of a prod from somewhere to set them moving. They're slow this year. Damned slow."

"What do they need? More rain, or more sun?"

"More heat. The ground is cold. We're on the north slope of the mountain here. It takes a while to warm it up."

"I see."

"Do you think you could manage that, Lofty? A bit of heat. Because, if you can, that will be the best field of Kerr Pinks in the country. Balls of flour. Waiting to melt between your teeth. And I'll give you a hundred-weight of the best of them." He laughed. Mirth in his tone, untainted by mockery or condescension. He expected nothing. He had survived sixty, seventy, years wresting his dinner from the inhospitable fields

122

on the side of this mountain. Nothing was likely to get the better of him now.

"But what we really need around here, Lofty, is women. Look at that countryside from here to the sea. What do you have? In every second house you have a bloody bachelor. Old bachelors. Young bachelors. And hardly a woman from the bridge in Ballisodare to the bridge at Ardnaree. Every one of those bachelors hungering for a woman. Just one woman for one night is what they pray for when they go on their knees, most of them, believe me. It's not the crops and the cattle that's on their minds at all, but women. Jesus, Lofty, if you can really work miracles, you'll get us a woman. One woman even, for the lot of us. That will do. We'll swap that for all that heaven can send. And we won't mind if the crops rot in the fields or the sheep perish on the mountain."

Before him he had the whole landscape of Tireragh. Laid out. Beautiful. Yet he looked on it with the detachment of a hangman. As though his heart were bound with steel for fear it might disintegrate, for fear it might soften, and then he would never be able to face the daily battle with his stubborn fields.

I let my eye wander from farmhouse to farmhouse, from cottage to cottage, and what he said was true: in a huge number of them were single men. Living alone. Living with brothers. Living with even more elderly parents. Few were the houses that had women. What he said about there not being a single woman in the whole barony was obviously an exaggeration, but there was too much of the truth in it for me to go quibbling.

And I knew what he was talking about. The hunger. Who knew it better than myself, for frig's sake?

There were women and girls in Tireragh. Of course there were. But very few. Most had left as soon as they were of age to look for a job. In Dublin. In England. In America. Further afield. Those that remained were outnumbered ten to one, maybe even twenty to one, by the men. You could see it at the dances in the Seafield, or in the Marine in Enniscrone. A straggly line of girls waiting to be asked out to dance, a battalion of men, rows upon rows, maybe five deep, about to advance on them as soon as the music started. Then the melee. Until the girls had all been picked off. All of them bar the few who didn't want to dance, or who hadn't been asked by the right person.

I was always in there. In the frigging rearguard. From about fourteen years of age onwards everyone went to dances. It was expected of you. It was normal. Not to go was definitely suspect. And it was also expected of you to speak in glowing terms of the experience the next day. I abhorred the frigging dances. Few of us managed to get even a single dance in the course of the night. Myself. I was guaranteed failure. Never, ever, succeeded in getting a frigging dance. It wasn't for total lack of trying. I always took up a place in the back row when the men lined up for the charge. And so it was always the girls who were left that I ended up asking. All I got from them was a decisive shake of the head, accompanied by an embarrassed flush if I happened to know them.

The hunger. That's what drew us back, week after week, despite all the ignoring and all the insult and all the hurt pride. Just to look at the girls in their light dresses. And to dream that one day we would meet someone who would dance with us. The hunger. I knew all about it. I knew what Peter was talking about. Every summer when John Curley's daughter returned from England, all dolled up, with short skirts and low blouses, she set the whole countryside on fire. There were moans and there were groans. But there was sweet frig all we could do about it. And if the normal young fellows had no chance, what hope for me? Yes I knew all about the same frigging hunger.

124

But at least now I had something in my life to distract me from such pain. My business, my new-found respect, were a powerful antidote, but the constant activity was probably best of all.

And talking of respect, the fact that I could read was now being cited as evidence either of another miracle or of my supernatural powers. Everyone knew I had left the national school still unable to read or write my own name. Now I took delight in showing that I could read road-signs, notices, or the names of the pamphlets I was selling. I enjoyed going in to the newsagents to buy comics. And the people marvelled at such achievement.

People were making similar assumptions when they became aware of my store of local knowledge - that I had acquired it overnight and by strange means. I was now being consulted frequently when people were at a loss. For instance the woman who was going around trying to trace a man by the name of Kavanagh who had left the area some time in the last century. She was frustrated. Had failed to unearth any information whatsoever. When she was about to give up, someone sent her in my direction. A job for the miracle worker, I suppose. She was a very pleasant woman. Well spoken. Easy personality. As a result I had no difficulty talking to her. I suggested he might be one of the Keaveneys, because some of the posh Keaveneys at one time changed their name to Kavanagh. That seemed to her worth investigating, and she went off excited. Two days later she came up to me on the street in Dromore West and gave me a big hug. She had located the man in the parish register without difficulty. I was right.

I was also right the time the American came looking for his roots, as he said. His great-grandfather had come from the parish of Easkey, and the poor man was distraught when he found that the name, John Conway, was as common as cow-dung in the parish. Again, when all else had failed he was sent to me. He approached me when I was manning the stall at the fair day in Easkey. He was a very personable man, and I took to him quite well. I agreed to meet him the following morning in the lounge of the Seafield Hotel. Over tea and scones he gave me the details of his grandfather. All he knew was the name, the townland where he was born, and the fact that he had emigrated to the United States with his brother, Frank, just after the Great Famine. There were dozens of John Conways in the parish records, so he could not figure out which of them was his ancestor. The only other clue he had was a garbled name for the townland, but no one was able to identify which townland it was. I listened carefully while he repeated the name that had passed from one generation to the next within his family over in the United States as the location of their home. After hearing it about three times, I recognised it, an old Irish name for a townland between Easkey and Rathlee, one that had gone out of use. But I had heard the old people use it once or twice. And so I was able to identify his cousins for him. And there were indeed cousins, still occupying the same small farm. And they had cousins too, so many it took him a long time to write them all down. He was stunned. As the interview progressed he became more and more respectful. He had obviously heard of me by reputation, and thought he was talking to some kind of oracle.

The talk of miracles and supernatural events evidently brought me to the attention of the Bishop. There were rumours and hints that I was being investigated. At first I was amused and flattered that the forces of the Creator were seeing me as a threat. But then I imagined the confrontation, the possible consequences. What if they banned me from trading outside the churches, or at the missions? Then I was not so exultant. Frigging worried, I was.

I sensed that the investigation had begun when I noticed a middle-aged man turning up regularly at my stops. He didn't buy anything. Didn't pray at the statue. He just loitered among the crowds. Watching. When I examined him closely, I convinced myself that he was a priest out of uniform.

He watched other people going aboard the van, saw them kneeling to pray before the lighted statue, saw them leaving gifts and donations on the floor of the van in thanksgiving for favours they reckoned they had received. He followed me on days I visited houses in out-of-the-way places. Once or twice he came up to the stall and spoke to me. Nothing profound. Just small-talk about the trade in religious goods. Apart from my suspicion that he was a spy, apart from my anxiety as a result, he was not the kind of person I could have talked to anyway. Starchy stiff. You know the type. Looked out of character without his collar. No wonder our exchanges were limited in scope and style.

After a couple of weeks of his constant appearances, I saw him no more. I was relieved. And I was right . He was a priest. And sent by the Bishop to investigate the miraculous happenings in Tireragh. News filtered back. People loved subterfuge. Too good to keep quiet. With all the rumours and twisted tales, I could not make out what exactly he had reported to the Bishop. But nothing more happened. According to the speculation of the clergy who took tea with my mother and aunt, he had advised the Bishop that it was all harmless. Innocent. That it would disappear with the first bad harvest, or with a collapse in the farm prices.

11

D O YOU BELIEVE IN GHOSTS? I WAS OFTEN thinking that ghosts might well be those people on the reverse journey. You know. From the wall of the tar-barrel back to the centre. Traversing the same little patch of time and place, but in a different form, in a different direction. What do you think? Over and back across the Creator's tar-barrel. And I wondered if I would sometime meet my father as our two ripples overlapped.

Soon I too will be on the reverse journey. After I hit the wall. And if we meet then, it will be as ghosts. Both of us. Will we have anything to say to one another then? Frig all, I suppose. The weather won't be bothering us. Perhaps we will be speculating as to how long more we will be held captive, like the Children of Lir, until the alarm sounds to herald the breaking of the flood-waters.

Perhaps we will just be moaning about our condition. Lamenting the power of the Creator. His duplicity. His perversity.

Even though the encounter with the Bishop's man passed off uneventfully, it still demonstrated how vigilant were the forces of the Creator. Not just the church. But the churches. All of them. Governments too. With their armies and their police and their officials. Men. Nearly always. With their conflicts and their competition. Their wars and their eternal frigging rivalries. Their self-importance. Always generating a distraction for fear of peace and quiet. For fear of giving people time to think for themselves. Always on guard against an intrusion by the Mother of God.

Always on guard.

Did men make a pact with the Creator? I wondered. Were they brought up to the mountains too? Shown all the kingdoms of the Earth. Theirs. In return for homage, sole and undivided. Did they accept the deal? Turn their backs on the Mother of God? Betray the female half of the population? Gain a world which they could operate only on the basis of conflict and competition and hatred? A world which the Creator could keep under his thumb by promoting constant strife, sowing confusion constantly. Probably. Most probably. There was no other explanation.

And yet. Strange as it may seem. Despite their relentless enterprise. I was sure I could sense her presence everywhere. Not in churches. Especially not in churches. But in the fields, where the corncrake was rasping out her joy, in the hedges where the woodbine was billowing its own wild incense, in the unsolicited wave of the hand from a passer-by. Yes. In spite of the conspiracy of the priests, and the governments, and the bankers, and the soldiers, there was a spirit abroad which could not be destroyed, even if it was constantly suppressed. There were times when I was beginning to believe it was the world of conflict and competition and hatred built by the Creator that was brittle and unstable. Hence the vehemence with which they shored it up. And one day that world would surely collapse, like a makeshift dam before the power of the great flood. Of all that I was now convinced.

And so my belief in the value of what I was doing did not weaken. The magic had not dissipated, as the Bishop's spy had forecast, with the autumn, nor with the spring. Long spells of unrelenting rain did not wash away people's faith in the statue, nor did a sustained drought wither the enthusiasm of those who came to pray before the shrine. Another year. Greener grass in the pasture. Taller stalks from potato drills. Ewes filling the hillside with bleating lambs, and sows littering bonhams in multitudes in the stable yards. And my red van threading its way around the countryside was regarded as central to this cycle of fertility, like the rising sun, or the spring rain. And as the people prospered I prospered.

After the Bishop's man gave me the clearance, I seemed to gain even greater respectability. Even the priests passing me at the church gate began to show me a little deference. It wasn't respect, neither was it condescension. It was a sort of uncomfortable recognition. They didn't treat me as normal. Hardly anybody did, for frig's sake. Well, Peter Kilduff and his like did, but then maybe they were as odd as I was. Maybe that was why I was so much at ease with them. Anyway. My presence was being acknowledged even by the frigging magpies.

And the people. They now seemed to regard me as some kind of holy man. But I didn't feel like a holy man. In fact I was very uncomfortable with the idea of having any such status. I would have been easier if people had continued to regard me as an outsider. I was not on the side of the Creator, and I was afraid I might be sucked over. Afraid I might be drawn into the ranks of the enemy by stealth or by default. As a result, I began to cultivate Stephen Hanlon's strategy of not going into church at all. Even when I was not trading, I would loiter outside in the yard during mass time. Not that people seemed to pay any heed. Either they regarded it as another eccentricity of mine, which could be ignored, or they were of the opinion that I was so holy already, I did not need to go to mass like everyone else. So much for my efforts to break my frigging image of holiness.

It was this odd special status of mine which brought me an invitation to go on the diocesan pilgrimage to Lourdes. Before, I probably would not have been allowed to participate in such a pilgrimage, unless, of course, I was being brought as an invalid by some responsible adult. Now, a delegation of three serious-featured men arrived at the house to ask if I would grace the pilgrimage with my presence. They were so serious about it, I felt like laughing.

They realised how great an undertaking this would be for me, they said. A half-wit, they might have added, but didn't. That was why they came to the house to discuss it with my mother and my aunt present, rather than simply approaching me by myself in the street. It would be a privilege to have me along. My devotion to Our Lady, they said, was legendary. My presence would encourage others to go, would ensure the success of the pilgrimage. Anything that encouraged people to go to Lourdes, and to dedicate themselves to Our Lady had to be good, they said.

It sounded good to me. Even though my opinion was scarcely being asked. The discussion was conducted between the three men on the one hand and my mother and aunt on the other, as if I wasn't there, or as if I wasn't capable of grasping the strands of the conversation, or as if I couldn't answer for myself. Just because I was listening with my mouth open. Anyway. It sounded good. A flight on an aeroplane. Five days in Paris on the way out. Five days in Lourdes. A night in Paris on the way back. Coach drives through the length of France. Very exciting. And a chance to study my own line of business in another country. Might come back with new ideas. Especially from Lourdes.

My mother and aunt professed to being anxious. Worried. Not at all sure that it was safe to let me off on such a long and complicated journey. Especially as I had never been away from home before. John Byrne was the leader of the delegation. Spokesman. Probably elected because the sombre expression on his face stood out even against the sombre expressions of the other two. It was a face in which the outbreak of a smile might look sacrilegious.

They had anticipated the misgivings of the two ladies, he said. Had given it much thought. Could assure them that any misgivings they had were totally unnecessary. There would be no problem. The three of them were travelling as a group and I would make up a fourth member. The whole pilgrimage was being organised for the diocese by the Legion of Mary, and they were all in the council of the local praesidium. Dependable people. They would be scrupulous in ensuring my safety.

They went over the travel arrangements for the third time. They had their own thoughts about the stop-over in Paris, but the trip would not be commercially viable without this incentive for the less devout. The positive aspect of the stop-over was that it would afford Legionnaires like themselves an opportunity of engaging in their contact work, rescuing souls. No opportunity should be missed. And this was clearly such an opportunity. Of course, the mass of people wanted the stop-over included as a bit of a holiday. And there was no harm in that, no harm at all, if it enticed them to go to Lourdes. The three of them would not, of course, be indulging themselves in Paris. A bit of sight-seeing during the day, naturally. But, like good soldiers of the Legion, they would spend their evenings doing their contact work, wresting hostages from the clutches of the Adversary, spreading devotion to the Queen of Heaven.

By the time John Byrne had finished his play the two women were convinced not only that I should go, but that it would be morally questionable not to support such a valiant effort to rescue these trapped souls from the clutches of the Devil. It was nothing less than a crusade, they repeated to each other enthusiastically long after John Byrne and his friends had left.

I was delighted to be going. I had earned a lot of money on my business and had spent very little. I was itching to enjoy myself. And this seemed a very appropriate way of enjoying myself. An appropriate way of spending my money, considering how I had earned it.

A pilgrimage to Lourdes. To see the original of my grotto. A pilgrimage to Lourdes. The very words sounded exotic. I could put no pictures on those words. None. Except, of course, a picture of the Grotto. I had seen it often enough, had modelled my own shrine on it. To behold it in reality was a prospect that teased my imagination to the limits of excitement. And there had to be stalls there. Pilgrims converging from all corners of the earth. There had to be stalls. And I might get some new ideas.

I had never been out of the country before. Never travelled on an aeroplane. In truth I had been in Dublin only a few times. On day-trips with my mother and aunt. Yes, my excitement, the tension of anticipation, was therefore almost unbearable. I drove along in the van taking the two sides of the road, in a waltz which was out of kilter with the tune I was humming. But it was sheer harmony to me. I found it difficult to tot the simplest additions on the calculator. Some of the events I had intended covering I overlooked, and left clusters of people standing at holy-wells all over the place. When I visited the wholesaler I could not recall what items I needed to order. I tried abandoning the business for the duration, but that was even more unbearable with so much time for thinking in the vacancy of home.

With great difficulty I managed to while away the three weeks to the morning of departure. We gathered outside the chapel, the local contingent, and were collected by a coach. I had a new hold-all in which my suit and my carefully ironed shirts were packed. Along with all the other things my mother and aunt thought necessary for this foray into Europe. They were both hovering about. John Byrne and his two companions arrived and took me under their wing, once more reassuring the women about my safety, once more declaring that it was a very great privilege to have me along. I sat beside John Byrne in the coach and he gave me the window seat. The other two, Peter Henry and Harry Murphy sat behind us. Harry had the window seat too but didn't display much interest in the countryside.

There was nothing new for us to see, anyway, until we reached the town of Ballina. We pulled up and parked outside the cathedral, and here there was certainly something to see. About twenty coaches in a line. All facing in the one direction. People parading up and down. Talking to each other. Loading cases on to the coaches.

"Are these all for the pilgrimage?" I asked John Byrne.

"Every one of them," he replied proudly. "Every one of them. We will be travelling in convoy from here to Dublin Airport. By the time we get there, the whole of Ireland will know that the Diocese of Killala is on a pilgrimage to Lourdes. And it might encourage the people who see us to go and organise one of their own. It's important to give the example."

There was much counting of heads and checking of seats, and packing in of late-comers to the empty seats. But eventually we got away. And John Byrne was right. It was impressive to see twenty coaches in a long file moving across the open countryside. Like an army on the move.

By the time we reached the airport, I felt I had already departed from the familiar world. Was moving through a world as strange and fresh as that of a dream. You know the feeling. Can you imagine, therefore, the effect on me of the flight in the aeroplane?

Again my companions gave me a window seat. So that I could watch the little disk of earth, watch the runway begin to move backwards as the floor lurched and moved underneath us. The sudden whirl as the runway disappeared and we were soaring. Soaring. What a feeling. What an invention, the aeroplane. The fields and the roads and the houses dwindling.

Darkening. I felt like whooping. Then the clouds. All about us. Exhilarating. Then we were above them. Still soaring. Plains of cloud underneath. Plains upon plains. And all the plains deserted. How many times had I wondered about the Ascension into Heaven. And here it was. In reality. I was being assumed into the heavens. Into a new world. In a state of absolute exhilaration.

The sense of liberation. I was laughing my head off. Laughing at the world of clouds underneath me, so dense I could imagine a van coming driving across it. But empty, undiscovered. Laughing. Laughing at the lot of us, soaring upwards and upwards. As if we might indeed eventually land in heaven, if we kept going.

You are familiar with all of this, no doubt. Have probably experienced it a hundred times. But, you must remember, I was twenty years of age and this was my first time to fly. My first time to leave the ground. My first time to be totally clear of the country and of the jurisdiction of my mother. And I loved the feeling.

12

DEATH IS A WALL. OPAQUE, GREY. GREY as a deep deep twilight. But impenetrable. Tinted with red. Very frigging appropriate. The red of my life about to be splattered all over that wall like a dash of spray paint. But now that I have seen it, now that I have recognised it for what it is – the wall of my particular tar-barrel – I realise that I dread it no longer. It is intimately mine. My destiny. My limit. Is this strange? Is it natural for the victim to form a relationship with the instrument of his murder, once the deed is inevitable? The poised knife? The pointed gun? Does the drowning man embrace the waves that smother him, once he has sunk beyond hope? Perhaps so. Yes, I really do think so. Because this moment is beyond regret, or anger, or anxiety. Death stares at me from the wall through ruddy eyes. Tiny drops of red in the grey wall. Grey as twilight. Opaque.

Paris. How can I even attempt to describe the effect that Paris had on me? The four of us were rooming together, John, Harry, Peter, and myself. It was a huge room with four single beds lined up with the heads against one wall. On the opposite side was a row of tall windows, windows that stretched from the floor to the ceiling, and the ceiling was the highest I'd ever seen in a room. Along the other two walls were wardrobes and dressing tables. Plenty of space to move around. But the crowning feature of the room was the magnificent balcony. You opened back the windows like doors and walked out on to the balcony. Below you, Paris. Wonderful.

Most of the pilgrims were billeted in a different part of the city. Over near the Eiffel Tower, everyone explained. Only a handful of Legion activists were deployed in this hotel. It was strategically located for the work they were going to do in the evenings, that was the plan, they kept reiterating.

They made me memorise the name of the hotel, in case I got lost. Ho – tel Oo – neek, Roo San Den – ee. I was to stay close to them during the day on the sight-seeing trips. In the evenings I was to stay close to the hotel, or stay in the room until they got back. But, just in case, they also wrote down the address for me and stuck it in my breast pocket, Hotel Unic, 133 Rue St. Denis, advising me to show it to a policeman if I ever got lost.

I had no intention of getting lost. It was novel enough for me just to be there. To be in that room in the middle of Paris, with the balcony over the street, where I could look down and see the teeming activity underneath. No, I didn't need to wander an inch from that balcony.

The night we arrived we had our dinner at the hotel and then we went walking through the streets. Up Montmartre. To see the Sacre-Coeur. It was magnificent. The church on the top a luminous white. And the rows and rows of steps leading up to it, all illuminated, all standing out against the dark sky. Magnificent. The church was closed, so we couldn't go inside. But my companions were moved to recite three Hail Marys, standing together under the wall of the church, looking back across the whole of Paris.

The next day, and all of the following days, we trudged around the city, under and over the bridges of the Seine, up the Champs-Elysees, around the Arc de Triomphe, up the elevators to the top of the Eiffel Tower. And we came back in the evenings exhausted. At least I was. Had a rest. Had our dinner.

From the second night on, John Byrne and his fellow-soldiers of the Legion set about their campaign of rescuing souls. When they mentioned this campaign originally it had not engaged my curiosity to any great extent. I had assumed it was some dull prayer routine. But from the snatches of conversation I overheard in the hotel room or over dinner, I deduced that it was somewhat more interesting, and I became attentive.

"What do we say to them?" Harry asked.

"Just start off by talking normally," replied John.

"And if they have no English?"

"They all have some English. Apparently they need it for the business. You know, to talk to the tourists."

"What does 'talking normally' mean?" enquired Peter. "Discussing the weather?"

"Discussing whatever you like. I have never done this before any more that you have. I've just talked to blokes who did it in Dublin. So we'll just take the ball whatever way it bounces."

But, apart from snatches such as that, they did not talk about their project in any detail. At least not in front of me.

I watched them get ready in the room that second night. John, tall, pale-faced, thin, ever so serious. So frigging serious I still felt like laughing at him. But I liked him. There was nothing pompous, or insincere, about John Byrne, as there was about so many of the pious men I knew. Harry and Peter were likeable as well, obviously committed, but obviously not so intensely as John. Harry was small and plump with jet-black curly hair. Peter Henry was a little older than the other two and was going a little bald. They dressed up in their dark suits with white shirts and dark ties, the way they would have dressed back home if they were going to a funeral..

Fully decked out, they stood silently looking at each other in the middle of the room. Then John Byrne blessed himself and prayed aloud: "I am all thine, my Queen, my mother, and all that I have is thine."

"Amen," chanted the other two.

138

John nodded to me as they were leaving the room. Solemn. Like men trying to hold their dignity even on their way to the gallows.

I was very taken with their little prayer. To the Mother of God. Direct. My heart had given a little leap, thinking that they too had discovered the truth. That their allegiance was to the Mother of God and not to her renegade son. But no. I felt that, like so many more, like Mrs Callaghan and all the Mrs Callaghans of the world, their devotion to the Mother of God was probably inspired by instinct, not by a clear understanding of the situation.

I went directly to the balcony to watch them emerge from the hotel entrance. To see which direction they were going. Hopeful of a glimpse of what they might be doing.

It was a sombre-looking trio that emerged into a street full of bright colours, full of loud noises, full of men strolling around casually in the most casual of clothes. Full of women.

And what women.

Let me try to tell you something about Paris. Okay, I realise that you probably know more about Paris than I do. A million times more, no doubt. Nevertheless, I want to try and explain something that you may not understand, that no doubt you do not understand. The day I stood on the slope of the mountain with Peter Kilduff, looking out over the world we knew, I understood what he was talking about when he complained that there wasn't a woman from one end of Tireragh to the other. I understood what he was saying, even though it wasn't literally true. But it was only when I walked the streets of Paris that I realised the significance of what he was saying. Realised that it was not really an exaggeration. Here in Paris I realised for the first time that half the population of the world really was female. Women. And that women, each and every one of them, were beautiful.

Everywhere I turned there were women. Young ones. Old ones. Every colour, shape, and size. But all beautiful.

I couldn't believe it at first. Couldn't understand how there could be so much beauty in the world. Couldn't understand how the whole heart of Paris could pulse with the vigour of womanhood. How the city streets, beautiful in themselves, seemed to serve merely as a backdrop to set off the beauty of the women.

My companions were pointing out famous buildings. And they were wonderful to look at. They really were. But I imagined that their very elegance was in some way derived from the proportions of the female body. Their domes. Their flying buttresses. Their ornate entrances. All a celebration of female beauty. And so, even as we explored the dark aisles of Notre Dame Cathedral, my eyes were on the voluptuous bodies of the women who were walking about even in such revered surroundings, with the lightest and scantest of clothes on them.

Have you ever been astonished, as I was in Paris, by the beauty of women? Have you ever stared hard at them? Noticed their delicate features. The little pucker of their lips. The dimple between the lips and the chin. The most beautiful landscape in the world, don't you think? Not to mention their bodies. The swell of their breasts, soft as the whisper of a breeze through the searching fingers of your imagination. The rhythm of their buttocks as they are walking along in front of you – lovelier than a mountain stream moaning over the curved stone of its bedrock. How beautiful. Have you ever noticed these things?

And afterwards. The palaces of kings, the paintings of famous artists, heroic monuments – I saw them all for what they were, pale imitations of the beauty of women. Ham-fisted attempts to capture that beauty, to hold it, to control it. As men try to do. Always men.

Just like their master. The Creator. Their little works. With their names underneath. Demanding recognition. Homage. Just like him. When all they were doing was going out trying to capture some of the beauty that was free and boundless around them. Trying to capture it, confine it, control it. Then pretending that they themselves were the sole begetters of this beauty. Like a child with a net, capturing a butterfly. Taking it home to show off. Look what I have.

Those were my reflections as I was walking the streets of Paris. Walking through these throngs of beautiful women. So close I could reach out and touch one of them. They passed so close in the crowded Metro that many times I was actually brushing against a woman. Brushing against her arm. Her hip. Even her soft breast. Could you believe that? I, Tommy Loftus, half-wit, so close to a beautiful woman. Unbelievable. At least it was until I came to Paris.

I was ever so curious about the work of the Legion. It was all so secretive, it had to be interesting. When I eventually managed an oblique enquiry, John Byrne explained, in his direct serious manner. Rue St Denis was notorious as a street where fallen women offered their bodies to men for money. Did I understand? It was called prostitution. And one of the chief tasks of the Legion was to rescue such women. To speak to them. To convince them that they should give up their way of sin and turn to Our Lady for salvation. Did I understand?

Of course I understood. I knew the facts of life, as they were called. Learned them in one lesson. A day that I was in my cousin's house. Jimmy's. As I have said, he was about a year older than me. I was about ten at this time. He revealed, in the presence of his mother, that I knew not the first thing about sex. Didn't know the birds from the bees. Wouldn't have recognised the same bees if they had stung me. Hadn't a clue as to how I had come into the world. Whereupon

141

his mother ordered Jimmy to take me outside and tell me all about it. Not to come back until he had told me everything.

The lesson was simple.

"Men have cocks," said Jimmy, giving me a belt in the groin in case I didn't know where my cock was. "Women have fannies." And he held up two fingers of his left hand, joined, to demonstrate the split. He raised the index finger of his right hand, held it horizontally, pushing it towards the split between the other two fingers. "The man puts his cock in the woman's fanny. Then the woman gets a baby in her belly. But it takes nine months to grow before it comes out. Now do you know?"

I nodded my head in appreciation. But I was still mystified.

"It's the same with animals. With everything," Jimmy continued. "Would you like to see a cow being bulled?"

"Yeah," I shouted enthusiastically. It definitely sounded interesting. We set off in a trot down the road.

"Pat William's bull is on the go all the time these days. It's a busy time with heifers in heat. That's when they're going mad for it. It's no use bringing them to the bull unless they're in heat.". Jimmy explained, in an even breath that I envied because I was puffing from the dint of the slow trot. "We'll have to hide in the bushes because he'll run us if he catches sight of us."

Pat William was a small dour old man who lived alone in a little hovel of a cottage. There was a thick hedgerow of trees, bushes, and scrub, all around his garden. This was where the bull was kept while he was in business. So we had no difficulty at all creeping into the hedgerow and worming our way into a concealed viewing position. The bull was munching at a bit of hay - the ground in the garden was all churned to mud, so there was no grass for him to eat, even though it was summer.

After a while we heard shouts, and the wallops of an ash plant, as Pat William and another man whom we recognised to be Frank Taylor, steered a frisky heifer into the garden. They were having difficulty, but eventually succeeded. And they closed the gate behind them. The heifer chased around the four sides of the garden as if she were looking for a way of escape. At first the bull munched away at the hay and didn't seem to notice her. Then he lifted his head and sniffed at the air. That did it. He began to follow the heifer around slowly. In no hurry.

In the mean time Pat William and Frank Taylor had come right around the garden until they were standing with their backs to us. They were locked in a very intense conversation. Almost arguing. Frank Taylor was giving out that he was dissatisfied. That this was the third time he had brought the heifer, the previous efforts having failed to put the heifer in calf.

"By jingoes, I don't know why that is," replied Pat William. "He usually hits the mark with the first shot. If not, he always scores with the second. I can't understand how it would take a third go. I can't understand that at all."

"It's a bloody nuisance. And now she'll be calving at the wrong time of the year for me." From the tone of his voice it was clear that Frank Taylor was annoyed and was blaming the bull.

The heifer slowed down, circling closer to the centre of the garden, until eventually herself and the bull were revolving in a slow waltz alongside each other, with the bull's nose to the heifer's backside. Then the heifer halted and the bull rose on her from behind, his great bulk, his heaving and pounding, threatening to grind the heifer into the mud. But didn't.

The moment the bull rose, Pat William approached the action. He was looking intently at the exercise. Shaking his head. He was not satisfied.

143

"It's not going in," he shouted to Frank Taylor, by way of explanation. He stood there watching, scratching his head, until the bull came down and the heifer ran free. "By jingoes, There's something wrong somewhere," he declared. "Catch her by the head."

Frank Taylor grabbed his heifer by the head and held her firmly. Pat William went to the other end which, up until now, I had thought was solely for the purpose of expelling dung and piss, but now understood to contain organs of a different nature. Pat William went examining her and poking her.

"If he goes any closer he'll have his nose up her arsehole," whispered Jimmy, and the two of us clamped our hands over our mouths to smother the giggles. "Ah, ha," exclaimed Pat William, with a note of satisfaction in his voice. He reached into his pocket, took out a penknife and unfolded the blade. He began to cut, and pull, and cut again at the heifer's behind, side-stepping around the garden to avoid the kicks of her hind-legs.

"There you are," he said at last, throwing away a piece of flesh he had cut off. "By jingoes, there was a blockage. But she should be as right as rain now. We'll give them a few minutes and let them at it again. " He wiped the blood from his pen-knife on the leg of his trousers and folded back the blade slowly.

"By God, Pat William is a bit of a surgeon and all," whispered Jimmy. And the two of us could no longer suppress the laughter.

"Well, ye little whelps," roared Pat William, as he advanced on the hedgerow with his ash plant. "Come out of there, ye little whelps." And he lashed out at the scrub with his stick.

But we quickly scuttled out of our hiding and ran to tell the world what we had seen.

Yes, that was how I had learned the facts of life, as they say. Animals rutting in the mud, for frig's sake. And I grew up to a world of men, a world of hunger and longing. Now you will understand a little better the impact that the streets of Paris had on me.

And Rue St Denis was a special street. Exotic. When my three companions emerged from the entrance of the hotel into the street, they stood for a moment, as if they were deciding which direction to go. They chose to go up the street, and I watched their incongruous figures as they slowly ambled along. There were women, many many women, just standing around on the street, or leaning against walls in very provocative poses. They were also very provocatively dressed, with short skirts displaying their bare thighs and low-cut blouses exposing a generous amount of their breasts. The men, who were sauntering about singly, or in twos and threes, were constantly stopping to talk to these women. Obviously these were the women that John Byrne was talking about. Fallen women, who were putting their bodies on the market. The problem was that they didn't look at all fallen to me. They looked angelic.

When the Legionaires had gone up the street a little way, they stopped and started talking to a girl who was loitering against a wall. She immediately perked up and took a couple of swaggering steps towards them. I watched closely. The three of them were around her. She with her ear projected. No doubt trying to understand them. They were obviously trying to converse in English. Then suddenly she turned on her heel and walked away from them, looking back over her shoulder, as if she had just received a highly bizarre proposition, and couldn't quite believe what had been said to her by these three strange men in dark suits. They looked after her for a moment also, then turned to proceed up the street. Finally, went out of sight in the crowd.

Alone on the balcony, I continued gazing down into the street. Exotic alright. All the different colours. I had never seen black people before. They fascinated me.

And the yellow and the brown people as well. Asian. Wherever they came from. The girls who were standing around were of all colours too. All beautiful. How far removed this was from the bull and the heifer rutting in the mud. How far removed from the dance-halls where the men had to elbow and jostle and sometimes fight each other just to get a frigging dance with a girl.

I wondered if these girls below me refused anybody. Did they take one look and decide that the man approaching them was too ugly. Or wasn't dressed in the right gear. Or had the gawky appearance of a half-wit. I wondered. Would they turn me down? Would they shake the head and turn away, pretending they hadn't really seen me? Or stare over my shoulder as if they had just spotted a long-lost friend? Did they really accept anyone who had the money? That thought sent excited pulses through my body and I leaned forward against the parapet to cool myself down.

Right below me, on the far side of the street, at the corner of a block, I saw a girl who held my attention. She was clearly loitering like the rest, but not so provocatively dressed, and not adopting such provocative poses. She was blonde and had this definite casual aura about her. She looked normal. And yet men were coming up to her and speaking to her. Like all the women of Paris, she was beautiful. And yet it was a different kind of beautiful. Attractive. She was wearing a white tee shirt and blue jeans. Okay, the tee-shirt was clinging to her body, showing off her breasts, and the jeans were stretched around her thighs. So, like the rest she was voluptuous. But she also appeared normal. You know what I mean.

After a while I saw her go off with a man, and I felt a twinge of jealousy. Regret. As if she should have waited for me.

The other girls on the street excited me as well. Especially the black girls. But she was the one I found attractive.

I brought out one of the chairs on to the balcony, and sat down. The sky was clear, the day still lingering above the street-lights, reluctant to go. Just as I was.

Eventually she re-appeared. Once more taking up the same position on the corner of the block. Was this her appointed place? My pulse throbbed. My emotions started rising. Down. I had to keep them down. Keep them under control.

It was getting darker now and the street was filling up with people. I could not see her as clearly as I had before. With the swell of people, she was drifting in and out of view. Sometimes I thought she was gone, only to be surprised at her reappearance when the crowd thinned again. But it was frustrating. Being unable to watch her. Properly.

Why not go down? The temptation triggered all kinds of fears and anxieties. What if? But she was so attractive. A closer look. So normal she might be Irish. And I would still be in view of the hotel. Couldn't get lost. Not even if I tried. And I wasn't going to try. To get lost. She was right across the street. It wasn't as if I was going to wander off. She was so normal. So attractive, she might be an Irish girl.

So down I went. Through the main door of the hotel I glanced to establish that she was still there. On the street I took a little detour. Couldn't be too blatant about it. Could I? Up the street a few yards, across, then back down the other side, looking into shop windows to appear as inconspicuous as possible. I reached the corner where she stood. Palpitations. Everywhere. My stomach in a knot. My breathing caught, as if I would never be able to gulp air again. I tried to glance at her. Obliquely. But her eyes were scouring the street, checking every passer-by. And she saw me. Jerked back her head to look at me directly. But I looked away immediately and sidled along past her. Flushed. Trembling. Wishing. Wishing I was not such a graceless lout. Wishing I was handsome, self-

147

assured, able to go up and talk to her. Wishing. Not to be forever creeping off like a mongrel dog that has had the spunk kicked out of him.

After walking along past four or five shop fronts I stopped, gazing intently into a window which displayed electrical goods. I glanced back. She was still there. I could not resist going back. One eye on the shop windows, the other on the girl. Trying to scrutinise her. By oblique glances.

Again her lively eye was darting all over the street. Her face alive too. When I had sidled up alongside her, her eye caught my glance. She turned quickly to me. Smiled. Eyes, lips, such as only angels should have.

"Do you want to fuck?"

A heavy-weight boxer levelling a punch straight into my midriff could not have winded me as that little question did. That matter-of-fact question. That little question, put with an ease that was foreign to my world. The enormity of that question.

I stood still. Staring at her. Stunned. No doubt an expression of horror on my face.

"No?" she asked in a pert little manner.

I remained stock still. When I made no response she gave her shoulder a light shrug, as much as to say: Ah, well.

Have you ever noticed how beautiful a woman's shoulders are? Delicate. The curve up to her neck, up to the lobe of her ear. Beautiful.

She was certainly not Irish. Her few words were heavily accented, carefully articulated, as if practised, rehearsed. As if these few words were the most important in the whole of the English language. She certainly wasn't Irish. An Irish girl would never have asked me a question like that. An Irish girl would have crossed the frigging street when she saw me coming.

I must have been standing there for a long time, looking at her, because, when I came to, I found her examining me with similar curiosity. I gave a flustered smile and continued up the street, going well out of view before I crossed over and slunk back into the hotel.

I threw myself down on the bed in a state of utter dejection. Confusion. Disgusted with myself that I was not yet able to cope with a situation like this. Absolutely disgusted. But there were sensations of pleasure woven through my reflections on the encounter. She had offered herself to me. To me. I could hardly believe it. Going over her words again and again in my head. Wondering if there could have been another interpretation. Some meaning obscured from people like me. Could she have meant something different? Did she really address those words to me? Me. Tommy Loftus. Lofty. Unimaginable that a beautiful girl would offer herself to me. Even if she was in business. Even if she was expecting to be paid. Surely she would find more enjoyable ways of earning her money. That was me. No wonder I was lacking in poise. Whenever a girl looked in my direction, I always glanced behind to see who she was looking at. It was what I was used to. Years of conditioning. So how could I have been prepared for this? Oh, I loved Paris. And yet it was more than Paris I loved, for now I definitely saw it only as a background to this wonderful manifestation of love and beauty. Yes, I was more convinced than ever that there was a great spirit of love and beauty abroad in the world and that it could come only from a being higher and more noble than the Creator. There was no other explanation. It had to come from the Mother of God.

Girls. As long as I remember, I had been in love with one girl or another. A love that occupied my mind and engaged my aching passion. Totally. While it lasted. Until the fire was consumed in the next conflagration. A greater one than before.

And even now, as I was lying on a bed in Paris, in the midst of an ocean of female beauty, after being propositioned by a daughter of pleasure, my mind was going back to the Tobercurry girl.

I never spoke to her. You're not frigging surprised at that, are you? She came to the stall one day in the company of her father when I was doing the rounds with Stephen Hanlon. We were set up in the field in Culleens the day of the Gymkhana. Crowds around. Lots of hawkers along with ourselves. Horse boxes scattered all over the field. Children running around, in great danger of being trodden on by a horse – but weren't. Loud speakers marshalling competitors. You know the scene. We were quite busy.

Suddenly she was standing there. Looking over the display on the stall. Black hair in loose wavy curls. Pale. Dark eyes. I immediately sensed that she was accompanying the man who was engaged in a friendly conversation with Stephen. Old friends, who haven't seen each other for years, that type of conversation.

She was conscious that I was staring at her. I knew that, but I couldn't stop. She blushed a little and smiled. Smiled without looking at me. Smiled while she picked up a figurine of St Anthony and examined it closely. Turning it over and over in her hands, as if it was some masterpiece that deserved close scrutiny. There was a warmth and luminosity about her smile which I had never witnessed before and have never witnessed since. And she was smiling because I was staring at her. She didn't seem to mind. Seemed pleased. But didn't turn to me. Maybe just as well.

When her father had finished talking to Stephen, she replaced the figurine on the stall. Still smiling. Her eyes still averted. She walked off slowly, following the man, who kept firing back his last remarks towards Stephen until he was lost in the crowd.

"Who are those people?" I asked Stephen.

"That's an old friend of mine from out Tobercurry way. And it must have been his daughter he had with him." We were busy and he said no more.

So she was from Tobercurry. That much was tangible. Helped to fix her in my mind. And I secretly pocketed the figurine of St Anthony which she had handled with such interest. Touching it gave me a feeling of closeness to her. I kept it in my pocket day in day out. Until the day I was given full possession of the van.

The first thing I did the following morning, the First of November, Feast of All Saints, was to glue the figurine of St Anthony on to the dashboard of the van. It was so small and fragile, I was afraid it might not be secure in a free-standing position. So I moved it forward until it was resting against the windscreen. St Anthony's tonsured head made perfect contact with the sloped windscreen, and so I glued him by the feet to the dash and by the back of the head to the windscreen. Now it was secure. Now nothing would remove it save an act of God. Strange phrase that. My relationship with the Creator was such that I couldn't trust him to lay off. Still.

I could now sit back and admire it. I could still fondle it, running my fingers all over it. I could squeeze two of my fingers in between it and the windscreen. I could even glance at it when I was driving along.

And I could dream of the Tobercurry girl. Hope that I would meet her again. Watch out for her when I was travelling the roads. Search for her face among the crowded streets of Sligo whenever I went to the wholesalers.

Tobercurry. A name that had resonances too from my childhood. My father talked of a man he knew in Tobercurry. A friend. Fellow competitor on the athletics field. Lived in the town of Tobercurry. A carpenter by trade. Had a workshop behind the house. Charlie Mannion, his name. And he talked of taking a trip out to Tobercurry to see Charlie Mannion. A long journey on a bike, it would take all day. But he would take me along. As soon as I was old enough to sit on the carrier.

Out the Lake road. Once we reached the Lake the climbing would be over. Downhill from there on.

We never got to Tobercurry. When I took over the van I indulged my curiosity by driving out the Lake road. The top of the mountain gap was the most desolate place I had ever seen. I pulled up at the shore of the Lake and looked at the mountains and the shadow of the clouds sweeping over the surface of the water, and the humble straggle of road taking its leave at the far end of the Lake to make its way down the other side into the town of Tobercurry.

I never went further than the Lake. Even after I had seen this girl and had a further reason to go down and explore that region, I could not do it. I had been thinking about it too long. Imagining the journey with my father. What it might have been. Now thinking of the girl. Of meeting her and having nothing to say. Same old frigging story. My head full of longing and desire, a longing and desire I was ill equipped to soothe. Yes, the Creator had ingenious ways of torturing us alright, with dreams of happiness.

13

THE NECKLACE OF LIGHTS WAS BEGINNING to glisten all around the rim of Sligo Bay. Lights were coming on in clusters, in Strandhill, in Rosses Point. Other villages to the north. Grange, Cliffoney, perhaps. Glistening feebly through the grey twilight. Out at sea, Innismurray was beginning to merge into the all-eroding dusk.

This was something else I was going to miss. The necklace of lights. I loved them. From the day I got my glasses and saw the lights around the bay for the first time. The dots of light on the side of the mountain. I was always fascinated. There's something about a light in the distance at night, don't you think? Mysterious. Suggestive of life being lived. Suggestive of possibility. Has it that effect on you? When you see a village across the bay during daylight, you see only houses, buildings. But when you see a light or a cluster of lights in the darkness, you imagine people, people you have never met, and wonder who they are and what they are up to. Is it like that for you?

Aughris was looming. There was silence in the back, but that was just as disconcerting as the noise and I had to keep my thoughts concentrated. Had to stay preoccupied so that I would not be dwelling on what might be happening in the back. So that I would not be thinking of her. Thinking of Michelle.

It was on my second meeting with her that I found out her name was Michelle.

The gallant officers of the Easkey Praesidium of the Legion of Mary had put on their battle clothes again. For the second foray. They looked grimmer. Even more silent than usual. From the few comments they made, it was clear that they had not

153

enjoyed success the first night. They were in the wrong war, they said. Soldiers on horseback charging against artillery. Still. Soldiers had to do what soldiers had to do. Before they opened the room door to leave, they again stood with bowed heads while John Byrne intoned: "I am all thine, my Queen, my mother, and all that I have is thine." "Amen" the others whispered.

As soon as the door closed behind them, I ran to the balcony. But not to watch them this time. To scan the streets for her. It was a while before she appeared, but appear she did. Same place. Same style. Same girl. I quickly locked the room door and descended to the street. Breathless. For fear someone would get to her before I did.

Same routine. Up the street. Across. Back down the other side. Trying to pretend I was out for a casual stroll. Heart pumping. Brain numb. As frigging always. Again her eyes darting up and down the street. Her warm smile alight to all-comers. When I approached she glanced at me, and I held her glance. Slowly approached. Smiled. Or gave some sort of twitch, no doubt, to indicate recognition. Her smile lit up a little more. She nodded.

"Hi. I see you yesterday. Yes?"

I halted near her. Desperately searching for a few words. One word. Desperately trying to control the tumult inside me. Desperately trying to project a normal image. Failing on every count.

But I couldn't go on failing. Flustering. Foostering. I hated it. It revolted me. And the advice of Stephen Hanlon, ever present, but sometimes obscured like a signpost in a mist, came glaring at me. Glaring at me. Switch off the feelings. Switch on the brain. Switch on the brain. Switch off the feelings, for frig's sake. And I took a deep breath.

"Yes. I'm in the hotel. That one." And I pointed across the road. Tried to erase that sound. The

154

sound of my voice. For fear I should freeze into silence, again.

"Uh, huh," she nodded.

Wishing she would ask me that question again. Wishing. Wishing she wouldn't. That earth-shaking question. What would I do, if she did ask it? Make a fool of myself, most likely. Not that it was an effort to achieve that. But she didn't ask. Already her eyes scanning the street again. On the watch. She had ruled me out. I was off the hook. Relief. Bitter, bitter disappointment. But, at least, the relief helped me to relax a little. The way she engaged me seemed to indicate that she was not shunning me. And I continued to stand there watching her. As if at any minute she might invite me to join her in a game of hopscotch.

"You are from England. Yes?"

"No, no," I shook my head. "Ireland."

"Ice-land. Cold." And she improvised a little shudder with her delicate shoulders.

"No. Ireland," I emphasised, laughing at her little demonstration of mimicry.

"Ah, Eerland," she nodded. "Rain. Yes?" And she fluttered her fingers downwards from the sky to suggest rain. I wasn't too sure about the Eer-land, but I was now certain she had got the country right.

"Yes. Rain," I agreed.

"What is your name?"

"They call me Lofty."

"Loftee. Nice name." She nodded approvingly.

I had never recognised anything particularly nice about it, but her liking it made a difference. I was waiting for her to introduce herself. But she didn't. Continued to run her eye over every male passer-by. I felt strangely at ease in her presence, and managed to muster up the courage to ask her:

"What is your name?" I had done it. I couldn't believe it. Couldn't believe it. And I didn't want to vomit at the sound of my own voice either.

155

She looked at me squarely for a moment. Then laughed. "They call me Michelle," she replied, mimicing my answer, laughing again. But there was no mockery in her laughter, just a kind of playful mirth, and I laughed too.

Michelle. What a beautiful, beautiful name. But I didn't say so. I had succeeded thus far beyond my wildest expectations. No point in overstepping now. No point in ruining everything.

Again there was an easy silence between us, and I began to glance up and down the street in her manner, as if watching out for a suitable customer for her.

"You like Paris?" she asked after a while, without looking at me.

"Yes. Very nice. We are going to Lourdes," I replied, then panicked a little, thinking she might not be impressed. Lourdes. Might not be exactly her territory.

But she shot me a warm smile that immediately dissipated my panic.

"Lourdes. Holy." And she brought her hands together in a praying pose, casting her eyes towards heaven. It was so funny I had to laugh. And she laughed too. I noticed how lovely her hands were. White. Perfectly shaped. Have you ever noticed that about a woman's hands, how beautiful they are? Sensitive. By comparison, men have crude hands. A bit like dung forks. Wouldn't you agree?

Then the inevitable happened. A man approached her. I cannot recall anything about him, because my eyes were on her as she took a few steps forward to talk to him. I did not look at him, but he must have been tall, because she was facing up at him, all earnest in conversation. They were talking in French, so I did not catch any of their words. But she turned to me before she left and gave me a warm smile and a nod.

And I was left alone. Plunged back into the pit of torments. Back where I belonged. Jealousy. Yes.

Disgust with myself. Yes. Fear that I would never see her again. Longing. If only. If only. Lust. I would give the world to be doing with her what that man was no doubt doing with her at that moment. But I didn't need to give the world. Just money. And I had tons of money. I could have paid her anything she asked, and still have more left than I had the wit to spend. A lost opportunity. A lost opportunity.

Yet when I was back lying on my bed, I tried to find consolation in the reflection that I had actually talked to her. That I had actually stood on the street and engaged her in conversation.

Every now and then I got up and went to the balcony to search for her. But she did not return that night.

When John Byrne and his friends came back they were extremely glum, and were discussing the futility of their exercise. Discussing whether it was worth going out the following night at all. I prayed that they would not change their plans. Prayed to all the saints to give them the strength to carry on. All the saints whose statues and pictures I had sold by the dozen. They owed me one. One more night was all I was asking. And the opportunity of seeing Michelle again.

The saints must have heard me. Must have agreed they owed me a favour. Because the following evening, when we went up to the room after dinner, Harry Murphy, to his eternal credit, piped up.

"Let's give it one more try, lads."

And the other two, to their eternal credit, lifted their downcast faces, and said, "We might as well."

Sweeter words were never heard nor spoken. I was overjoyed. But tried not to show it. Tried not to betray my excitement until the three cavaliers had forayed abroad once more.

Then to the balcony. And, joy of joys, there she was on the corner. As if she were waiting for me. I cut the routine this time and crossed the road in a bee-line towards her.

She smiled ever so warmly as she greeted me. As if I were an old friend. Yes, it did seem as if her face lit up at the recognition.

"Hi," she said.

"Hi," I replied, echoing her, for it was not our normal greeting back home.

"You are in Paris yet?"

"Yes."

Once more I was totally at ease in her company even though we were not saying much.

"You leave for Lourdes soon?"

"The day after tomorrow."

"The day after tomorrow. Yes," she repeated, as she was teasing out the meaning. "Then you will be a holy man." And she gave her impish laugh.

"I don't think so."

"What do you do in Eerland?"

"Ireland."

"Yes?"

"We call it Ire-land. That's how we say it."

"Oh!"

"I sell things. Holy pictures. Statues of saints. That kind of thing."

"You have a shop?"

"No. A van. And a stall that I set up behind the van."

"Ah. Like in the market?"

"Yes. Sometimes I set up in the markets and the fairs. But mostly outside churches."

"You are a holy man."

"No. I'm not."

By then a customer that she had been eyeing had come up to talk to her.

"Excuse," she said politely. There was a lovely tone of familiarity in the way she excused herself. As if we were old friends talking. Needless to say, I did not regard the intrusion so benignly, and hoped the man would go away.

158

I was studying her hair while she was talking to the man. As I have said, it was blonde. Heavy texture with a sheen off it. There were darker shades through it. Not a different colour. Just deeper shades of blonde, if you know what I mean. And it dropped loosely about her shoulders.

Dismay. She had come to an arrangement with the man. And turned to me with an exaggerated doleful look.

"I must go."

"Bye," I whispered.

I went back to the hotel room and sprawled on the bed. Remembering her hair. Concentrating on it. Trying to etch an image of it on to my brain. So that it would not fade. Would not disappear. A woman's hair is beautiful. Don't you agree? It would be satisfying just to run my fingers through her hair. My fingers probing. Deep into her hair. Until my finger tips were caressing her scalp. Astray in the forest of her heavy blonde hair. But, even as I was stroking her hair in my fantasy, the image was fading and I had to recite to myself its characteristics, so that I could rebuild the image in my mind.

I grew impatient. Kept going to the balcony. What I needed was to see Michelle again. To look at her hair. To see how it parted over her forehead. To examine how it contrived to darken within its deeper recesses. Then to move on to her eyebrows. I could recall nothing of her eyebrows, what colour were they? What shape? I had no image of them whatsoever. I had to see her again. To study these things. To memorise them. Otherwise she would fade entirely.

After about an hour she re-appeared at the corner. My heart leaped. Stopped. Started galloping again at runaway pace. And I was off. Down the stairs. As if the hotel were on fire.

She smiled when she saw me. "Loftee." I liked her pronunciation, so I did not correct it.

"Hi."

"You have girls in Ire-land. Yes?"

I knew what she meant but my frigging inhibitions steered me off on a tangent. "Not many girls. Lots of men. Nearly all men."

"Lots of men. I should be there." She exaggerated a wistful look. I loved her face, her features. Constantly changing. So expressive, it made up for any deficit in her language. "Why lots of men, no girls?"

"In Ireland the girls leave to work in England or America . Sometimes in Dublin. Some of the men go too. But many stay to work on the farms. They're nearly all old."

"But these men have girls? They marry? Have wives?"

"No. There are no girls to marry , so the men are single mostly. Bachelors. Probably too poor to get married anyway. But they're good men. I like them. I call on them with my van."

"Why? They buy holy pictures every day?" When Michelle asked a question she did so with her shoulders. Her beautiful shoulders.

"Well, they buy different things. And I have a statue of the Virgin in the van. They like to pray before the statue."

"These men live alone. No girls. And you bring them a statue of the Virgin in your van." She was shaking her head with an incredulous look on her face, this time not improvised. "You should bring them a girl, Loftee. They need a girl, not a statue of the Virgin!"

I laughed at the idea and at her bemused expression. Then another frigging customer interrupted our conversation. Once more she was whisked away from me. And I was left alone on Rue St Denis looking at the place where she had been. I had forgotten to look at her eyebrows and I was annoyed with myself. I could not complete the image of her face

160

without noting the shape and colour of her eyebrows.

"A write-off," declared John Byrne, on his return. "Wasting our time. We'd be as well off banging our heads off the Eiffel Tower. Or getting drunk, like everyone else in this damned city."

Poor John. I liked him. And Harry. And Peter. The Queen that they served was my Queen too. Of that I was sure. But they would not have shared my opinion of the Creator. Of that I was also sure. So I said nothing. Simpler that way.

14

HAD THE CREATOR A DIFFERENT TAR-barrel for every individual? Or a different tar-barrel for different places? Different nations even? Certainly the one he devised for us out here on the ledge of the world was as devious and nasty as could be conceived. Even by him. The craving for love, yet love denied. The craving for joy, yet joy denied. The eternal flame of need. Singeing. Scorching. Smouldering. Fanned to a furnace by an occasional illusion of hope and happiness.

Such was the Tobercurry girl for example. A phantom. I never spoke to her. She never even looked at me. Smiled, no doubt, but she might have been thinking of someone else when she was smiling. Very likely. If she had taken one look at my round face and hanging jaw, she wouldn't have been smiling. If she had taken one look at my fat ungainly body, she would have run away in horror. Yet, month after month, she was foremost in my mind. As if we were in some way lovers.

He certainly has cruel means of torture. The Creator. Maybe our bodies are our first tar-barrels. Tar-barrels within tar-barrels. In case we escape from one we're caught in another. But now I'm getting carried away. I must stop. Soon my puny ripple will meet the wall. And then I will know, or not know, as the case may be. Grab the moment for frig's sake. All you've got is a moment. But the moment can be a day, can be a lifetime.

When he looks down into the tar-barrel and sees his image there, is he pleased?

No. I must stop. Seize the moment. Darkness looms. As it loomed while I drove rapidly to Aughris. I needed the last of the light to illuminate my way to the top of the Head. To the Cor a dTonn. And so I eliminated any more thoughts of the countryside, fixed my eye on the road, and drove with determination.

One of the ways the Creator made our particular paradise a hell was by withdrawing the girls and the women from us. Letting us grow into adults without their company. Helping us to build our own mental barriers as a complement to his barriers. Yes, and we certainly co-operated with him to make our lives as nasty as possible. Didn't we?

I don't know what torture he contrived for the people of Paris. But it wasn't a scarcity of women. It appeared as if all the girls and women who had forsaken our northern lands, like swallows in autumn, had congregated in Paris. Going back over my experience of the city while we drove down through France in the coach, I had this very strong impression of Paris as populated entirely by women. I could recall no men. Don't you think that frigging strange? If I had noticed any, they had rapidly faded from my pictures of the city.

And the landmarks too. The famous bridges. The gigantic museums. All fading too. As if I had no more than flicked through somebody's album of photographs. All gone. However, I had feasted my eyes on every woman in Paris, and I had gone away with this powerful sense of the spirit of the place. And that spirit of the place was very much due to the concentration of so many women. So many beautiful women.

The Creator had a perverse frigging sense of humour alright. Even this visit to Paris on the pilgrimage must have been contrived to torture us further. But what would he do if I tried to subvert his schemes by bringing back some of this womanhood? By bringing back just one beautiful woman? That would put a twist on his sense of humour. As Michelle said, I should be bringing a girl around in the van, instead of a statue of the Virgin, if I wanted

163

to brighten up the lives of those lonely men. Yes, that would be one over on the Creator. And one up for his mother too. Wouldn't it?

I did not see Michelle again. On the last evening, John Byrne insisted on the four of us going to the Latin Quarter to sit in an open-air cafe and sip tea and mineral water. It would have been very pleasant but for the ache inside me. You know. The longing to see Michelle again. The awareness that she was probably at the corner opposite the hotel was gnawing at me. And I could be talking to her. Was there no end to torture? And as we sat back in the street café watching the people pass, it was her face I was looking out for. Occasionally my heart would leap when I imagined I saw her coming up the street. I would rise to greet her. Only to be disappointed. Michelle was in another street. No doubt watching the passers-by as well. But to her own purpose. To her own purpose.

It was the same in Lourdes. Despite the enormous sense of expectancy I had brought on this pilgrimage, I was unable to concentrate on anything that was happening on the way to Lourdes. When I got there I could not focus my mind on the stalls and shops selling a range of religious objects, bewildering in its variety. Nor on the Basilica, with its ceremonies in one foreign tongue after another. Nor even on the grotto that seemed so familiar because I had seen a thousand replicas of it. Wherever there was a crowd of people, my eyes were sifting through them, looking for a head of blonde hair, seeking to re-create the features that I doted on.

When I sat down to meals with the rest of the pilgrims from the diocese, I could not share their joviality. I was thinking of her. I was withdrawn. Downcast.

Standing before the Grotto, looking at the face of the Virgin, I noticed, for the first time, that she was a woman, that she was beautiful. It made sense of John Byrne's devotion, and Peter's, and Harry's. Yes in their way, and without knowing it, they too were devoted to the virgin mother of God. They just saw her differently. Got her confused with Mary the woman who bore Jesus.

But as I stared at her features, her beautiful features, they began to melt and coagulate into the features that I was desperately trying to retain in my mind. And the features I had tried to etch indelibly on my mind were being eroded by the features on the statue, the longer I stayed looking at it.

So I made a resolution. To stop looking at the statue. To stop looking at women among the crowds of pilgrims. To turn away whenever a woman passed me in the street. So that I could concentrate on the image of the one person I wanted to keep in my mind.

I tried it. Tried hard. But even that didn't work. I needed her presence. In the flesh. In reality. My frigging brain could not hold her image if she was not in front of me. And if I lost her image, I had nothing of her left. I was desperate. If her image faded, I would start filling in the picture from my imagination. Soon she too would become a phantom, like the Tobercurry girl. And my mind was already congested with phantoms. I needed a real girl, for frig's sake. This girl.

I suppose you find all of this difficult to understand. You are probably one of those who could be invited by the police to pick out somebody from an identity parade, somebody that you had seen very briefly maybe a year before. Not me. Not frigging me. I would probably fail to identify a man who had assaulted me an hour earlier.

I had to see her again. And there was hope. We were going back to the same hotel for our over-night in Paris on the journey home. Despite John Byrne's best efforts. He wanted to have us changed to the hotel in which the main body of the party was staying. Poor John. His disappointment was enormous. He had failed to rescue a single soul. I got the feeling that he didn't want to lay eyes on that street again if he could.

Not just defeated, I think he felt ludicrous, felt that the street itself would be mocking him. And I could sympathise with him.

But there was no escape for John. Bookings had been made. Money paid. No one wanted to swap with us. And I was delighted. At least, it left me with hope.

We checked in to the hotel in the late afternoon at the end of the long return journey across France. After dinner we sat around in the room, talking. We were exhausted. Nevertheless, Peter and Harry wanted to make use of their last night in Paris. Wanted to go out. John was reluctant. Back to Montmartre, they suggested. To climb the steps to the church. To look out over the glittering streets of Paris. To stand side by side under the wall of that church and say a prayer, the way they had done on the night we arrived. John was persuaded.

They did not include me in the planning, just assumed that I would tag along. And so they were surprised when I declared that I was too tired, had a headache, wanted to stay and rest. However, they accepted my withdrawal, with some words of concern for my well-being, and set out by themselves.

As soon as they shut the door, I was out on the balcony, scanning the street, mounting surveillance on the corner below. I didn't have to wait long until she appeared, but I did have to wait a few seconds to reassure myself absolutely that it was she. A mist of light rain obscured the view a little, and she was hugging the wall of the building for shelter. It was not her features, nor her clothes that I recognised her by. It was something deeper, an air, a presence, some kind of spirit of her that I had come to relate to. I delighted in that recognition.

Crossing the road directly towards her, my knees were weak, my heart pounding like the engine of a train. Tongue swelling. Mouth parching. The coward inside me screaming to go back. To go back to the security, the safety, of the hotel room. Before I made a fool of myself. But my weak knees kept plodding forward.

Because of the rain there were few people in the street, and she spotted me crossing the road. Her face bright with welcome.

"Loftee."

"I want to fuck."

As soon as the words were blurted, I was mortified. My face must have burned beyond crimson, must have gone into contortions. But I knew that if I did not say the words first, I would never say them. Would never have managed to bring around a conversation in a natural way to this point. Would have gone home again without knowing what consequence might follow the saying of those words.

If I looked like some gargoyle come to life in the rain, she didn't recoil. Didn't flinch. Looked surprised alright. With maybe a hint of disappointment, I thought. But the girl was so self-possessed. These reactions were mere flickers that disappeared as quickly as they had arisen.

"Okay, Loftee." And she stood a moment, looking at me. "Come with me. Okay?" And she turned slowly, pensively, to walk down the side-street where I had seen her go with the men before.

"Lourdes was good. Yes?" she asked as we walked along side-by-side .

"Yes. Good," I replied. I was drying-up. I could think of nothing to say. Nothing. My mind blank. Despite the hours of long intimate conversations I had conducted with her in my imagination over the days and the nights since I had last seen her. Despite the eloquent speeches I had rehearsed. If only we could pursue a relationship like this solely in the mind. It would be perfection. No inhibitions. Flowing speech. Absolute mutual understanding. Instead of these grunts and nods. Instead of the continual anxiety about the words spoken. Instead of the continual regret about the words left unspoken.

"Holy man now." She tried to resurrect the old joke, but I could do no more that respond with some sort of forced smile.

Isn't it perverse that sometimes we are tortured by the frustrating of our wishes, sometimes by the granting of them? Here I was walking towards the fulfilment of my dreams, and I was wracked by anxiety and self-doubt, wracked by pain as intense as I'd ever experienced. I had no pleasing qualities, so it was only a matter of time, moments maybe, until she was repelled by me. I had no skill in conversation, no good looks, no graceful manner. Why, oh why, did I inflict this situation on Michelle who might otherwise have carried away at least a warm impression of me.

The tension I was transmitting seemed to be undermining even her normal self-assurance. Or was she having second thoughts? One way or the other, she must have been as relieved as I was when we arrived in the lobby of a large building. A dour-looking giant of a black man standing in the centre of the lobby looked closely at us while Michelle went to the desk and said something to the bored-looking man acting as receptionist. She then turned to me almost apologetically and whispered, "Money." I pulled out a fistful of notes. She counted out so many, pushed them across the desk to the bored receptionist, and he slid a key back to her. She glanced at the number-tag and nodded to me to follow her up the stairs.

She opened the door of the room and looked around inside as if checking it out for spiders or cockroaches, a slight expression of disapproval, maybe disdain, on her face.

"Not very nice," she indicated the room by a nod of the head. Taking up a towel, she examined it to make sure it was clean, then mopped the tiny droplets of rain that clung to her face, her hair.

When she eventually turned her attention on me and looked me in the face, she burst out laughing.

"You look like you will be. . ." she drew her index finger across her throat to show what she meant. What I looked like. A man on his way to the gallows. Then she reached her finger under my chin and, with a pert little movement, sprung my chin up to close my gaping mouth. Then in the same movement she put the finger to her lips, planted a kiss on it, and transferred the kiss to the tip of my nose. It was the loveliest, most intimate gesture I had ever experienced. I felt close to her. Were I not so terrified, I would have relaxed on the spot.

She took me by the hand and drew me close to her.

"Here is my work place." She gave a light laugh as she nodded to the bed. "You like to open my buttons. Yes?" she turned her back to me. A row of buttons fastened her dress from behind.

I started opening her buttons from the top. Fumbling. My fingers stiff and useless. Watching the flesh of her neck as I exposed it. Watching the flesh on her shoulder-blades. The white strap of her bra. Right down to the small of her back. Until the last button was undone. The back of her dress resting on the rich curve of her buttocks. Just beneath my trembling hands. Almost breathless from excitement. Had to stand back a little because my cock was standing, straining, throbbing. She slipped her arms from the sleeves of her dress, dropped the dress, and stepped out of it. She kicked off her shoes. She stood before me in her bra and pants

She turned to face me, and came close. Slipped off my jacket and folded it over the back of a chair. Then began to open the buttons of my shirt, starting from my neck. Every nerve in my body tingling. Every muscle taut and stiff. My cock straining, throbbing. Her fingers steady, gentle. Her breasts brushing my chest. Little ripples in the muscles of her hips, her stomach, as she opened my buttons down to my belt and pulled the shirt free of my trousers. It seemed as if an ocean of warm flesh was opening up before me, inviting me to thaw my native frost, inviting me to bathe my native isolation in its soothing embrace.

As she was stooping to unbuckle my belt her breasts hung loose. Touching my chest. Her bent head brought her hair close to my face. I was breathing her perfume. Staring at the warm swell of her breasts. Feeling the movement of her knuckles on the taut muscles of my stomach as she worked on my belt. And all that intense tingling tautness of my body began to melt to flow. Began to flow from the lower reaches of my toes and feet. Began to flow from my forehead and the back of my of my neck. Began to flow from my finger-tips, up my arms. All over, tautness loosening. Melting, flowing. And these rivulets of melting tension converged on my groin. Running now with all the fury of an uncontainable flood. My groin straining like a dam unequal to the task of holding back a deluge. Dam burst. And the relentless flood teemed into my throbbing cock. Flowing to the tip. No hope now of restraining that pent-up fury. And it gushed through. Gushed. Gushed. The pent-up flood of a life-time's tension flowing now with unrestrained total ease.

I felt the warm flow easing down my leg. Soaking my underpants. I pulled back from Michelle. Mortified. I tried to glance down to check if it was soaking out through my trousers. I couldn't see. But it was only a matter of time. I grabbed the tails of my shirt to button them. To cover my embarrassment. My cock beginning to bow in shame.

She was taken aback.

"Something is wrong. Yes?"

Words stuck in my throat. I was no better now than that day I started school. No further on. An idiot then. An idiot now. Still wetting my pants. Was there no escape?

170

Escape. Now a more immediate objective.

"I have to go," I said.

She looked shocked as I grabbed my jacket from the back of the chair. Let it hang in front of me to conceal my ignominy, my failure.

"You did not pay for a girl before. Yes?"

I looked at the ground. Could I conceal nothing from her? Was she aware also that I had come-off all over my trousers? Probably. All she had to do, all anyone had to do, was give one look at me and they saw that I was a half-wit. The rest followed.

"No," I replied without lifting my eyes.

"Wait," she said. "Don't go." And she quickly slipped on her dress, deftly closed the buttons I had so laboriously opened. "We can talk. Yes? Rain tonight. Not nice on the street. Nobody out. And we can stay here for a little time." She pulled a comic expression of misery. " Rain. Like Ireland. Yes?" And she raised her eyebrows interrogatively, urging me to laugh.

I did smile. Nodded. Tried to fasten the buttons on my shirt with one hand while I still held my limp jacket in front of my crotch.

She went around the room. Looking. There wasn't much to see. There was an electric kettle and some mugs. She opened a jar.

"Tea?" She asked. "You like tea. Yes?"

" Yes."

She filled the little kettle from the tap at the handbasin and plugged it in. I quickly finished buttoning my shirt, and, while her back was turned, I examined my trousers. The damp had soaked through, but was not too obvious due to the deep colour of the cloth. In relief, I put on my jacket, and buttoned it to increase my cover.

Disgusted with myself. Disappointed. Despairing. Yet drained of tension. And it was the first time I ever had a girl make me a cup of tea. There was a sense of luxury about that, despite the debacle. A feeling of being pampered. And I was still with her. She wanted me there. Asked me to wait.

I pulled in a chair to the small table, and sat in tightly, while she put out two mugs, steaming with hot tea. There was no milk or sugar, and I never drank tea without milk and sugar at home. However.

"Tell me about Ire-land," she said as she pulled in the other chair to the opposite side of the table.

I was relaxing. Even my mind was beginning to clear. "It rains," I said, throwing my eyes up the way she had once done. And I smiled at her.

"It rains in Ireland. That is not news. Everyone knows that. Tell me about you."

Me? I was shocked. Why should she want to know about me? No one ever asked me a question like that before.

"Nothing much to tell. I live with my mother and my aunt. Just outside a village called Easkey. It's near the sea." I dried-up rapidly on that subject.

"Your father. He has left?"

"Dead. I think."

"Oh. I'm sorry." And there was genuine sympathy in her voice.

"It was a long time ago. When I was young."

"And you sell things from a van. Holy things."

I actually laughed. She had that kind of effect on me. "Not holy," I tried to explain. "Religious. Pictures and statues. That kind of thing. I drive around the country and stop at houses. People like to buy pictures and statues. They think they are . . . . lucky."

"People in the houses all men. Yes?" She laughed.

"Not all. Some houses have women. Old women mostly. Some men have wives and mothers. But an awful lot of men live alone."

"Mm. That would be a good place for me. Men living alone. Many girls on the street in Ire-land. Yes?"

"No. No girls. No streets. Not like the streets in Paris anyway."

"Men living alone, and no girls on the street." She exaggerated surprise. "I should be there."

I thought of Peter Kilduff and all the other men like him back in Tireragh. The hopeless hunger with which they looked out over the forlorn landscape. How they needed a Michelle. Deserved a Michelle. How a girl would transform their lives. Bring a beam of warmth into their frigid humdrum. Straight from the Mother of Love. Mother of Life. Queen of Heaven. I declared as quickly as the thought had come, "Yes, you should be there. Why don't you come to Ireland?"

She looked puzzled and amused at once. "But no streets. You say no streets in Ireland."

" I could bring you around in the van."

She laughed. "You put my bed in the van, and bring me to these men. Yes?"

"Yes." And I had a surge of enthusiasm for the idea. Felt it was right. Inspired. And, if it brought Michelle to Ireland, I was prepared to take any risk. But it was too much to hope for. Surely?

"Mad," she said. "That is mad, but sweet." And she reached her hand across the table and put it on top of mine. Bliss. "And you would be my manager. Yes?"

"Yes." I replied, not quite believing that this conversation was for earnest.

She was smiling. Almost to the point of laughing. But not at me. Not at me. With me. In joy. In happiness. She took out a packet of cigarettes and got up to search for an ashtray.

"I like you, Loftee. You make a good friend. You make a very good friend."

She lit her cigarette and began smoking. Sitting back, almost in contemplative mood. Still smiling. Thinking. Was she giving serious thought to the proposition?

The more I considered it, the more overwhelmed I was by the rightness of it. The more I was shocked by the enormity of it. It had all the signs of divine intervention. As the Mother of God had seen fit to cure Mrs Callaghan's cow, maybe she was now shedding a little warmth into the lives of the lonely men in Tireragh. And again using me to do it. I was the instrument of fate. No more. No less. And if I could assist her in undermining the schemes of her son, the Creator, then it was my duty, my moral duty, to co-operate.

Her cigarette smoke was billowing across the table. I loved the aroma. Breathed in her smoke, as if I had been suffocating in a dungeon and was now inhaling the fresh air on a mountaintop.

"Would you come?" I asked her again.

"You are serious. Yes?"

"Yes."

She was silent for a moment. Looking into space. Smiling.

"I will think about it. Good for me, perhaps. Yes, perhaps, very good for me. Who knows? I will think about it."

"I have to go back tomorrow."

"That is too bad. Not much time. I will think about it. We will be good friends, Loftee. Yes? Where will I stay? Hotels in Ire-land. Yes?"

"Yes, there are hotels in Ireland. You could stay in Sligo. It is a city. Well, a town anyway. There are hotels in it."

"Very good. But how do I go to Ire-land? Where do I see you?"

"You can get an aeroplane to Dublin, the same way as us. And then get a train to Sligo. I can meet you at the railway station in Sligo. I know it well. It's right beside the wholesalers."

"Sligo," she repeated, as if she liked the sound of the name.

"You could write to me and say when you are coming. I could meet you at the station," I urged.

174

She shook her head as she was stubbing out the butt of her cigarette. "I cannot write English. I speak a little. I cannot write it well."

I thought of my own extreme limitations when it came to reading or writing English, but said nothing of that. With a touch of pride in my own achievement, I suggested, "Just write the day and the time you will be arriving in Sligo and I will know to meet you."

"Okay. I will think about it. Write down your name and your address." She rummaged in her hand-bag and produced a piece of paper and a biro.

With pride and satisfaction I took the biro and paper from her and proceeded to write my name and address for her in big bold capital letters. Then realised that I would not be able to read her script if she wrote in joined hand-writing. I handed the paper to her, and while she looked at what I had written, I said:

"Can you print like that so I can read it."

She was absorbed in her thoughts.

"Yes. I will think about it," she said.

A bell tinkled inside the door. "Our time is up," she said. "I will take you back to your hotel."

15

DIFFERENT TAR-BARRELS? OR ONE GREAT tar-barrel? One great plonk of a pebble to set a single ripple in motion. One great ripple rolling out to the edge of the Universe. Then smack. Back again. Back to where it started. All contained. Controlled. And the Creator forever gazing down. Gazing at his own image. At first single, clear, perfect. Then shattered, fragmented, settling into twisted distortions. The way he wanted it. The way he liked it. Never the same. Never. Blink your eye: changed. Shift your angle: different. How he liked it. Confused. Divided. Whip up fervour. Demand homage. Spread fear and suspicion. Spread hatred. Incite violence, demand recognition. I am the Lord, thy God. Creator of Heaven and Earth. Bow down and adore me.

His poor mother mortified.

Perhaps we were all just flotsam on the surface of this great tar-barrel, waiting for the ripple to come? Waiting for it to raise us just a moment, then plunge us deeper, until it passes on to activate other lives. Activating a whole great circle of lives at once. Before the coming of the ripple all lolling about in isolation. Unconnected. Then suddenly all caught in the single powerful swell. Different parts of the Universe all caught in the same swell. All lifted above the surface long enough to catch a glimpse of the distorted image of the Creator. Afterwards, becalmed. Directionless. Waiting for the next ripple passing out or coming back.

Maybe so. Maybe so. But great and all as his single tar-barrel might be, it would be flooded and washed away in the great flood that was coming. That was my firm belief.

And yet, I inclined to think that he had us all trapped in separate tar-barrels, somehow. That feeling was particularly strong when I returned to Tireragh, when the full impact of the difference between the two places hit me. The contrast was so frigging enormous, it seemed that Paris had ceased to exist. Or, if it did still exist, it was so remote that it had no bearing whatsoever on our lives on this shelf of land between the mountains and northern sea.

For a start, they spoke a different language there. I couldn't understand a single word they said when they spoke in French, their own language. Strangely enough, I didn't reflect much on it while I was there. As I have explained, there were other aspects of the city that had me totally preoccupied. But when I returned home, this was an aspect that fascinated me. The fact that there was a city, a country, out there, speaking words that we could not understand. It lent support to the idea of different tar-barrels for different places. As I have said to you, I was always a good listener. Words fascinated me. For as long as I can remember. Back to when I was a child. Every new word that came my way I seized and rolled about in my mind like a shiny marble. Admiring it. In no hurry to find out the meaning. The meaning would come, eventually, when I heard the word used a few times. Until then, the word had mystery. Could mean anything. Could hold secrets of knowledge concealed from me so far. And often I was disappointed when the meaning arrived and the mystery took its leave.

My fascination continued, indeed increased, when I went to school and couldn't read nor write the words I knew so well. They became mysterious once again as if there were dimensions to words which I could never penetrate.

I could never figure out, for example, why a certain thing had one word only to describe it, cow, grass, milk, bread. Crisp. Clean. No attitude involved. In contrast there seemed to be an endless battery of words to describe a half-wit, as if the whole human race had dedicated its energy and resourcefulness to coming up with a more hurtful and derogatory term. And every one of them had been used on me. Fool. Amadan. Idiot. Eegit. Moron. Gom. Mug. Twit. Retard. Many more. Then, for variety, they coined phrases. Not the full shilling. A slate loose. Every single word or phrase sharpened to cut, to hurt, to maim.

My mother, being educated, used words that no one else used. And pronounced them properly. Idiot, not eegit. And they seemed sharper for being pronounced properly. Cut deeper. Like imbecile. She was the only one who ever used that term. So I never quite pieced together a definition of it. But I never needed to. Each syllable emitted from my mother's mouth like a poisoned arrow. Im-bess-eel. I didn't have to enquire what she meant.

What amazed me later was the way people failed to see the meaning in the words they used. Never thought about them. Assumed they meant something else. For example, the phrase I mentioned, Virgin Mother of God. What could be clearer than the meaning of that? Yet people didn't see it. Assumed it referred to Mary, the mother of Jesus, and thought no further.

Yes, words are strange. I was often caught myself, on the meanings of words. Got the wrong end of the stick. Completely. The result of not being able to talk to people. Generally.

Like the word, premature. Yes, premature. A good example.

I found it so excruciatingly difficult to ask anyone a question. To open my mouth at all. To hear my own voice. Doubly difficult to ask a sensitive question.

Nevertheless. One day I was sitting at the table in Jimmy's house. Eating dinner. His mother, father, two

178

sisters, were there as well. Casually, jocosely, in an attempt to conceal the seriousness of the question, I asked, "Why does my mother hate me?"

They all stopped eating, and looked at me and at each other with quizzical expressions. At the content of the question? At the fact that I had spoken at all? I didn't know. But Nora quickly took control.

"Ah, I wouldn't say she hates you. She's your mother, after all. She might have a bit of a problem, maybe. Because you were born premature."

The way she said it. Slowly. Reverently. "Pree mature." Sounded significant. And the sisters spluttered into their plates of spuds and cabbage and bacon. As if it was the funniest thing they had ever heard.

"Will you get on with your dinners, you two, and leave the boy alone. Or I'll give you a skelp that will leave you wondering what your mother has against you."

And that was the end of that. But I carried away the word, premature, to try and unravel its significance.

At first I assumed it explained my appearance. Something that happened at birth to make me look the way I did. I assumed that when my mother took one glance at me, she was repelled, forever. This assumption held up well, when later I heard the word being bandied about by farmers, referring to the animals, the little runts that were born before their due time. They were weak and scrawny, and often saved everyone a lot of bother by turning over and dying.

But later again, much later, I began to question my understanding of what Nora meant by "Pree-mature." It was still my favourite house to stop at, even though I was older and had the whole countryside to choose from. I loved to call in casually, the way I did when I was a child. I had finished with school at this stage, and Jimmy and his sisters had already followed the rest of the family to England.

One such day, Nora was there by herself and, when I had settled into the big armchair beside the range, I decided to probe a little deeper.

"When you said I was premature, Nora, what did you mean?"

She looked at me, puzzled.

"Do you mean years ago, when I said it?"

"Yes"

"For a minute there I thought I was doting, because I couldn't remember discussing that with you in recent times. But I remember now. That was a long time ago. And do you mean to say you haven't worked it out yet?"

"No."

She clicked her tongue as she did when chiding someone. And shook her head. But smiling.

"It's like this, your mother and father got married on Easter Monday and you were born during the summer holidays. It was put out that you were premature. But that was what they did in those days. They didn't like to admit that a woman was pregnant before she got married. It wouldn't do at all, in those days. Especially for a school teacher. She would have had to pack her bags. Go somewhere she wasn't known. That's the way it was."

I was stunned. For years I had been going around with the word premature in my head, and I had never worked out that simple implication, had never suspected that the word could be a curtain pulled across the truth.

"And there were plenty of young lassies put out at the time. They fancied your father. And naturally enough they thought your mother snared him by foul means."

That was the end of the conversation. I had nothing else to ask, and Nora rambled on about some other aspect of the old days, to which I gave scant attention. So my mother was pregnant with me for months before they were married. Did they marry because she was pregnant? Because she might lose her job? Yes, it was always the priests who managed the schools, and they would have had little sympathy for someone giving scandal like that.

And I wondered what kind of morass my father and mother had waded into.

Anyway. As I have said, all of that had been revealed to me through pursuing the meaning of the one word, premature.

I would have been á long time listening to the words in French, trying to puzzle them out. And now that I was back in Tireragh, the city of Paris, speaking a language that I did not understand, seemed to be a remote world. As if the people there were indeed contained in a very different tar-barrel. Or, if we were all flotsam on the surface of the one great tar-barrel, then we were at opposite ends of it. My experiences were different to theirs. Mrs Callaghan, the pilgrimage, a boy wetting his trousers on his first day at school, my father hovering over fields of sea-wrack, even the van hurtling towards this inevitable wall, all out there, drifting, very frigging different to the experiences of the people of Paris, waiting for the ripple which would make the link.

Maybe. But I was still inclined to believe that we all had our individual tar-barrels or, at least, that I had my own. Trapped forever in a life. Look at the way I was re-visited by the same experience. That night in Michelle's place. As if I was back in school again. The first day. Terrified. Was there no escape? From myself. From my body? From all the handicaps that the Creator had inflicted on me.

There was a while that I did begin to believe I could re-create myself in defiance. Re-create myself as a different person. Totally different. Starting when Stephen Hanlon taught me how to overcome my lack of arithmetic. When I taught myself how to read and write in a few months, something the teachers had failed to do in eight years. When I was returning from Lourdes. To Paris. To Michelle. Determined to see her. Determined to beat my mountainous inhibition. Determined to be a man. Determined.

But then I was reduced to a small boy again. Wasn't I? Reminded that I was in my tar-barrel. Out of which I should not presume to climb, nor jump, nor swim. Nor will myself.

But yet. There was hope. Had to be hope. The Mother of God. In pity. Sometimes. Cuffing aside her wilful son. Intervening. To shed a little love into the depths of the deepest darkest frigging tar-barrel.

And that was what happened. I got a letter. With a stamp which was undoubtedly French. My name printed in block capitals. My address. I opened it. Feeling nothing. The moment beyond feeling. Senses numb. A card. With a few words. Printed as I had asked her to do: SLIGO. SATURDAY 3 MAY 5.30pm – MICHELLE.

So she was coming.

I spelled out those few words a hundred times and more. Touched the paper. Smelled it. To make sure it was real. It was real.

I wanted to run out. Shout at the top of my voice. She is coming.

Then panic. Self-doubt. Anxiety. What was she expecting? Would it all be a fiasco? Given my history, it was bound to be a fiasco.

There were times when I felt the swell of fortune under me, lifting me, like some magical tide. My leaden experiences sinking like the dross they were. And then the tide would be sucked from under me, leaving me to wallow in the dross I foolishly thought I had jettisoned forever. As if the Creator had singled me out to toy with at his pleasure.

At night, in the clammy darkness of my room, I was haunted by the image of Michelle standing in front of me, in her bra and pants, loosening my shirt buttons.

Despite my tenacious concentration her features had begun to soften at the edges. However, the memory of her skin was fresh, and palpable, stark, teasing me, mocking me. And I reeled about in my tortured bed, screaming inside, screaming abuse at myself for having managed to fail when it must have been a million times easier to succeed. But that was me.

Just as well it was not long from the time I got the letter until the Saturday she was to arrive. I went to the railway station, each day I was in town, to establish that it was there. That I knew the way. That there was a train arriving from Dublin at 5.30 on a Saturday evening.

I thought of calling around to Peter Kilduff and my other favourites to tell them their fantasies were to be realised. But thought again. Better wait and see what Michelle wanted. A girl. A girl in Tireragh. Even if I did have to share her with every man in the barony. It was still a miracle.

My rounds in the van had become tedious. The people were still clamouring for my presence. Still buying my goods with their former appetite. But my heart wasn't in it anymore. Even when people came back to me in gratitude for saving their crops or their livestock, for curing their most chronic ailments, for rescuing them from pits of misfortune, I could feel neither enthusiasm nor satisfaction. My mind was on one thing now. One person. And every other consideration had been consigned to the dusty drawers of the irrelevant.

And so the painful wait. Two floating twigs, drifting slowly towards one another. Ever so slowly. Two worlds. About to touch.

Even though there were crowds alighting from the train I spotted her as soon as she stepped on to the platform. She put down a large case on the ground and then went back on to the train. By the time I reached the spot she had lugged another heavy case off and landed it beside the first. Then she looked up and saw me approaching. Her lovely face lit up.

"Loftee. You are here."

She threw her arms around me, and hugged me to her. Then kissed me, first on one cheek, then on the other. Held me back to look at me. With her impish finger she flicked up my chin to snap my mouth closed.

And I had no words. My mind blank. But it didn't seem to matter. She seemed to understand how I felt. How delighted I was to see her again. Speech was unnecessary.

I carried her two cases down the platform and out to the van which I had parked close by. The weight in them suggested she must have brought all her possessions, suggested she was planning a long visit. Maybe she would stay.

"This is your van. Yes?"

She stood admiring it as if it were one of those fancy sports cars. She walked all around it. "Lovely."

I put her cases into the back, and opened the passenger door of the cab for her. The van had always been special. Always. But now it was transformed. Different. She was sitting there. Beside me. In the cab.

"Where do you want to go?" I asked her.

"Drive until I see the city. Then we look for a hotel. Okay? "

"Okay."

I drove around the rectangle of streets that formed the centre of the town. Then down the side-streets. She declared her admiration for the appearance of the town and its setting.

"Beautiful." She slowly articulated each syllable of the word.

Then we looked for a hotel. After driving around the streets again, she chose a small hotel down near the docks. Discreetly tucked into the side streets, it was obviously a perfect choice. I would never have picked it out, but when she did, I could see why. And no doubt cheaper than the big hotels on the main streets.

I lugged her cases up to the room she booked.

"Not bad. Yes?" She turned her raised eyebrows towards me after she had examined the room and checked the view of the docks from the window. "It will be okay. For now."

It was tiny, to be honest. There were two armchairs either side of a coffee table. But no cooking facilities. A door led to an adjoining bathroom and toilet.

We sat down in the two armchairs and stretched our legs.

"You are well, Loftee?" she asked. "You have been busy. Yes?"

"Yes. Busy," I replied. "First Communions. Confirmations. A lot of that kind of thing."

"Ireland is a holy country. Yes?" she asked, laughing her lightly mocking laugh.

"Well, religion is popular, anyway. Just as well for me."

"But there will be demand for a girl. Yes?"

It was like a dart suddenly piercing the quick of my heart. I would have preferred to ignore why she had come. To imagine she had come because of me. But reality had to be endured. Confronted.

"Yes. I'm sure there will be. Great demand."

"And you will bring me in your van. Yes?"

"Yes. I have it all washed out." I was almost gruff. But emotion ran deep. Ran wild. And inhibition, like a wet blanket, smothering the flames of emotion. What a frigging struggle there? I did want to bring her as a gift, a very special gift, to Peter Kilduff and all the other hungry men of the seven parishes. But I also very sincerely wanted to keep her to myself.

Impossible. She did not come to be with me. She came for her business. And the best chance I had of keeping her here was to ensure that her business thrived. So I had to forget about myself and think of the great favour I was doing for Peter and his likes. Think about that, yes and enjoy the company of a beautiful woman for as long as I could make it last.

"The men?" she asked after a silence. "They are old? How old?"

"Some are old. Some are not so old. All are bachelors."

"Bachelors?"

"You know. Not married."

"All the men are not married."

"There are plenty of married men. But we won't go near them."

She looked perplexed. "No married men. But married men were my best clients in Paris."

"We'll have enough bachelors to be going on with. Wait and see."

My scruples would not have allowed me to involve married men. They had women. It would be wrong. What I felt was right was to bring the warmth of a woman to those who had never experienced it. I felt I had some mandate to do that. From the Mother of God. To bring a little female warmth into the cold world of these men.

"Okay, Loftee. You are my manager. You decide. Okay?"

And she reached over, put her hand on top of my hand, and pressed it gently. Fondly. Her female warmth bestowed on me. Her smile. Impish. Trying to lift my spirits by the power of her expressive features. For such moments the torture of sharing her was bearable.

16

HAVE YOU EVER CONSIDERED HOW significant to us is the place where we were born and reared? Maybe it is part of the frigging trap. Keeping us rooted. In the one location. Forever wanting to escape, forever wanting to remain. Frigging peculiar alright, don't you think? And then the way a particular place can keep haunting you. As Aughris did with me.

Aughris was not my favourite place, not by a long shot. I could see how it might be special to a thousand other people. Not to me. Maybe because of the Cor a dTonn experience. That might have affected my impression. And why wouldn't it have?

Do you know Aughris? Maybe not. Unless you had business there, you might not know it even existed. As you drive along the main road to Sligo you would hardly notice that the coastline takes a detour away from you. You would not notice, because it returns so quickly. It is only when you leave the main road and take one of the by-roads that you realise what a stretch of countryside there is sweeping towards the Head. And there is a whole network of by-roads linking houses and villages, wandering hither and thither, and making their way back to the main road as the humour hits them. A bit of a maze really. But I had travelled these roads in the van hawking my religious wares. I had travelled them again with Michelle as I had some very good customers among these scattered farms.

But I had never gone back to the Cor a dTonn. After that visit with my mother and the nun. Never wanted to go back. Never wanted to be reminded of those dreams. Still felt the pain of being disillusioned. Still nursed the anger at the being who had caused my grief. And the problem I had as I drove into that network of by-roads in the thickening darkness was that I did not know where the path to the Cor a dTonn was located. I remembered crossing fields. That was all. So I now had to search for a causeway to the cliff-top.

I had a rough idea of where the cliff was located, and drove slowly along the road watching out for a boreen or a cart-track which might lead me where I wanted to go.

A car came up behind me, its headlights fully on. The light dazzled me and I had to move my eyes out of the lines of the mirrors. The glare made it difficult to continue scouring the walls and hedgerows to my left-hand side. I pulled to the side to let the car pass. But it didn't pass. And its headlights were still glaring. I slowed down more and tightened in to the ditch. But the car behind still didn't pass. The road was narrow without doubt, but anyone who was used to driving on those by-roads should have had no difficulty passing me out I was going so slow and was so tight to the side.

Then I began to panic. Perhaps the word was out. Perhaps His Reverence had had some important engagement, like entertaining the missioners. Perhaps someone spotted him getting into the back of my van. If he was reported missing, perhaps they were now after me, tracking me down to question me about his sudden disappearance. They might have regarded my abrupt departure as suspicious.

Because I could neither see, nor concentrate on, the side of the road, I was about to pull in fully and stop. Force him or her or them to pass me by. But, if it really was people tracking me, they would then have me cornered. So, instead, I put my foot down, speeded up, and drove on. The car behind speeded up too and stayed on my tail. I was now really worried. When I came to a crossroads, I took a right turn heading back towards the main road where I would be able to make a run for it. Glanced in my mirror. I almost shouted with relief. The car had driven on straight. They were not after me. At least not yet.

I didn't want to stop and turn around. Still too terrified. Anyway that might have attracted attention. Instead I drove around the by-roads in a square until I was back again on the stretch that was closest to the cliffs. Once more craning my neck and straining my eyes in search of the way to the Cor a dTonn.

Failed to locate it on that stretch of road. Now pitch frigging dark. Drove up to the old village of Aughris. The deserted village. The grey derelict shells of houses looked ghostly in the darkness. I crept along, watching for a path or a gate that might provide a way to the cliff tops. No luck. I pulled up on the grassy street of one of the ruins and halted. Had to turn around anyway. Cul-de-sac. That was French. I wondered if they were speaking French in the back. Wouldn't be surprised. Wouldn't be surprised if His Reverence knew a bit of French.

No sign of anyone around, so I turned off the engine. Knocked off the lights too. Even if they were out looking for me, no one would find me here. Not until dawn anyway.

Not a sound from the back. Neither French nor English. Were they gone to frigging sleep? Or had they killed one another? I listened. Wished they would make some noise. I didn't want to be plunging over the cliff with two corpses in the back. That would be frigging unnecessary. Not a sound. Not even breathing. Were they at it again? Maybe they were. Making the most of the opportunity. No use wasting a chance that has been dropped in your lap. This thought helped to whet the edge of my bitterness.

I hopped out of the van and walked up and down the village. Searching. It had been a lively place once. A hundred years ago. Even less. And it had a rich history too. Aughris. Used to have a monastery. It was from here that the monks went to

189

Innishmurray. Sister institutions. Over and back. Even though Innishmurray was closer to the north Sligo coast. Now that was an interesting place. Innishmurray. I had never been out. Always wanted to go. Especially to see the Cursing Stones.

Have you ever heard of the Cursing Stones? Those are special stones which you rotate anti-clockwise while you recite a prayer to bring down a curse on your enemy. I always wanted to do that. Try it out. Never more than now. If I had one of those stones now, I could do a job on His Reverence. Turn him into a hedgehog. Or a donkey. Yes, a donkey would be good. He would have a chance to wear a collar again. Then sell him to the tinkers for a small consideration. Nothing much. A couple of tin cans, perhaps. Yes, that would be good. It would save me the bother of a plunge. Save the cost of a good van too.

Yes, a few cursing stones would come in very handy. And maybe that could be the next commodity I could go hawking around the countryside. The next service I could provide. 'Good morning, ma'am. Anyone you want to curse this morning, ma'am?' Well, why not? I had started out selling rosary beads, and had gone a long way. Why not go a bit further?

I had scoured the village, peering over gates and fences. Now convinced that it was a dead end as well as a cul-de-sac. No causeway here across the fields to the cliff-top. Yet there had to be some kind of a path, somewhere. I had no recollection whatsoever of where we left the car that time I came here as a child. No recollection of where we had crossed the fields. It was a right frigging puzzle alright.

I walked down the lane to the junction with the by-road. More than the village was deserted. The whole frigging countryside was deserted. If I had chanced on any man I would certainly have asked him. No point in thinking of risk at this stage. Nothing to lose now.

But no one came. No sign of life in either direction. So I picked the road to the left and set off walking slowly in that direction. Still not a soul on the road. The stars were beginning to fill up the sky. No moon. Perfect night for a plunge. Came to the crossroads. Then remembered that a short distance ahead was a pub, the Beach Bar. Why not? I was bound to get all the directions I wanted there.

A small enough crowd inside. All men, maybe ten or twelve. I looked around. They were all huddled in groups, busy, talking. I went to the bar and caught the barman's eye.

"Can you tell me where the Cor a dTonn is?"

He looked at me in slight surprise, as he pulled the tap and held a pint glass under the swirling beer. "Do you mean how to get to it?"

"Yes."

He concentrated on filling the glass. Then landed it up on the counter. "Do you see that old fellow over there? The one with the cap. He owns land up near the Cor a dTonn. He's the best one to give you directions."

"Okay. Thanks."

I went over to the table where three men were sitting. There was a discussion going on, so they didn't notice me standing beside them. Waiting. For a break in the conversation. But there was no pause. They appeared a little intoxicated as well.

When I felt I had waited as long as politeness required, I tapped him on the shoulder. The old man with the cap.

"Sorry for interrupting. But I want to know the way to the Cor a dTonn, and the barman said you were the best one to ask."

He looked at me vacantly. It was immediately obvious that he was more than a little intoxicated.

"He said you own the land beside it," I continued.

"I do."

191

I stood there expecting an answer, and he was sitting there looking at me, examining me, as if I were the man from Mars.

"Now I know who you are," he declared eventually. "You're the gasur who goes around selling the medals. Am I right?"

"Yes."

"Of course I'm right. I knew straight away it was you. Sit down there now, like a good gasur, and have a drink with us."

"No thanks, I won't have a drink, I'm alright," I replied as I sat down on the vacant chair at their table.

"Mick, bring the gasur a glass of porter," he shouted to the barman.

"Honestly, I'm alright, thanks," I protested.

"Of course you're alright. And the line of business you're in, you're bound to be alright. Not like the rest of us. Not like me anyway. Do you know what age I am? Go on. Give a guess."

I looked at him. He had a strong wiry physique, but that weather-beaten face had been taking the wind and the sun for a long long time. He looked surely eighty. But he probably wanted to be flattered if he was bringing up his age. And it was in my interest to humour him if I wanted to get the information I needed.

"Seventy," I said.

"Isn't that amazing?" He slapped his knee in a show of delight. "I ask that same question of everybody. And everybody gives me the same answer. About seventy. But do you know what? I'll be eighty at the end of next month. That's what I'll be. Without a word of a lie. So amn't I a great man for my age when everybody puts me at seventy or thereabouts. Young fellow, you'll have a drink with us, and I'll tell you everything you want to know about the Cor a dTonn."

17

WHEN YOU LOOK DOWN INTO A TAR-barrel on a calm day the disk of water below is like a round mirror. The water absolutely flat and smooth. And you look at your reflection until you have studied every ugly feature of it. When you can bear to look no longer, you drop a tiny pebble into the centre of the disk. Plop. And the circular wave starts on its way. Strong at first. Clean. Clear. Full of purpose. Then it hits the wall and rebounds, meeting the pursuing waves. Weaving through them. Trying to gather its force back to the point where it started. Being hampered and weakened by its own pursuing waves still emerging from the centre. I told you about this before. How frigging fascinating it was to study.

But what happens to your reflection during all this is also very interesting. It wavers and distorts at first. Then breaks up totally until it is all in fragments. And the thought struck me that maybe the problem is that the Creator himself isn't so happy with what he sees when he looks down into the tar-barrel. Maybe he too feels flawed. An impostor. Inadequate. Feels as if, when all is said and done, he is merely playing around with the plasticine he has nicked from his mother.

Insecure. The only way he can convince himself of his own power is by making his creatures suffer. It would explain a lot. Wouldn't it? Why he fragments his image until it is unrecognisable. Maybe he is as disturbed as the rest of us, can't handle his guilt. Maybe when his mother sent her other son she was trying to redeem him, trying to redeem the Creator. That made more sense, don't you think. Jesus was sent into the world to redeem the frigging Creator himself, to show his brother the error of his ways. To win him back from his cruel preoccupations. Restore him to the goodness and the love which is the natural state of existence. And that is the way Jesus was to save mankind.

But it didn't frigging work, did it? Jesus became man and took upon himself the suffering of mankind in order to move his brother to shame. But the Creator was not moved. Even the sight of his tortured and dying brother didn't touch him. And if that didn't move him, the suffering of mankind certainly won't.

So I came to the conclusion that it was only right to thwart him at every frigging turn. To oppose him and all his schemes against the innocent of the world. To open up a breach wherever possible and allow through the healing flow of his mother's love.

I felt I was indeed opening such a breach in bringing Michelle to Tireragh. Felt good about it when I thought of it in this light. I was bringing to the famished lives of my friends the experience of woman. The only experience capable of soothing the pain of their hunger. The experience of warmth, of beauty. The experience of love. If only for a moment.

But the joy I felt driving her out to Tireragh for the first time was very much qualified by my own need of her. My hunger was as great as theirs. Greater, I'm sure. I wanted her for myself. Would have given every penny I owned to turn back to the hotel and keep her to myself. But that was not the bargain. And as always I was too frigging bashful to advance my own cause.

So I had to be satisfied with the consolation that I was doing this as a great favour for my friends. Making this huge sacrifice. Giving them a present of what was most precious to me.

Mixed feelings alright, don't you think? A pathetically scrambled mind? I'm not looking for frigging pity, you know. I just want you to understand how it was. Confused emotions? Certainly. Stephen Hanlon would have been appalled at the chaos of thoughts and feelings that now reduced my brain to mush. And try as I could, I could not restore any kind of order or detachment there.

I had adapted the back of the van for the alternative use. Had bought a mattress and a heavy multi-coloured counter-pane. All the stock and the statue of the Virgin I had removed and stored in the shed. No problem on that front as I kept the shed locked and neither my mother nor my aunt ever went near it. The lights I kept, but got a set of red bulbs to achieve a warmer feeling. It looked well with the arc of red lights at the head of the mattress. I was pleased with my work. And I could restore it for its original purpose without difficulty. Michelle too was impressed. And amused.

"You are a genius," she declared. Not what I was used to being called. Not by a long shot.

Despite the warring inclinations that were tearing at me, I really was brimming with excited expectation as I drove on up through Tireragh, up towards the mountains, straight to Peter Kilduff's house. I had told nobody about Michelle, so this was going to be a surprise.

Peter was out in his cabbage garden when I called. He came towards me, wading through the rows of green leaves, a head of cabbage in the crook of his arm.

"I haven't seen you in a while." He welcomed me with a broad smile.

"Been busy."

"Keep up the visits. Keep up the visits. We depend on you for our luck, you know."

"Hope everything is alright."

"Yeah," he said, with a long slow exhalation on the word. "Everything is alright. Maybe it's just the company we need."

"I know. I know. We talked about it before."

"We did. And no doubt we'll talk about it again. And we'll be talking about it until they put us in the box and fasten down the lid. But talk won't do much good. Will it?"

"Talk is no good at all," I said, trying to conceal my amusement. "And it's no good dreaming either. We need to do something about it."

By this time I had followed him into his kitchen, where he threw the head of cabbage unceremoniously on to the kitchen table and wiped the clay from his hand on the leg of his trousers.

"You're absolutely right, Lofty. But I'm afraid that in this corner of the world we'll have to settle for our dreams."

"Still, we can keep hoping that our dreams will come true."

"We can indeed, Lofty. Keep hoping. To the end of our days."

"Would you like to have a look in the van?" I tried to be as nonchalant as possible.

He laughed. "You're right, Lofty. It's saying a prayer I should be, at my age, instead of indulging in dreams. But you'd never know: maybe you'd work another miracle and make one of these dreams come true."

We walked out to the van together. He still hadn't detected anything unusual in my manner or voice, despite the absolute torrent of feelings I was trying to bottle inside me. I said nothing to him, but opened the back door of the van, took down the step for him, and stood back to let him enter. When he had gone in, I closed the door behind him.

Then I released the flood of emotion. Standing alone on the roadway I laughed into my clasped hand. I ran away from the van so that my laughing could not be heard when it gushed through my fingers. No hand could hold it now, and I let it flow freely. Laughed at the joke I had played on my loveable friend, Peter Kilduff, imagining his reaction when he found himself with Michelle instead of the shrine and the statues and the pictures of the saints. Laughed in sheer joy for the fulfilment of his dreams, the realisation of all his wishes, the soothing of his painful longing, the feeding of his deep deep hunger. Laughed until the tears were pouring down my face. And when I had finished laughing, the tears were still pouring down my frigging face. But the tears were for me.

By the time Peter Kilduff re-emerged from the back of the van, I was drained of all the excess of emotion. In control of myself. When he had his feet on the ground he looked back at the van, the doors of which had swung shut. He looked dazed. The enjoyment of the joke returned to me.

"Did that really happen?" He looked at me with a broad smile on his face, but sounded as if he was really looking for an answer to that question.

"Just a dream come true," I replied, smiling back at him.

"Where did she come from?"

"Ask me no questions, I'll tell you no lies." I trotted out a saying that had been currency in the school yard when I was a child. I had arranged with Michelle that we would give information to no one, that we would tell no one how we met. I did not want people to know the use I had made of the pilgrimage to Lourdes.

"Well, Lofty, all I can say is, you're a miracle worker sure enough. Wait a minute, will you? When you've enjoyed the tune, you have to pay the piper." And he went off into the house to get his money.

I tapped on the back door of the van. Like a stranger. Before I opened it. To see if she was alright.

She nodded her head. "He needed a girl, okay. He needs practice too." She laughed. Then she crinkled her nose and upper lip. "He does not have a bath. No?"

I had forgotten about that. These men washed their faces once a week before going to mass. That was the extent of their washing.

Peter returned, and I let him go back in to Michelle. That was another of our arrangements. That she

197

would look after the money. At the end of the day we were going to divide it in equal shares. We were partners. I was her manager. They had a different word for it on the streets, she said. It was not a nice word, but it suited the men in question.

I walked back with Peter to the door of his cottage. He was beaming with pleasure. Still mesmerised.

"Would you like me to call again?"

"How about tomorrow?"

"No, not tomorrow. There are other people I want to call on. But I'll be back. Two conditions."

"If there were twenty two, I would still agree to them. What are they?"

"You tell no one about this. And the next time you are washed. Have a bath."

"Of course I agree. But when will you be back?"

"I don't know."

"Then how do I know when to get washed?"

I shrugged my shoulders. I couldn't help him on that one.

"Never mind," he said. "I'll wash myself every day. Just in case."

"It would be no harm," I agreed. "Just in case."

I was closing his garden gate when he called after me.

"Lofty"

I looked around. He was standing framed in his doorway, as if he were posing for a picture. He opened his mouth to say something, then closed it again, and gave me the most emphatic thumb up.

There were a thousand Peter Kilduffs scattered all over Tireragh and it became my objective to reach every one of them. Old codgers who in all their lives had got no closer to a woman than to eye her across the aisle at mass on Sunday. Young men in their prime whose natural mates had all migrated to the cities, to England, to America. Hungry men all, whose cottages were the very picture of want, neglected shacks with discoloured walls, and windows grown opaque with dirt.

These were the people I loved, my people, and I threw myself fervently into the task of bringing a little beauty and love and satisfaction into their lives. And they responded. Just like Peter Kilduff. As if I had brought heaven to them in the back of a van. Grateful beyond bounds. Almost worshipping me. And I re-doubled my efforts. To get to more of them. To get to them more often.

And how they were transformed. Almost overnight. The same conditions were laid down for all. They had to observe total secrecy, they had to wash every day. Just in case. They suddenly took an interest in their appearance. Bought new clothes for wearing on Sundays, wore their Sunday clothes during the week, dumped their old rags. Lingered around their cottages, just in case, instead of going to the pub. And their cottages too were brightening up. Windows cleaned here. New curtains there. Paths and streets cleared of weeds. A new coat of paint on the walls here, slates replaced on a leaky roof there.

All was changed. I suppose they had to be doing some frigging thing while they were waiting at home day and night just in case the red van called. But it was more than that. They appeared happier. Taking pride in themselves. Making their houses more attractive, as if they were expecting an important guest. Which they were of course, but she never got out from the back of the van.

And it went further than their houses, their appearance. They were taking better care of their farms as well. Minding their sheep and their cattle as they had never minded them before. Weeded their potato drills, where heretofore the heads of thistles would be vying with the potato stalks for the thin ration of sunlight.

They were thriving. And credit was being heaped on me and on the van. More miracles. More examples of our powers.

I suppressed all other thoughts, all other emotions, and concentrated on this objective. Took satisfaction from the obvious good I was doing.

Back in the hotel in the evenings, Michelle and I. We talked. As friends. As work-mates. As partners. After I had driven her home. Easy conversation. About trivial events. Making little jokes about people. She mimicking certain individuals for my amusement. Dividing out the money, as if we were doing no more than selling apples. It was like that. Normal. Innocent.

What happened in the privacy of the van we did not discuss.

We worked at a prodigious rate. It was as if Michelle too was imbued with the spirit of our objective. Anxious to allay as much of the pain of humanity as she possibly could. But we could not work every day. I had to keep up the front of dealing in religious goods. And so, whenever she decided she was tired or not feeling well, I loaded up the van with the statue and my array of pictures and souvenirs of Confirmation Day, and headed out on my traditional rounds.

But it was very tricky managing both operations, getting the balance right, and I was inclined to include more of the Michelle days. Until a crisis occurred.

I was driving along a by-road in the parish of Templeboy one day, with Michelle in the back, when I was stopped by a crowd of six to eight people, mainly women.

Mrs Conway, mother of ten, standing squarely in the middle of the road, like a bulldog bitch, was their ring-leader and their mouth-piece.

"We want to know why you aren't stopping off at our houses any more."

"Been busy," I replied, my feet poised over the clutch and throttle in case they made an attempt to open the back door. In case I needed to force a quick get-away.

"That's not good enough, Lofty. That's not good enough at all. You have a responsibility to everyone.

But it's obvious now that there's an element of favouritism creeping into your service. And that's not fair, Lofty. That's not fair. You're calling regularly to every sheet-mickey in the parish, but not to us."

"Every what?"

"Every bloody sheet-mickey. Every good for nothing bachelor. Sure we can see it as plain as daylight. And you're giving them a fierce amount of time before the statue. All that praying is doing wonders for them, but it's leaving us trailing in their wake. And they're going around with smirks on their faces, all done up like tailors' dummies, scrubbing their houses as if they had Yanks coming, shovelling dung while they're dressed in a collar and tie. The rest of us need the help of the angels in heaven as well as they do."

"And the publicans aren't pleased either, one bit," butted in her husband, Patcheen Conway. "They haven't seen sight of these boyos for weeks. And they used to spend their lives inside in the public houses. Aye and spend more than their lives, they spent every last penny they had on drink. Now the pubs are empty and the publicans are close to being in Stubbs."

I wanted to say, 'frig the publicans', but I didn't want to start a row. I said nothing. Just continued to face them down.

"You've been up to John Joe Carter just now. We saw you," continued the bulldog bitch. "So why don't you pull in now, like a good young fellow, and let us pray before the statue and pick out a few tokens. We can do ourselves some good, and you can profit from us just as well as you can from John Joe Carter and his likes."

"Can't."

"Why not?"

"It's not lucky." It was the first thing that came into my mind. Blurted out without any thought. So I had not anticipated its deadly effect. She was plainly rattled. Taken aback. Puzzled. Impressed.

"Why not?"

I enjoyed seeing her in disarray. Enjoyed the unaccustomed feeling of superiority. I took my time replying. Took time to think it out. Slowly. Calmly. Stephen Hanlon would have been proud of me.

"Days it's lucky to call on bachelors. Days its lucky to call on married people, families. It's like that. And it can be very unlucky if you get the days wrong. As it happened, there were a lot of days for bachelors lately. But that could change soon, and we could have a run of days for married people."

"Is that so? I hadn't realised that." I had her on a leash now, the bulldog bitch, and she was lapping my fingers.

"Another thing I've found out is that it's not good to stop on the road. Not lucky. So from now on I can only call to houses."

"Is that so?" she parroted. "And what about the stall outside the church?"

"That's different. That's okay. That's always lucky."

"I see."

"The best thing for you to do is to go home and wait for me. The first good day for married people, I'll call on you. That's a promise."

"Alright, Lofty, we'll do that. We'll be waiting for you. And God bless you."

"And you too. And all of you."

They fell to, and I drove on, absolutely exhilarated at the way I had handled the crisis. I felt like cheering, like whistling. But I was afraid of attracting attention. I had to be careful. Especially when I had Michelle in the back.

Still, I decided that we would have to divide the days more evenly. More days with the religious goods and the shrine. More days for the frigging married people.

But there were days when we did neither. Days when I would arrive to collect Michelle, and she

202

would be in her dark mood, cursing under her breath in a language that wasn't English, and didn't sound like French either. Her eyes full of anger, aggression. They were bad days for her. But, in a way, they were wonderful days for me. Never once did she look at me with anger or hostility. It was always clear that I was not included among what annoyed her, what depressed her. No, I was on her side. We were in it together, whatever it was. And she would even hug me when she was in these moods. Hold me, as if I were her sole comfort at such times. And she would say: "Loftee, we go somewhere today. Not work."

And on those delicious days she would make up sandwiches, fill up a thermos flask with coffee. We would buy buns or biscuits. Then head off in a totally different direction. Riding side by side in the cab. There was no danger of being seen by people from Tireragh once we headed north out of Sligo town. They never ventured beyond the town itself. So here it was perfectly safe for us to travel together. No one to ask questions. No one to raise an inquisitive eyebrow. No one to report that he had seen Lofty driving out the Bundoran road with a gorgeous blonde in the van. No, we were free. Michelle was able to lift the gloom. To forget. Marvelling at the countryside every turn of the road.

When the weather was good we went to the beach. Strandhill. Rosses Point. Once even as far north as Rossnowlagh. Places I had never been to before. Places that were bustling with leisure, with people enjoying themselves. People lying in the sunshine. Lying on the sand. Paddling in the water. And we did all these things too. Watched children digging holes, building walls in the sand, with brightly coloured shovels and even more brightly coloured buckets. Gaiety. That was what was in the atmosphere. And we joined in as if it were our birthright.

How beautiful it was to be lying beside Michelle on a sandy beach, sharing a rug with her, as if we were on a date, taking a sandwich when she shared them out, holding a cup of coffee while she poured the milk. Homely little things that we did together without having to discuss them. Such days were blissful, with the sun shining down assertively between banks of white fluffy clouds. Shining on Michelle in her shorts and her brightly coloured blouses. Shining on me in my incongruous heavy brown jacket and my equally incongruous corduroy trousers. Shining.

On other days, when the sun was not quite so assertive, we drove inland, to explore places I had always wanted to see, but had been reluctant to visit on my own.

One such trip brought us up along the river, the Garravogue, to Lough Gill. Were you ever at Lough Gill? It was frigging magical. I had often heard how beautiful it was, but still it exceeded my expectations. The first landmark we stopped at was Tobbernalt, a holy well to beat all holy wells. The spring itself was a real gusher, with a cut-stone surround, and it took a wide deep free-flowing stream to drain the overflow down into the lake. It was set in a grove on the side of a hill, with a grotto cut out of the rocks, and stone steps up and down. My kind of place. There was a slab of rock which had been used as a mass rock during Penal Days. Might have been an altar in earlier Pagan times too. Huge trees, beech, oak, sycamore, provided a wonderful cover over our heads. I could have waited there all day. And Michelle too was entranced.

"You could pray here. You could be holy here," she commented in approval.

"You could be happy here too, " I replied. "If you didn't have to go back to the world."

"Yes," she nodded, looking around, tightening her brow.

But we couldn't stay there forever. We had to move on. Bliss to have her in the front, beside me, instead of hidden in the back. Bliss to be sharing with her the experience of seeing these places for the first time. Bliss to hear her oohing and aahing at every new sight.

A short distance down the road we came to Dooney Rock. I parked the van in a lay-by that was carved out of a wood, and we got out to have a look. We started climbing the rock. More a small hill than a rock. It rose up from the shore of the Lake, hundreds of feet, carrying a stretch of the wood on its back. We kept climbing. It got steeper. She grabbed my hand when she was slipping, and I supported her. When we reached the flat top I was still holding her hand and the whole lake with its wooded islands opened out below us.

A woman's hand is a beautiful thing. So delicate. So vulnerable. Just as she was. Whistling in surprise at the sweep of lake, the wooded islands, like gigantic emeralds set on a bed of deep deep blue. Her eyes misty.

"In Europe I have not seen a place like this." And she meant it, her voice was so deliberate, her words slow.

"How much of Europe have you seen?" I asked casually.

Immediately her misty expression became clouded. Darkened. An edge of indignation on her voice. "Europe is not beautiful. Not beautiful like this."

She would say no more. And instinctively I held back when I felt her soul was raw. A few times I had asked her questions like that, wondering exactly where she had come from, what her family was like, what she had done before I met her. But I had found out nothing. She warded off these attempted intrusions very definitely. She was silent, private, although she did not appear offended by my curiosity. And so I probed no further. Happy to be standing beside her, holding her hand, looking out over the most beautiful place in Europe.

18

HAVE YOU EVER IMAGINED WHAT IT IS like to be born ugly, I mean really frigging ugly? A round fat face with round thick glasses parked on your nose permanently. A mouth that falls open automatically as soon as you think of something other than keeping your mouth closed. A body that is in keeping with that hallowe'en turnip of a head. Small, fat, awkward. Have you ever thought of what it would be like to be born into a body like that? To be trapped inside a body like that and yet to have all the needs and ambitions and desires of a normal person. Add to the minus side, if you like, a defective frigging brain. One that has a different wiring system to every other brain, but has the same instruction manual, as Stephen Hanlon pointed out. How would you like to stare down into a tar-barrel and see all of that staring back at you? How?

How would you like to be forever on the outside? How would you like to have people take for granted that because you are ugly and defective and odd you have no need to love and be loved like everyone else?

Have you ever stood staring at an old whin bush on the side of a hill, and dreamed of becoming a prince or a millionaire with fancy houses and fancy cars, a woman at your feet worshipping you?

Have you ever looked at a blackthorn bush being wracked by the wind? I mean really looked. Stared at it so long that you might have been standing there for a minute or an hour or a year? Watched how the wind combs out the sprigs and leaves? How the wind heaves and drags at it, as if it is testing the roots for grip? Watched how the bush cowers away from the wind, leaving its exposed back to become callused and

206

gnarled from the constant lashing? Have you ever looked at an old blackthorn bush long enough to notice things like that?

Have you ever tried to concentrate so hard on such an old thorn bush or whin being wracked by the wind in order to shut out the pain inside yourself? In order to forget about yourself and your awkwardness and your ugliness that has left you outside, waiting. In order to forget about this defective brain which cannot tell you whether a girl likes you or whether she is merely not so repelled as everyone else. A brain which cannot tell you whether you should be queuing up with your money in your fist like everyone else instead of standing outside watching an old whin bush slowly turning brown or an old blackthorn trembling before every onslaught of the wind.

I have seen such things. Have watched them endlessly while I was waiting for Michelle to finish with yet another customer. Wishing I could be in there. Wishing I could keep her to myself. Wishing we could head off to the beach every day instead of pursuing these interminable rounds. Questioning whether I should ever have made a gift of her womanhood to my friends. Then reflecting that they were as much in need of her comfort as I was. Then reflecting that she would not be here at all were it not for the business arrangement.

Sometimes she would notice that I was as wracked as an old blackthorn in the wind, give me a peck on the cheek, a hug, and I would try to conceal it again. Yes, but feel the frigging pain even more acutely. Sometimes she would look at me and say, "we have done enough. Yes?"

One such evening we were covering an area on the road out towards Lough Easkey. When I stuck my head through the back door of the van, she looked at me, thought a while, and said:

"There is a nice place we can go. Yes?"

I knew what she meant. Somewhere like the beach at Rosses Point. Somewhere like the valley of Glencar with its waterfalls tumbling from the side of Ben Bulben. Somewhere we could ramble together without the fear of being seen. But we were now in Tireragh, and she had to stay concealed in the back of the van.

Then I thought of the Lake, and said, "yes, there is a place we can go". And I sat in and drove. Drove up the mountain slope. Leaving the houses behind. And the farms. And the green fields.

When the slope levelled out, the Lake was in front of me. There was a little side-road along the edge of the water, not so much a road as a track of gravel and stones that might have been shovelled off the back of a lorry. But it was good enough to drive on, and it enabled me to park the van well away from the straggle of road that wound its way along the other side of the lake, and up across the mountain again. The saying was that even a snipe would need a motor car to follow that road across the mountains. There was no house for miles and the only movement was the lazy nosing of the sheep among the rocks for the scant tufts of grass.

When she got out from the back of the van, Michelle was stunned by the landscape. She shaded her eyes with her hands, partly to adjust to the light, partly to scan the horizon.

"Where are we? This is beautiful," she exclaimed.

"The Lake," I replied.

She walked about among the crags, pressing the ground with her feet. It had an unusual spongy, springy feel where there were layers of dried reeds underneath.

"Look," she pointed with her finger and traced the course of a little stream that had etched a path down the slope of the mountain and cascaded over the steep rocks just above the lake shore.

"Look," I responded, pointing at a hill on the other side of the lake that stood ominously in a dark shadow cast by a huge cloud that was drifting across an otherwise blue sky.

"Lovely."

We walked along the shore picking up bits of warped branches that were dried out and bleached by the weather, tossing them into the water, watching them bob about in the tiny waves that creased the surface of the Lake.

When we came to a little cove that had a gravely beach, she whipped off her shoes and waded out knee-deep into the brown water. I sat on a stone watching her paddle about delightedly in the murky little waves that washed over her ankles and flapped against her shins and the slender calves of her legs.

Have you ever noticed how beautiful are the ankles of a woman? John Patrick Murphy, an old man whom I visited as a child, an old man with a long life-time of observing such things, once declared that he could judge a woman by her ankles alone. The rest of her physique was always in harmony with the shape of her ankles, as was her character and temperament. Yes, you could tell everything from the close scrutiny of a woman's ankles. It was the regret of his own life that he had not taken to the road with a travelling woman who had the most beautiful ankles in the world. Slender as those of a race-horse. Yes, that travelling woman had the breeding of a thoroughbred wherever she got it. The regret of his life that he had not taken to the road with her.

He could have been right, you know. If one person can read your life from the palm of your hand, why can't another do the same by looking at your ankles? Especially a man like John Patrick who had made a life-time study of it. I suppose you would have to be a woman though. I don't know if he looked at men's ankles in the same way. Probably not. I never heard him make any claim for men's ankles.

He would probably want to take to the road with Michelle. If he saw her paddling in the water of Lough

Easkey. Stepping carefully. Revealing her slender ankles in flashes above the bog-brown waves. Slender as those of a race-horse. Indeed. Indeed. Thoroughbred. Wherever she got it. He would want to take to the road with Michelle. If he were still alive.

The feeling of remoteness lulled me from my usual anxious watchfulness when we were in Tireragh. And so I had not noticed the white Volkswagen Beetle come bobbing and dipping over the road on the approach from Tobercurry.

"Quick," I shouted when I spotted it on a brow as it negotiated the stretch along the Lake.

"Hide."

In a wink the car had disappeared again into a hollow. She rushed to the shore and crouched behind a boulder. The car re-appeared, slowed down when it approached the nearest point to where the van was parked, and I could see the driver craning his neck as he scrutinised me. Maloney, the cattle-jobber. On his way home from a fair or a mart somewhere. As he passed by, about a hundred yards from where I was sitting, nonchalantly as it were, he favoured me with a stiff salute.

I heard the stories going the rounds later that when Maloney crossed down into Tireragh and hit the pubs there, he claimed he had just witnessed an apparition. He claimed he had seen me on the shore of the Lake. I was in a trance. Gazing at a beautiful woman who was walking on the water. But, by the time he got close, she had disappeared.

Relief. Maloney's story was being repeated in mockery of the man. He was permanently drunk. So the apparition was put down to the effects of alcohol. To the horrors. It was an hallucination that was more than predictable. It was inevitable. And I was relieved. The last thing I needed now was more attention.

19

HAVE YOU EVER WATCHED RAIN FALLING on a tar-barrel? Interesting. First of all, you drop the pebble in the centre, get the ripples going. Then watch the rain-drops. Fall. But they don't affect the course of the ripple. Not to the extent that you can notice anyway. Just something from the outside. From nowhere, a tiny injection. The ripple absorbs the raindrop with ease. And yet it is extra. From nowhere. A little injection.

I should have discovered drink before. All my life I had lived in terror of my own voice. Afraid of it. From the time I was a child. Afraid of the heap of contempt that would come tumbling down on me the minute I opened my mouth. The heap of ridicule. And so I learned early to keep my mouth shut. Less chance of making a fool of myself.

But drink. A little something from the outside. From nowhere. Like a raindrop falling on a ripple. Natural, but extraordinary. I should have discovered it before. It should have happened to me before. Whatever. It wasn't as if there was a scarcity of it in my environment. But it had never engaged my attention. I suppose I had always thought it made people more foolish. Like Maloney, the cattle jobber. Befuddled their brains. And my brain was befuddled enough. I could not afford to become more foolish than I was. Drink was not for me. Of course I had never reasoned it out like that, given it a second's consideration even. All of those thoughts were there without my ever having worked them out.

How wrong I was about drink. How wrong. The first glass of Guinness in the Beach Bar went down reluctantly, like medicine you force yourself to take for reasons quite unrelated to the attraction of the exercise itself. But, quickly, I had adjusted to the taste. Once the anaesthetic forces had been unleashed, the taste-buds were the first to be side-lined. The tangled mesh, the barbed fences of tension and pain were then under assault.

More glasses followed as each of the men called for a round in his turn. Each of them included me. And I was beginning to enjoy the effects of alcohol. To enjoy the sweeping away of age-old ramparts. To enjoy the sweeping away of those defence works which, I think, had made me a prisoner as much as the circle of the besieging forces ever had. All being swept away.

The cycle of rounds turned on me. I was self-conscious, uneasy. But it turned out to be as simple as a nod to the bar-man, as simple as putting a fiver in his fist when he plonked the drinks on the table in front of us.

It was a lot more difficult to get the information I wanted out of Frank, the man who owned the land over which I had to pass if I was to drive to the sum-mit of Aughris Head, if I was to find my way to the Cor a dTonn.

"I am the last person to have been born in the vil-lage of Aughris," he said. " Would you believe that?"

I would have been prepared to believe anything he told me, if he would also tell me how to get access to his mangy acres so that I could get on with the busi-ness of snuffing myself.

"Deserted. These seventy years." The other men nodded sympathetically.

"It was a cosy place in the old days," said the one called Paddy, in a tone that suggested they had tra-versed this subject before and there was little juice left to be chewed out of this particular cut of tobacco. It was a ritual conversation, the kind I had listened to over and over on my visits to old people.

"How many families would have been there in the old days?" asked Paddy, as if he had not heard the answer to the question a thousand times.

"There must have been a good dozen anyway," replied Frank as if it was the first time he had been asked the question and had to work out the answer. "Some of the houses were already empty when I was a child. But the Kellys were still there, and the O'Haras and the Maloneys. They all left in my time. Ended up in Chicago, most of them.

"But who did the other houses belong to?" asked Paddy. Had I not been in a hurry, anxious, worried, I would have enjoyed this ritual conversation, enjoyed listening to the well worn facts being re-told like decades of the rosary. However, the alcohol was now making an onslaught on even my most immediate anxieties, and I was slowly being drawn into the circle of talk.

"Well, one of them belonged to old Pat Healy. He had gone to live with his nephew back in Skreen in my time, but he used to cycle over every day to have a look around and count the cattle."

"That's only five of them accounted for."

"Well, one of the houses belonged to the Killawees, but there was no land going with it, so they never came near the place. Another belonged to the Laings, but they had sold the house and the four acres that went with it to Mike Kelly when they were leaving for America."

"There must have been more than that. You said yourself that there was a good dozen houses there in the old days."

"What about the McDermotts," I piped in. Quite naturally. As if I belonged to the circle of conversation. "There were McDermotts living in Aughris one time." The drink had loosened my tongue. Had washed away my inhibitions. And it felt great. Then the quick backlash of panic as self-consciousness returned, briefly, tentatively.

The three men stared at me in surprise and silence. It was as if they had been addressed by the corpse at a wake. Eventually Frank raised his bushy eyebrows.

"What McDermotts are you talking about?" He looked at the other men. This was not part of the ritual. He was supposed to be asked questions to which he knew the answers. To which the questioner also already knew the answers. The path was well-worn, there were ground-rules. Deviations were not expected. And were not easily tolerated. He was clearly irritated at being tested on the knowledge that people were merely expected to admire. "There were no McDermotts there in my time, and I never heard tell of any McDermotts from the village of Aughris."

All my life I had been waiting for this. To wade into a conversation in which I had the knowledge on my side. Like playing cards with a handful of trumps. Before this night I would have been itching and straining to join, but would have been terrified of interjecting, even when I had the knowledge that was sought. Now, thanks to the power of drink, there were no restraints on me anymore.

"There was a man called Teddy McDermott from the village of Aughris," I declared with authority. "He was a thatcher by trade, and he played the flute. He was a great favourite wherever he went. And whenever he finished a job there was a hooley in the house that night. MacDermott played jigs and reels and hornpipes on the flute, and people gathered in to dance on the flag-stones. And he played and they danced until the cock was crowing in the yard outside the next morning."

"And when was that? Sure, there haven't been thatchers around since St.Patrick was a gasur", Frank was rising. Indignant.

"I don't know when. But I do know he was there. I often heard the old people talking about him. Teddy MacDermott. From Aughris. He played the flute. And people loved to see him coming because they knew that, as soon as the work was finished, there would be a hooley."

Frank scratched his head, and fidgeted. The other two were laughing at the way he was discomfited. He was the old man of the community and had gained status from his knowledge of the past.

"It's true," I emphasised. "He was a thatcher by trade. He was always summoned by people up our way. Whenever they had a roof needed a new coat of thatch."

"Maybe you're right," said Frank in a sullen voice. "Maybe there was such a man. But I never heard tell of him." And he ended that conversation by nodding to the barman for another round of drinks.

I was exultant at winning the argument, at winning an argument for the first time in my life. And I felt cocky enough to be indignant that Teddy McDermott was forgotten by his own people. He was as clear in my mind as any of the three men in front of me. Clearer because I would forget them the moment I walked out the door, whereas I knew Teddy McDermott inside out and upside down. Had walked the roads of Tireragh with him in my imagination from the time Long Tom Forde first narrated the story of the thatcher from Aughris. Had watched him deftly weaving the straw and the sallies. Had listened to his music in the kitchen after the floor had been cleared and the forms and settle beds had been packed with eager neighbours. Yes, I knew Teddy MacDermott from the talk of Tom Forde and other people. And they all claimed he was from Aughris. But here I was in the middle of Aughris people, and they never heard of him? What kind of empty heads had they?

I drank faster in the huffed silence. With relish. Drank the fresh glass that Frank had bought. Still thinking of Teddy MacDermott. Was there nobody to recall how he would arrive with his donkey and cart, and unload the long troughs he used for steeping the sally rods. How the children would crowd around him but he would never get annoyed, and never hunt them out of the way, except when the hot water was being poured on the sally rods in the timber trough.

When I asked Long Tom what had happened to MacDermott, he said that the thatcher had the misfortune to fall in love with a girl above in Kilglass, daughter of a well-to-do farmer whose house he was working on. He asked her to marry him, and she was willing, but her father scorned a match with a landless journeyman thatcher. And that was that. MacDermott was so put-out by this disrespect for his trade and his way of life that he packed it in. He set off walking to Derry and signed on for free transportation to Australia. Nothing was ever heard of him after.

"And what else do you know about Aughris?" asked Frank, sulky, hoping to turn the tables on me, to show up the limitations of my knowledge.

But he did not realise that the drink had just liberated my tongue, my voice, my self-confidence, and I was not going to be put down so easily that night. Or ever again. Drink is a wonderful thing.

"Did you hear about the monks in Aughris?"

"There was a monastery here in the old days," agreed Paddy, nodding his head, and looking around the others for agreement.

"They went out to Innishmurray, where they set up another monastery, where they had cursing stones," I added.

"Everyone has heard of the Cursing Stones of Innishmurray" scoffed Frank. "Sure aren't they bringing boatloads of tourists out to see them these days."

"But did you know that they brought those Cursing Stones with them from Aughris?"

I was now departing from the history that I had gathered in my years of listening to the old people. I was now launching into pure fabrication. Make-believe. Fantasy. But the effect on the three men was a treat to witness. They suddenly gave me their total and lively attention. It was as if they had suddenly been electrified.

"They brought the Cursing Stones with them when they were banished from Aughris. Banished from Ireland. You see the monks had a terrible secret. Terrible but true. That God, the so-called Father, Creator of Heaven and Earth, is an impostor."

It was more than a treat. It was a feast. They were staring at me with their mouths agape, the way I had stared at every fool in the past. They were stunned. Speechless.

"They had discovered that this Creator was the son of the real god, and that she was a woman. Mother of God, as they say. She had three sons, the Creator, Jesus, and the Holy Ghost. The Creator was a craftsman always making something, but jealous, always needing credit and praise for everything he made. And when he made the world, he pretended to mankind that he was the only God. No mention of his mother, after she gave him life and love, and the wherewithal to construct his world. So, the Creator was the one who revolted. This was the terrible secret that the monks of Aughris had discovered. That the Creator and Satan are one and the same."

Frank almost choked on a mouthful of stout and spat it back into the glass to clear his mouth. "What kind of shit are you talking?"

"It's true, you know. And the monks in Aughris discovered it all those years ago. So instead of praying to God, they developed a ritual of cursing the Creator. By turning the stones anti-clockwise they were reversing the motions of nature, the motions of the sun, the moon, and the stars. All the things that he had created. And they fixed their minds on his Heavenly Mother instead, who is the real source of love and life."

Frank was rising from his seat. His weather-beaten face was now a reddish-purple, and I took pleasure in watching his fit of rage. "There was never the likes of that in Aughris," he declared.

"There was." I knew I was driving the knife home. And I offered it up to Teddy MacDermott who had been ignominiously forgotten in his own village. "Until the Bishop heard about it, and then the monks were banished to Innishmurray, where they could do what they liked. And they kept on turning the Cursing Stones for a thousand years afterwards."

Frank was now standing up and had adopted a belligerent pose, which was comical in such an old man. "Are you trying to tell us that the monks in Aughris thought that God and the Devil were one and the same?"

"That's what they discovered, and it's true if you frigging think about it." I knew I was provoking him to the point where he might hit me. But I didn't care. I was ecstatic to be arguing in a way I had always dreamed of arguing. Ecstatic to be anaesthetised against feelings which had always afflicted me in these situations.

Frank spat on the floor. "Let me tell you, young fellow, that you are the most perverted get I have ever come across. God the same as the Devil. Let me tell you, son, that He is up there, and you are answerable to Him. He has the whole world in the palm of His hand. And He has you in the palm of His hand too, whether you like it or not. And what He does with you is His business. But let me tell you this, you little snot-nosed cur, you had better shift yourself fast out of this pub and out of Aughris. Because if I ever catch you in these parts again, it isn't the way to the Cor a dTonn I'll be showing you. I'll be taking you by the scruff of the bloody neck and chucking you over the Cor a dTonn. Now shift your arse while you still have one."

I looked at the other men. They had adopted hostile attitudes as well. And everyone in the pub was staring at us, because Frank had raised his voice to the point where he was roaring his final remarks at me.

So there was no choice. I drank the last of my Guinness and headed for the door.

I felt I was walking on clouds, so lightly and easily did I move among the lounge tables and the low stools. But as soon as I opened the door, and got a blast of fresh cold air, my stomach seemed to do a somersault and a rush of nausea spread through my body. I felt the contents of my stomach welling at my throat and I ran across the yard to a low wall where I disgorged the weight of Guinness into a patch of grass on the other side.

Then I sat down on this low wall. My head was spinning. Or rather the whole world was spinning around me. Yes, it was I who was fixed and everything else, the pub, the yard, the beach, the stars, all were in a very powerful spin around me. That made me even sicker, but I no longer had anything to disgorge.

Eventually the spin swirled to a halt and I lay sprawled on the little wall, a hand on either side planted on the cold stone to keep me upright. I kept trying to focus on things, but they kept moving. The stars. The white wall. The pub itself. And it took a while for things to settle.

I felt like lying down. Had an almost irresistible urge to lie out flat on the wall and go to sleep. But I couldn't do that. What if I didn't wake in time and someone were to come across the van? Once dawn broke it would be very conspicuous parked there in the deserted village. Very suspicious. It would attract immediate attention. So I forced myself to remain upright.

And the self-esteem that I had gained in overcoming my inhibitions in the conversation inside quickly evaporated out here in the yard among the nausea and the vomit and the overwhelming frigging tiredness.

One comment from the conversation, though, kept ringing in my ear. 'he has you in the palm of his hand', setting off little reverberations. When everything else settled I turned my attention to this. To what I was doing. Is this what he wanted? Was I walking into his trap by killing those who had offended me. It was certainly his style. Don't you think?

Not like Jesus. Turn the other cheek and all that. Definitely. Jesus was out to undermine him and everything he stood for. But the Creator wasn't undermined that easily. Too clever. He hijacked Jesus. Got the old scribes and pharisees to take over the Church. And nothing changed. They even set themselves up as the sole interpreters of the message of Jesus. Neat one that. Told people what to think of Jesus. Maybe Jesus even said: 'Mother, Mother, why hast thou forsaken me'. But these boys would quickly draw the line. Can't have that. God is a man. A creator. Competitor. Aggressive. Jealous. Demanding recognition. Like any other good man. And they made Jesus's church the same as the old church of the Jews. In there fighting and hating and murdering like the rest of them.

So what was I doing?

Hating and murdering, like the rest of them? Playing into his hand. Betraying his mother. After she sent her loving son in a vain attempt to redeem the world by redeeming her renegade son who had made it. The suffering of Jesus was meant to reflect the suffering of the world, reflect it right up into the face of the Creator. Reflect it from the depths of the tar-barrel smack up into his eyes as he was gazing down to admire his handiwork. But was he moved? Not at all.

And yet. The only way to deny him satisfaction was to reject his ways. To insist on loving in his world of hostility. To refuse to compete in his world of competition. To court anonymity with the same dedication as he and his followers show in their demand for praise and glory and recognition.

And I had to be careful not to play into his hands. Had to make sure I was not doing his will.

The door of the pub opened and I heard voices. They were going home. The customers. I had to move or I might have another confrontation with Frank and his mates. My feet were steadier now. My head clearer. My stomach empty. I even felt hungry. Realised I hadn't eaten all day. The by-road was so dark I had to be careful not to trip or fall as I hurried along.

Had to get off the frigging road before anyone saw me. Had to get back to the deserted village.

The van was as silent and as dark as the sky overhead when I returned. I paused. Sat against the front bumper. To reflect. Was I about to do the right thing? I was. Couldn't have it on my conscience that I did the will of the Creator. Couldn't go down thinking that I'd acted as he would have done. Thinking of his having one long final laugh as I plunged from the top of the cliff. And the wail of the Cor a dTonn would be heard on the far side of the Ox Mountains alright. My wail. His laughter. Wasn't going to have that. Not by a long frigging shot.

I went to the back door of the van. Unlocked it and threw it open. Then I waited. Unafraid. Alert.

The black figure of His Reverence quickly emerged. Arrogant. Flying his tattered dignity like a flag. Didn't acknowledge my presence. Stormed off as soon as his feet hit the ground. Off into the night.

Michelle came out more slowly. I didn't move to assist her, as I normally would have done. She peered at me through the darkness. Trying to assess the situation. She looked tired and puzzled. But she was nimble and hopped down on the ground. She came closer. I still didn't make any move.

"You have made an enemy, Loftee," she said shaking her head and nodding in the direction His Reverence had disappeared.

"Good," I grunted. Nothing could do more for my self-esteem than to have such a man as an enemy. Yes, he was the enemy alright.

"Why did you do it Loftee?" she asked, a disarming innocence and perplexity in her voice.

"Why did you do it?" I parroted back. "A priest. Especially him. He spends half his life in my mother's parlour."

"I did not know that, Loftee. I knew he was a priest, yes. Priests should be holy. But in Paris many clients are priests."

"It's not because he's supposed to be holy, and isn't. That's not what matters. What matters is that he's..." I searched for a word, but couldn't find one, and at the risk of sounding ridiculous, I continued, "he's the enemy."

"I did not know that, Loftee. I did not know. You opened the door. He came in. I thought he was another client."

"I didn't open the door. He did. Before I could stop him."

"I am so sorry, Loftee. So sorry you are upset. He was the first to come in today. The first in three days. I thought he was a client."

Now I had begun to feel ridiculous. I had not given any thought to her perspective. Of course she would have thought I was ushering in another customer. What else could she have thought? I was glad of the darkness hiding my embarrassment.

Seeing her with the priest was a shock. But then it would have been a shock to have seen her with anybody. That was the frigging trouble if I was honest about it. And it was true that I hadn't taken a single customer for three days. I just couldn't bring myself around to it.

"What is happening, Loftee?" she asked, with genuine hurt puzzlement in her voice that pierced me to the quick.

What was happening? I was frigging well in love with her. That was what was happening. And try as I did, I could not continue to share her with anyone. I

222

had been driving up to the gates of my best customers, but couldn't bring myself to stop. Over a couple of weeks I had reduced a thriving business down to nothing. I made excuses to Michelle. Told her that the men were not at home. That the novelty was wearing off. While the same poor men were left standing at their gates, with their tongues hanging out, as the red van passed them by.

I ended up driving Michelle around the roads of Tireragh in the back of the van, stopping for no one. Frequently driving out to the Lake so that we could be together, alone. Don't get me wrong - I had tried to force myself to continue our former rounds. Had even driven up to Peter Kilduff's house and parked outside his front gate. Had watched poor old Peter through the open door readying himself. But before he came out I drove off again. I passed by the houses of hundreds that I had called on regularly over the weeks, and I knew they would have seen me. But I didn't care. Couldn't stop.

Now looking back, the thought crossed my mind that maybe it was one of those disgruntled customers who had betrayed me to His Reverence. Peter Kilduff? Not Peter. Probably not any of the others either. Deliberately anyway. They too had probably recognised it was at an end - the great escape attempt, the attempted break-out. The mission was on. So they decided to confess their transgressions. Very likely.

Yes, that was what had happened. After weeks of bringing Michelle around to the lonely and isolated bachelors of Tireragh, after weeks of standing outside the van staring at whin bushes while their loneliness was being dissipated. I could no longer continue giving her. I wanted her for myself and for myself alone. Wanted to take her away and place the mountain of my love at her feet, before her eyes. Wanted to escape with her into that mountain. Wanted to build a hut on top of that mountain, far from pestering intruders.

Where I could mind her. Where we could be happy. But I could not find the words nor the way to tell her. And I ended up driving around like a fool and pretending to her that I could locate no customers. An unlikely story after weeks of feverish demand for her services.

And it was while I was driving around in this quandary that I was stopped by His Reverence. Now do you understand why I reacted as I did? Can you understand me? At all?

It was she who broke the heavy silence.

"He gives me one day to leave. Just one day," she said quietly.

"What?"

"I must leave the country or he will tell the police."

"The bastard. Will he tell them what he was up to himself?"

"He says you will go the jail, Loftee, if I do not leave."

I laughed coldly. Standing there in the darkness, with nothing but millions of stars looking on, with the anaesthetic powers of the alcohol wearing off, the world felt like a distorted place, and the idea of going to jail seemed bizarre rather that terrifying.

"And if they send me to jail, what will they do to him? What will they do to you? Hang the two of you?"

"I believe him, Loftee. You must listen. He says the law is against pimps. They will do nothing to me. But they will put you in jail for getting clients and earning money."

"Fine then. If they can do nothing to you, that's fine. Let him report me."

"I cannot let them put you in jail, Loftee. I cannot let them do that."

"Why not?"

And I ached for her to say something extraordinary, something tender. A declaration. Any indication that she felt for me as I felt for her.

She took the few steps that separated us, slid her hand under my arm, laid her head on my shoulder, and said very lowly, very tenderly, very sincerely: "Because you are the best friend I ever have."

It was beautiful, but it was not what I wanted to hear. I would have preferred to hear her say: you are an out-and-out bastard, but I love you. Something like that. Anything like that. Still.

"You are the only man who was good to me. I have a long story. Very long. With many problems. I cannot be reported to the police either or I have more trouble. I have a long story, and I will tell you, but not here. We go to the Lake, the lake in the mountains. I would like to see it again. I would like to be there with you one last time."

"Alright."

She was in a dilemma for a moment, not knowing whether to go in the front or into the back. But I opened the passenger door of the cab very decisively for her. It was over, so there was no point in being secretive anymore. It was over, and I wanted her to travel in the cab with me and drive through Tireragh for this one time without fear or shame.

20

WHEN THE THUNDER PEALS ACROSS THE sky, is it the annoyance of the Creator at our failure to honour him, or is it the laugh of the Creator at our efforts to thwart him? Who knows? Whether I was pleasing him by releasing his lap-dog, whether I was annoying him by rejecting his way, I do not know. There might have been thunder, but I didn't hear it. Anyway, I was glad I had seen the error of my ways. Just in time too. Well, I hadn't been making much progress in finding a road to the top of a cliff anyway. But that was my stupidity. My incompetence. Nothing to do with what I wanted. If there had been a cliff handy I would have driven over it, believe me. And the Creator would have been delighted. Absolutely frigging delighted. Just what he would have done himself. If your enemies offend you, hang them up by the balls from meat hooks. Just to show who's boss. Just to show them who should be honoured and respected. Yes, I had been right in the palm of his hand and didn't realise it.

I was relieved I had seen it in time. Thanks to old Frank's outburst. He has you in the palm of his hand, he said. Maybe he had, but I didn't have to accept his right to prod me and poke me for his own amusement.

I don't have to tremble for his gratification. I don't even have to acknowledge him. There was someone higher than him, someone to whom he owed everything, owed life itself. Someone whom he tried to obscure, even obliterate, for his own glorification. His mother. Mother of God. The real source of life and love. He was a sham. But still her son. Still one of the three divine persons. There are three divine persons in one God. He was the eldest. But she the one God.

226

The first. Embracing her three sons. Accepting all that they do. The bad as well as the good. She feels responsible. Even asked her faithful and loving son, her second, to undergo the suffering of humanity. To embarrass his brother. To redeem him. And to tell the people the good news that the ways of the Creator were not the ways of God. That love and generosity and self-sacrifice were superior to hatred and competition and self-glorification. The good news that the day would come when our heavenly mother would tolerate his petulant ways no longer and would flood his tar-barrels to the brim, to overflowing, flood his whole creation with one gigantic swell of love. And then he would be seen for what he was. He would be seen to be no more than a clever designer, no more than an able craftsman. A wayward son who rejected the love of his mother and tried to fill the vacuum in his soul by creating beings to worship him, to honour him, to satisfy his need for recognition. Yes, that was him alright.

I felt almost sorry for him. It is easy to feel sorry for someone, for anyone, for everyone, when you have a woman's head resting on your shoulder. Have you ever experienced that? Have you ever bathed your face in the pool of a woman's hair? Felt the strands of a woman's hair flow like rivulets across your forehead, your nose, your lips? Taken a deep deep breath heavy with the odour of her perfume? It was my unspeakable joy to experience all of that when she asked me to put my arm around her, to hold her. After I had parked the van in the old spot on the shore of Lough Easkey.

Awkwardly I put my arm over her shoulders and she snuggled in to me so close my face was in her hair. I held her shoulder tightly with my hand. Her body was so lithe and light, it seemed as if she would disintegrate, disappear, if I didn't keep a firm grip on her. And a firm grip I held.

Dawn had begun to dissolve the solid darkness of the sky, of the clouds, over the other side of the Lake, over the gap in the mountains, over Tobercurry.

And in halting phrases and half-phrases she began to tell me her story.

"My name, it is not Michelle. But I think you know that. No? And I am not from France. I was born in a country behind the great wall. My family still live there. They do not like to live there, but it is their home. And they cannot get out. When the War finished they tried to get out. To Austria. To Germany. Thousands and thousands of people. But the Russian soldiers stopped them at the border. Made them go back. My parents had to go back. They were sorry they did not get to the West. And such people were not popular in our country any more. When I was growing up, they always talked about the West and getting to the West. They hoped their children would get to the West some day.

"I had three brothers, all older than me. Our parents made us learn French and English, so that we would be successful when we got to the West. And we sometimes spoke German at home.

"I was not happy growing up in our country. I wanted to go to the West. I wanted to be an actress. I wanted to be in the movies. You know the way. Like every kid, I suppose.

"When I was seventeen, eighteen, I was involved with boys. With men. You know the way. And I was acting. In plays. And I learn that if you want a good part in a play, you sleep with the director. Simple. I talk always about getting to the West. To be an actress. To be a big success. Everyone says, you cannot get to the West. No one gets across the Border. They shoot people who try. But I say I will get out if I have to fuck every border guard in the country.

"Then one man, he says he can get me to the West. He knows people. But I will need more than to fuck border guards. It costs money. A lot of money. But I was pretty, I was smart. He says I will go a long way. He says I can be an actress in the West.

"But my family was poor. They had no money. So this man said he had contacts. He knew people. They would loan the money and I could pay back when I got to the West. When I got a job.

"I agreed to this. I wanted to go to the West. I wanted to be an actress. I wanted to be famous. I wanted to wear nice clothes and have a nice apartment. They got me papers and one day they took me to the Border in a car. Three other people were in the car. Three men. Me, I was terrified. There were so many stories. Of people trying to escape. And here I am at the checkpoint, trying to escape to the West. Of people being killed. I expected the guard to point his gun at me. I could not believe it. The border-guard, he just looked at my papers, he looked at me, he said nothing. He looked at the papers the men showed him. He said nothing. He just waved us on. And we were in the West.

"They took me to Paris. They said it was easier to become an actress in Paris. They told me how much money I owed them. It was huge. They said not to worry, that it was easy to earn such money in the West.

"They gave me a room and a little money. They said I should look for a job. But they told me I had to be careful, very careful, because of my false papers. They told me I must get some money to pay them back. They needed the money fast. I went around the city, but I was terrified to ask for a job. I was afraid I would be in trouble with the police. They told me that if my false papers were discovered I would be in trouble with the police, and I would have them in trouble too. They would not like that.

"Every time these men came back they were more angry. They said I must pay back the money or something not nice would happen to me. They said that something not nice would happen to my family, if it was known I was gone to the West. They came back one day with another man called Henri. They said Henri would give me work and I must take it.

"Henri, he was nice to me. He said he was my friend. He said I can work for him and earn money. A lot of money. And I can pay back the men. It would not take long. And maybe I could get more of my family out to the West.

"Henri was a pimp. He taught me how to work on the streets. I did not like it. I was not an actress. It was not a proper job. But I was earning money. And I thought, very soon I will pay these men, then I will do what I want.

"The men, they collected my money from Henri. When I thought I had paid off a lot of money I asked them, how much is left. And they told me I owed nearly as much still. I said I paid you. It should be less. But they said there is interest on the money. Interest. So I still owed them a lot of money. And Henri, he advised me not to fight with them, not to argue with them. They could be very ugly. You know. They could hurt me. And I was terrified.

"That is the way it was when you came to Paris, Loftee. It did not matter how much I paid them, they said I still have to pay more. Interest. And when you said, come to Ireland, I thought, yes, this is a way to escape. So I ran away to Ireland.

"You are my best friend, Loftee. You are the only man who helped me. Everyone else. Pooh.

"They did not help me. They helped themselves. Only you, Loftee. Only you have helped me.

"That is why I must not get you in trouble with the police. I too must not get in trouble with the police. They must not find out where I am. I must not be sent back to Paris. They will get me. They have connections everywhere. Those men. And they will be nasty. Very nasty." And she shivered.

I listened to her story with gripped breath. With my arm around her, her head resting on my chest, I was in a state of numb excitement. Yet I listened to every word she spoke with total concentration. And when a tear trickled down her cheek I pressed my mouth close, to capture it, to taste the delicious bitterness of that salty tear. Little did she know how I too wanted to take advantage of her. And now I felt guilty. Frigging guilty. Ashamed. Men had used her and abused her. Badly. Very badly. And had I not been spancelled by my own handicap I would have used her and abused her too.

Why was it so? Why was a man's brain so driven by lust? His judgement so clouded? Was it all part of the Creator's scheme to confuse and obstruct men in their search for love? That was certainly a possible explanation. He was frigging bloody-minded, wasn't he?

Yes. Even the way he matched people in lust who were not matched in love. Yes, and sealed that match with all the solemnity of his frigging institutions. Till death us do part. A neat trick. And when they suffer, he laughs, laughs till the sky and the earth are ready to crack. What a joke. What a fast one to pull on his mother. Shows he is the clever one, the important one, the Creator. Cannot be bested. Not my her and her simplicity anyway. Not by her and her thoughtless giving of love. Not by his suffering brother either. Nor his younger brother with his bright beams of inspiration. Nothing clever in that. And whenever men or women in their tar-barrels get too preoccupied with love, a quick whiff of lust is enough to lead them off on a wild goose chase.

Yes he had us all in the palm of his hand. And by the scruff of the balls too, for that matter.

She was silent for a little while and I was able to focus my attention on her. On her hair that flowed all over my face when I inclined my head forward. On her shoulders that I was holding firmly to me in a tight clasp. On her body that was lithe and trembling on the seat beside me while the dawn grew in confidence out over Tobercurry.

"What will you do?" I asked her eventually. Dreading the answer.

"I think I would like to go to Germany. On that day we passed through the check-point, we were driving through the most beautiful country I had ever seen. So peaceful. There were little villages with duck-ponds and trees. There were towns with shops. There were castles on top of hills. And I asked the men where this was. They said it is Germany. And I wanted to get out and live in Germany. I have money now, thanks to you, Loftee. I can make a life in Germany. I can get a job. A proper job. No streets. And the men, they will not find me there. You have saved me from them, Loftee. You have freed me. And I will not forget you. I will think of you every day I live."

I might have derived some satisfaction from this declaration were it not for the agony I was suffering at the thought of her leaving. And I could say nothing. Tongue-tied as usual. As frigging usual. The declarations I myself wished to make, all stuck in my craw.

"You will drive me to the station, Loftee. Yes?"

"Of course," was all I could frigging mumble from the floods and storms of thoughts and feelings and words that were raging inside me.

21

HOW DIFFERENT IS EVERYBODY'S TAR-barrel. But nevertheless a tar-barrel. Michelle's was a beautiful body, just as mine was an ugly one. Frigging ironic don't you think? All my life I hump around this burden of my own grossness, dreaming of beauty, and wishing, wishing, wishing. While Michelle was endowed with all the beauty that I lacked, that I coveted. But that turned out to be her burden. Her handicap. Her un-doing. You have to hand it to the Creator, there is no surpassing him for the clever twist. He doesn't just put in the knife, he dazzles you with the jewels on the hilt at the same time.

And the pair of us brought together by her beauty and my ugliness, brought so close for a moment we could have been the white and the yoke of the one egg, now to be separated by another clever twist. Was there no end to his ingenuity? No end to his machinations?

I was numb. With grief, I suppose. Bringing her back to Sligo. Hovering about while she packed her bags. And the words that I wanted to speak all caught inside me.

She had fallen silent too. I believed her when she said I was the first person she had told her story to. Yes. And now she too was quiet. Was she expecting a reaction from me? Was she, too, screaming inside? Screaming silently? Or did she tell me her story because I was a good listener? Like everyone else, did she find me convenient when she needed to talk? I didn't know. I didn't frigging know.

Probably. Who would have the slightest interest in me anyway? That kind of interest. Looking like something a farmer would gather on the top of a fork and he cleaning the stable yard.

And yet. For a glorious moment. An hour. Maybe two or three. Whatever. I held her. Close to me. Bathing my face in the pool of her hair. Watching the dawn break. The sun rise. Over Lough Easkey. Watching the crags and the whins and the heather on the side of the mountain stir forth from the slumbering darkness. While she told me her story.

Yes, I have known heaven. And that has made hell so much more difficult to bear.

I drove her to the station. Numb. Silent. Helped to tuck her cases neatly on the train. Then out. On to the platform. The two of us. Looking at each other. So much to say. So little ability to say it.

The attendant started to bang the doors of the train closed. Time to go. And still no words spoken.

In her fashion she pulled a face mimicing regret, loneliness, sorrow. You know the kind of face. Comical. And I smiled. Hoping to convey as much. I should have cried, but the frigging tears were jammed as tight as the frigging words.

She reached up her arms. Hugged me. Kissed me on one cheek. Then on the other.

"Goodbye, Loftee," she said, as she stepped back on the train. Softly. But I could hear her voice breaking.

The train shuddered and began to move. She was going. Leaving.

And I felt the tears loosening, running freely down my face. She was gone and I hadn't even said goodbye. Said nothing, for frig's sake. Dumb as a stake. What must she think? I could have asked her to write. So I would know she was okay. So I would know where she was. So we might have a chance of meeting again. Sometime. But nothing. I had said nothing. Hadn't even told her that I loved her.

As the train bended out of sight I wheeled around to leave, and bumped into a dust bin. I lashed out at the bin with my foot. Hurried out of the station.

The world was waiting for me outside. Cold. As if an arctic wind was breathing from the very pavements. This was the world without Michelle. Cold and bleak. It was not a world I wanted to be in. I needed her. Needed her back.

If I had spoken some words? Would she have stayed? If I had spoken some words? Would she have invited me to go with her? To Germany. Anywhere. We could have survived together. Now I would never know. All because I had not spoken some words.

And the words were trapped in my brain. Mocking me. Burning like ice. I would never be free of them. Because I had not spoken then when I had the chance.

I had reached the van. I sat in. Turned the key. The words. The words. I had to speak the words. So that she would know. That I loved her. Even if she was only amused. Or embarrassed. Even if she pitied me. I had to speak the words.

There was a chance. A final chance. The track was poor. The train was slow. Rolled along timidly for the early part of the journey. The first stop Collooney. I could reach Collooney as soon as the train. If I hurried.

And I hurried. Drove like a maniac out of the town, out the road. Do you know the road? It winds along towards the village of Ballisodare, never far from the railway line. By the time I reached Ballisodare I could see the rump of the train poking furtively behind the houses.

I tried to go faster. Tore through the village. Spun left after the bridge and headed for Collooney. Do you know the road between Ballisodare and Collooney? Again it twists and turns. It converges on the railway line, then veers off, converges again. As if it is involved in some kind of crazy waltz.

I could see the train. Despite the meanderings of the road and the slow purposeful directness of the railway line, I was making progress. Catching up. The train would stop for a few minutes in Collooney. Without doubt, I would be in time. I kept hurrying. I would see Michelle. I would speak the words. Perhaps go with her. To Germany. Wherever. Or persuade her to stay.

There is a stretch of the road which nuzzles close under the railway line. You know the stretch. A slope of birch saplings between them. That is all. It was there that I finally caught up with the train. I was so excited. To be within a few yards of her again. I was so close I could see the passengers inside the carriages. Just above me. And I strained to try and pick out Michelle. I knew where she was sitting. Midway down the train. And, yes, I spotted her.

I started screaming. Not silently. As loud as I was able to scream. I love you. That is what I was screaming. Michelle, I love you. And I started waving. And banging on the windscreen. At first she was looking down and didn't see me. Then she glanced out the window, casually, and spotted me. She jumped up and held her face to the window. Her two hands up against the glass. Flat. You know the way. And I was waving at her and screaming at the top of my voice. Michelle, I love you. And I was ecstatic because Collooney was only a short distance ahead. And I would easily overtake the train.

That is what I thought. I had my foot pressed to the floor on the throttle. Going as hard as the old van could move. Faster than I had ever dared go before.

And then. You know the story. You know the stretch of road. Immediately after the straight bit along the railway line, the road gives a few very quick twists. Like the flicks and kicks of a beached eel trying to shake off its captor.

I managed the first twist. I stayed on the road for the second twist even though I had already lost control of the van. The final twist brings the road in under the railway bridge. A viciously sharp twist. And the cut-stone wall of the bridge loomed straight in front of me.

I could hear the relentless throb of the iron wheels overhead. The train pushing on to Collooney and Boyle. To Mullingar and Dublin. Bringing her on her way to Germany. Germany.

The train has passed now and all is silent. I have stopped screaming. Not in terror. But in total calm. I realise I have one moment left before the impact. But a moment is a day, is a life-time. I am calm, utterly calm. I clear my mind totally. And then it fills with the deep deep consciousness of all I know, all I have learned from the old men and the old women, the history of my people since time began. Such is a moment of sheer calm. This moment of sheer calm.

Now I look at the wall. Directly. Closely. The wall is there in front of me. I can see every stone, carefully hewn, carefully placed, waiting for me all this time. And I can see the grain in each stone. And the grain is tinted with red. I am not afraid. And I am proud of myself that I am not afraid. It feels as if I can make this moment last forever. Hold that wall at bay forever. By sheer concentration. Power of mind. Poised in the moment of about to die.

My attention is drawn from the wall by a conscious glance at the little figurine of St Anthony glued to the dash. Glued by his tonsure to the windscreen. And I recall the oblique smile of the girl from Tobercurry. Luminous. Transparent. I realise that, when the wall strikes, the figurine will suffer the first blow. So I shoot out my hand. Grab the figurine. It is as if this lapse of concentration has allowed the wall to come pounding through the windscreen. I feel the first impact on my fist, on my knuckles. Hard. Solid. Determined.

Maybe all this time I have been looking too closely and too long at the tar-barrel from the inside. Maybe death has nothing at all to do with the ripple hitting the wall of the barrel. Maybe death comes from the outside instead, ploughing through the barriers. Emphatic. Random. As this wall has now come ploughing through my windscreen. Maybe this is her work. Her intervention. Maybe it is she who is gashing open the tar-barrel. From the outside.

Spilling the drop of trapped water.

Have you ever thought about the water trapped in the bottom of a tar-barrel? How that drop of water can never be at peace until it finds its way to the sea. It is in its very nature to seek union with the sea. Did you ever think about that? If you were to tip out the water, what happens is that you set that drop of water off on a journey. Down into a drain, perhaps. Off into a stream. And the stream flows into a river somewhere. And the river will never stop flowing until it reaches the sea.

Yes, maybe, when all is said and done, that that is what death is. Her. Smashing through the side of the tar-barrel. To release the drop of trapped water. To let it run free. On its journey to the ocean.

Of course the Creator would resist. Does resist. Doesn't give in as easily as that. Captures the water again. In another tar-barrel. In a pool, or in a pond. In a lake. In frigging anything. Anywhere. To hold it as long as possible from running down to the sea. Out of his power. Back to his mother. And I imagine he finally ends up like a frantic child on the beach erecting barricades of sand to try and hold back the relentless flow of the stream, even as the tide is relentlessly rising to meet it.

Yes. Maybe. Wherever she gashes open a tar-barrel, wherever she frees a drop of water to start its journey, it will continue flowing until it reaches the sea. Even from the other side of the Mountain, even from Tobercurry, the flow may be in a different direction, to start with, but it will eventually end up in the sea joining all the other streams. And sometime, even away in Germany, a tar-barrel will be breached, a drop of water will be set free to flow, will go on flowing until it reaches the very same sea, until it mixes its waters in the ocean along with the streams flowing from the other side of the Ox Mountains, with the streams flowing from Tireragh, with the bit of a trickle gathering at the bottom of a stone wall under a railway bridge on the road to Collooney.